Kissing Owen Darcy

Arlys Avery

Kissing Owen Darcy

An enemies to lovers, clean teen
romance
based on Jane Austen's novel
Pride and Prejudice.

Arlys Avery

To all the girls who have their friend's backs,
and to all the women who have mine.

1

"'It is a truth universally acknowledged, that a single Jane Austen heroine, living in modern days, would have good fortune and totally dominate in high school,'" I read to Amber as she looked at my laptop in disgust and slammed her locker door.

"Ellie, no. That is the lamest opening to a presentation ever. No way Ms. Lemon will believe I wrote it," said Amber Raine, the senior class's vote for Most Beautiful person and my vote for Meanest Project Partner ever.

"You didn't write it. I did," I said, obviously feeling reckless. One didn't question Amber, especially as a freshman.

"Hey Ellie, you got this! Final report!" cheered Catt as she and Emma hustled past. "We have Econ and then freedom! Woo hoo!"

"See you after?" asked Emma, glaring at Amber and using her raised eyebrow to ask, "do you need me to handle her?"

I shook my head no and smiled, "see you after" before turning back to the Homecoming Queen with daggers in her eyes.

"What did you say to me?" snarled Amber, not even

registering that my friends had spoken, much less that they existed.

"I only meant that Ms. Lemon told me I had to do the presentation so I could get public speaking credit. You were supposed to do the research. You even picked our topic."

"Feminism in 19th century England through Jane Austen's literary lens," she recited.

"I picked it because it sounded easy, and you are supposed to be some Jane Austen expert. Look, I forgive you. And I will do our presentation justice. Ms. Lemon gets it. I have a better stage presence. I am going to be a famous meteorite, after all. The camera loves me," she said with beauty queen poses and sweeping jet-stream hand gestures.

"Ummm, you mean meteorologist?" I asked.

"'Weather Girl' is not very gender-neutral, but you know what I mean," said Amber, totally missing the point.

"We were supposed to do this together," I said, sounding too loud in the newly quiet hallway.

Amber grabbed my arm and pulled me across the hall into the empty science lab, nearly growling in my face. "I am the senior, the one with a life, and I need to pass this class," she spat. "I do not have time to work with a freshman who is scared of her own shadow and wears stupid shoes," she said, taking her hand off my arm and putting on her plastic smile again as a group of giddy juniors passed by.

"I like these sneakers…," I said, pulling at my skirt and checking my reflection on the black screen of my phone.

"You may be smart, but I know you are going to get in there, and take one look at all those senior boys in the back row and freeze up, again, like you did with the Monsters in Literature presentation. They are cute but get a grip. They are just boys."

"I'm not scared of my shadow, or those guys," I mumbled as I pulled myself up to my full five-foot-four and tightened my high ponytail.

"Whatever. Let's just get this over with. Give me something smart to say to introduce it and then you can take over."

"Ummm, how about you say the title and then say, 'Jane Austen fought against social conventions the best way she could in her day, by creating heroines who were intelligent and spoke their minds,'" I said.

"Okay, I got it," said Amber, showing me her pen-marked hand.

"Amber, can we please practice just once? This is the only free period we have together today. You toggle the slides from here," I said, pointing to the arrow buttons. "Ms. Lemon will think you did all the research and you will pass. This is my last class of the year. Your last class in all of high school."

The bell sounded, making both of us jump. The clanging echoed in the empty hall for just a moment before streams of high schoolers flooded out in the hall, laughing, high-fiving, and bursting with the buzz of excitement that only imminent summer vacation could bring.

"Sorry kid, I'll wing it. My hot boyfriend is coming this way. When you have one, you'll understand the priorities," said Amber as she strutted away wearing her plastic smile and flinging herself into the arms of the perfect Ken to her Barbie. Watching them kiss and laugh in front of their friends, so comfortably, made my already edgy stomach drop. Maybe Amber was right. If I had a boyfriend, then maybe I wouldn't care about getting straight A's or doing well on speeches.

All thoughts of boys were jostled out of me as I got an enthusiastic hug of my own. My bestie Marni, dressed in her typical boho-chic style, grabbed my shoulders and said, "It is a new moon tonight and Jupiter has aligned with Mars;

meaning your presentation will be perfect and Ms. Lemon will give you the internship. The planets don't lie."

"The internship… I had forgotten. I mean, I forgot to worry about that," I said, with widening eyes. "I need that internship. If I want to be taken seriously by colleges as a community advocate, I HAVE to. It's my thing. I don't have another thing." I could feel myself getting hotter and talking faster, and my voice sounded higher than usual.

"No, no, no, no you don't!" Marni said as she started shaking my shoulders. "Ellie, stop."

"I shouldn't have worn these shoes. Amber said they were stupid."

"Your shoes? They aren't stupid, you are just freaking. Take a deep breath…"

"Breath," I said with a faraway look.

"Come on," Marni said, shaking me again. "The planets don't lie. You can do this. It has already happened. Visualize the success. You are sunshine and yellow… you've got this!"

"I'm yellow, I've got this," is what I tried to say, but my throat locked up and my entire body was radiating cold and hot at the same time. I remembered standing on the high dive at the pool the year I turned eight. I had been excited when climbing the ladder, but the moment the lifeguard whistled at me to hurry and I noticed the big kids jeering, I couldn't remember why this seemed fun. It was so high up and then I couldn't move.

The hallway noise was dissipating, and Ms. Lemon came to the door.

"Come on ladies, get to class. Ellie, come in. I am looking forward to your presentation."

"I think I broke her," Marni said to Ms. Lemon as I zombie-walked into Brit Lit. and the door shut behind me with solid

4

finality.

It felt like the entire room was looking at me as I walked to my seat, but that was impossible because I was invisible. I was the only freshman in a senior class of the beautiful people where Amber and her latest "Ken" reigned. Most knew my older sister, Jade. She was a junior. She was shy but well-liked, so if they noticed me at all, they called me "little Jade" or "little Gardiner." When I signed up for this class, I liked British literature and Ms. Lemon enough that I didn't care about the rest of the class until it came time for the presentations.

Each time I stood up to give a presentation, I drowned in a wave of fear. I could see myself reflected in the critical eyes of my classmates. They saw a beige nothing of a person with brown hair and brown eyes. I had no cool personality traits, no quirky fashion sense, nor interesting hobbies. I made good grades, had fantastic friends, and I loved Jane Austen's books, but those things weren't enough to be someone in high school.

I liked the idea of being chosen to work at the new community center and help people. Ms. Lemon was the chairman of the committee renovating the center, and she would recommend a student to do the outreach program. When Ms. Lemon found out I tutored at the center a few times a week, she suggested I apply. My parents were excited because it would look good on my college resume and I was excited because it would give me a "thing." Finally, something to call mine. I would be a community advocate... whatever that meant.

While Seth and Tiffany were doing their presentation on "The Four Major Themes of the Christmas Carol, are we all Scrooge?" I was happily dreaming of an audience of people smiling up at me as I cut a ceremonial yellow ribbon with giant scissors. I was welcoming my admirers into the newly renovated Community Center when "That Creep Benji That

Teases Me in Brit Lit.," Benji Wyman, leaned forward and whispered in my ear.

"Hey little Gardiner, are you dreaming about me?"

I sat bolt upright and heard Benji snicker. A multitude of thoughts swirled in my brain. "Why do you now need to notice my existence?" and "#metoo you Neanderthal!" and "I don't know why embarrassing me is so fun for him." and "Crap, why is my face so hot?" While my mental tornado whirled around Benji, I heard Ms. Lemon clear her throat.

"Thank you both. That was great. And the little sick boy 'what's-his-face' was Tiny Tim. Okay, last group, Amber and Ellie, you are up," said Ms. Lemon.

My face and neck, having flushed red when tickled by Benji's breath, suddenly lost all color. Thankfully, Amber being Amber, bounded up to the front, grabbing everyone's attention as I walked past her to log on to the wireless projector and start the presentation. I tried not to, but I looked over at Benji. He winked at me and yelled "woo-hoo," and elbowed his buddy, which, of course, Amber thought was for her, so she smiled broadly at her admirers.

I stood next to Amber, looking like her unsophisticated kid sister, and took a deep breath. She took a quick look at her hand, then said our title and the line I had given her, projecting it out like a Broadway star. She then looked pointedly at me, and so did the rest of the room. Some of the baseball players in the back chanted "su-mmer, su-mmer, su-mmer…" very low, and I cleared my throat and nodded to Amber to start the slides. "Su-mmer, su-mmer, su-mmer…"

I looked at my shoes. Amber was right. These shoes are stupid. Why had I worn them? I looked up and saw Amber glaring at me. I opened my mouth, and I tried to make a sound come out and tried to remember why I was standing up there, but it didn't work, my voice just did not work.

"Okay, everyone, stop with the chanting. You are still on my time. Ellie, take a deep breath and begin," said Ms. Lemon with the slightest edge of concern.

I tried again. I closed my eyes for a second. When I opened them, I saw all the faces ready to burst out laughing. I closed my mouth and looked at Amber for help.

Amber looked at me pityingly and pushed me toward the laptop. I toggled the keys, and she began reading along with the presentation, making no sense, but charming the class. She really was great in front of an audience, and I was not bad at stifling my tears as I advanced the slides.

I came out of my self-pity fog when Amber finished and bowed to applause minutes before the last bell rang. Cheers got louder in the room and down the hall as carefree students filed out of their classrooms; a boisterous river flowing out to the parking lot and into summer. I powered down my laptop and went back to my desk to grab my bag.

"Ellie, I need to talk to you, if you would stay for a minute?" asked Ms. Lemon.

"Happy summer, you guys. Stay safe. Stay out of jail!" Ms. Lemon yelled to the last of the retreating backs.

"I'm sorry," I mumbled when I felt her gaze on me.

"Ellie, what am I going to do with you?" she asked, and I knew she didn't need an answer. "Okay, here is the deal. I cannot give you the public speaking credit. You didn't make it through any of the presentations we had. So, you will have to take public speaking next year with the rest of your sophomore class."

"Sorry. I did the research; I knew the material. I just got stuck, again," I said, looking down and feeling ashamed of myself.

"I know you did the research. I recognize your work. But I

asked you to let Amber do it. You were to focus on presenting."

"I couldn't get her to even meet with me," I said, feeling like a tattletale even though she totally deserved it.

"I'm not mad you didn't give a speech," she said as she ran her hands through her hair as if to summon patience out of her auburn locks. "I'm concerned because you are so capable. One day you will see, you are every bit as strong as these fictional heroines you idolize. But in your current state, I cannot recommend you to the Community Board for the internship."

"Oh, but, no, please," I said, feeling the sting of the disappointment turn to panic. "I need to have that internship. Everyone is so excited about it. I am excited about doing outreach and helping people."

"If you can't actually reach out, how can you do the outreach?" she asked.

"I can go to speech therapy, or summer school, or...," I said as she paused for a long moment, looking at me. She looked at me for so long that I wasn't sure she was going to say anything else until her eyes lit up with an idea.

"No need. You, Ellie, are going to lean on those quirky friends of yours and they will help you," she said, a smile growing on her face. "Yup, you will be fine. Do what you do best, study, and lean into Jane Austen and your friends," she said. Warming to her idea and sounding determined, Ms. Lemon put a final binder in her backpack and flung it over her shoulder.

"You need to do what your presentation said, and be one of those intelligent, outspoken women who believed in themselves enough to stand against any foe, even a glowering Mr. Darcy!" Ms. Lemon said, smiling at me. "You have until the August 15th fund-raiser to get confident speaking in front of an audience, because you, my dear, will be M.C.ing with me on stage in front of the whole town!"

"I what?" I said, stunned.

"Yup, if you want that internship, fight for it. Show the Board, and me, you can speak comfortably in public. So, young lady, get it together. You have two months! Now get out of my classroom, I am on vacation!" said Ms. Lemon, ushering me out and flipping off the lights.

"I can do this, I have two months," was what I was muttering as I walked out the front door of the school toward four sympathetic faces.

"How did it go?" asked Ava in her soothing voice.

"My shooting star wish last night was to go one day without public humiliation. Today was not that day," I said.

"There is always tomorrow?" offered Catt in her ever-positive way.

"You are right, I guess. Tomorrow couldn't be worse," I stupidly said.

"Shooting star wishes come true," chimed Marni, "so at least you know one embarrassment-free day is coming!"

I smiled and looked around at this group of four amazing friends who have been my ride-or-die since first grade. So few people get to grow up with one good friend, much less four. I was so lucky. Even on my worst day, I had them.

"El, you were muttering you have two months. To what?" asked Emma.

"Well… we all have homework from Ms. Lemon. We have two months to get me ready to speak on stage in front of the whole town."

"Ahhhhhhhhhhhhhh!" they all screamed.

"I know!!!!" I laugh-screamed back.

"We are going to need more than two months!" said Emma with wide eyes.

9

"We are going to need ice cream!" said Catt.

"What we need is our first pool day to plan," said Marni. "My house, tomorrow. I'll message the time."

"And eat ice cream?" asked Catt.

"Let's go get ice cream now to celebrate… we just survived freshmen year!" I said, feeling happier than I had all day.

2

The morning light found me where it often did; a brown curtain of hair hanging off of my bed, legs up on my wall, reading my favorite book. Turning the page, I found the quote I had been looking for. "This is what I should have said to her yesterday," I said out loud and began melodramatically reading. "I am only resolved to act in that manner, which will constitute my happiness, without reference to you, Amber Raine, and you stupid boys," I lowered my book and glared at the imaginary classroom in front of me, "now shut your faces so I can do my presentation!"

"Ellie, are you still fighting with Amber?" my sister, Jade, asked, coming into my room, looking very upside down.

"I just want a do-over, so I was rereading my personal guidebook for inspiration. For next time."

"Your guidebook is *Pride and Prejudice*?" mused Jade.

"It's like you hardly know me. Your favorite sister?" I said as I flipped right side up and off the bed.

"Only sister," corrected Jade.

"Only sister, who has idolized all things, Jane Austen, since birth." I swept my arm toward the top tier of my bookshelf, where I had displayed the five remaining Jane Austen novels in order of publication.

"Well, since you are my favorite sister, I do know you and I know something is bothering you; more than just Amber. It is the first day of summer. You would normally be pestering me to go walking or planning a trip to see Aunt Cassie in the city, yet here I find you, all upside down. What's really going on?" Jade asked, sitting on the bed beside me.

I paused for a long minute. I was not sure how to explain what I was feeling and finally asked, "What's wrong with me?"

"What do you mean? Nothing is wrong with you," asked Jade.

"I mean, like why do girls like Amber and those older boys get to me? I can talk in front of people most of the time, like a normal person. It's just sometimes I get frozen in place."

"It used to happen when you were little and Aunt Catherine would come to visit. I think some people just make you feel mad or judged, and it closes up your voice," noted Jade.

"Oh, yeah, I hated her, she was always telling us her other "nieces were soooo beautiful, sooooo accomplished, blah blah blah..." I said in my puke-face voice.

"You imitate her so well," Jade said, smiling and pushing her shoulder to mine. "That is a good example. Her opinion means nothing. She is a grouchy old lady, but you took it inside and couldn't do our *A Christmas Carol* reading that year. I think you just need to realize what mom and dad, me, and your friends already know. You are awesome and it doesn't matter what other people think, only what you think."

"I guess so," I said, still not knowing how to fix it.

Jade stood up and took *Pride and Prejudice* from my hand. "So why is this your personal guidebook?"

"Jane Austen created women who didn't get pushed

around, and I need to figure out how they did it. How I become more like Lizzy Bennet and less like Ellie Gardiner."

"You want me to call you Lizzy? It is still part of your name?" said Jade as we walked together into our shared bathroom; her searching the drawers for a hair tie as I began brushing my teeth.

"Here, just take one of these," I offered my left arm and its array of hair ties and bracelets.

"How are you reading and brushing your teeth at the same time?" Jade asked.

"I'm at the best part, well, second-best part. Lady stupid De Bourgh has cornered Elizabeth and keeps insulting her." I held up my pointer finger, rinsed, and spit before continuing to read. "Elizabeth says, 'You can now have nothing farther to say. You have insulted me in every possible method. I must beg to return to the house.'"

"It's not really a strong comeback," Jade pointed out.

"No, but she stood up for herself. She said to this scary woman, 'I am not putting up with this. Peace out.'"

"Peace out?" Jade smiled. "I get it. You want to stop being pushed around."

"What time do you want to leave? I told Eden I would walk over with you. We are going to start on our college essays," said Jade.

"Almost ready," I said as I grabbed my pink sparkly phone. "I'll meet you out front in ten?"

Group Msg: The Invisibles
Ellie: So ready, bathing suit, books, bullet journal,
         new attitude… check!
Catt: Yay! Summer! Bikini emoji
Marni: Wait, books? puke emoji

Marni: Oh, for project Make Ellie, EB! Got it!
        Celebrate emoji
Ava: Making sandwiches, might be 10 min late.
Catt: Yay Snacks!!!! heart emoji
Emma: Made our summer playlist! Hey, heard cute boys
        were moving in by you, E.
Ellie: Srsly? Double pink heart emoji. Dibs on
        blue raft SYS

I pulled on my favorite denim overall shorts over my
bathing suit and shoved *Pride and Prejudice* and a handful of
other books into my backpack. It was important to start
research with peer review works and I was determined, after
my talk with Jade, to understand my freezing up problem. I
finished a quick side braid and headed out the front door.

When I opened the door, my normally tranquil
neighborhood was in utter chaos. I had a stress-dream right
before final exams where I was pushed onto a stage, in the
middle of a play I didn't know, as hundreds of eyes stared at
me expectantly from the audience. This moment was kinda
like that, except I was fully awake, and fully clothed.

Nearly jogging across our lawn and looking at me hungrily
was the neighborhood gossip circle. My mother, as the group's
unofficial president, was leading them straight toward me.
They were pointing and giggling to a large moving van driving
away down the street saying, "if I were only ten years, oh,
okay, twenty, years younger" and "such charming
grandchildren" and "single and so handsome." They were
being so loud I was sure whomever they were talking about
could hear every word. I could feel my face getting hot.
Meanwhile, off to the left, the Garcias had stopped packing
their kids in the car to look over at all the commotion. I think
little Natalie was blowing raspberries my way, as she liked to

do. At the same moment, across the street, I saw poor old Magoo, the blind terrier, sneaking off his porch, heading toward the chaos with a gleeful trot.

"Oh, it's you. Ellie, where is Jade?" my loving mother asked as she nearly shoved me out of the doorway. "The new neighbor is seventeen and single," she giddily sang. "He will definitely need to get a look at Jade!"

"I'm heading to Marni's."

"Fine, fine," she impatiently said as she passed. "Jaaaade!"

Her shove had the effect of unfreezing the entire neighborhood. Everyone went back to what they were doing, and I jogged across the lawn to scoop up old Magoo before he wandered into the street.

"Oh, Mr. Magoo, who's the good doggy? Didn't you know, Magoo? It is a truth universally acknowledged that a single cute boy, new to our neighborhood, would definitely need a girlfriend!" I laughed while kissing his muzzle. "Poor Jade. You're so lucky to be a dog. Let's get you inside."

Knocking on the door, I yelled, "Hi, Mrs. Norman. I brought Mr. Magoo home."

"Oh, thank you, dear," chimed a slender, grey-haired woman as she swung open the door. "I don't know how he sneaks past me, but he must have gotten out when I got the newspaper. You know, you look lovelier every time I see you, Miss Ellie."

"No disrespect, Mrs. Norman, but you don't have your glasses on," I smiled. "But seriously, Jade is the pretty one, I'm the studious one."

"I know your mother always says that, but it's nonsense. Jade is lovely. She looks like your mother. That's why she favors her, but you hear me, young lady, you are just as pretty. And you have the most important part. You have a sparkle. A sense of fun, and a naughty streak!"

"I should have never told you about us toilet-papering the Conleys. But they gave out erasers for Halloween," I laughed.

"It's our secret dear!" said Mrs. Norman. "Can you come in for some iced tea?"

I pointed across the street to the usually obedient Jade, now sneaking out the side door of our house. "Looks like my ride is here, rain check?" I asked, as I waved bye to Mrs. Norman and ran to catch up with my sister.

3

I yell-whispered "Jade, wait up!" which made her jump and made me laugh. She was so genuinely good that this brief moment of rebellion was a new experience for her. Sneaking out before mother and company could force her to take cookies to the new family or some other fake-sounding ploy, made her nervous.

We have both found it is just easier to let our mom plot her latest scheme and stay out of the way as best we can. Through each embarrassing intrigue, we always knew she loved us. She could just be a lot, so we rarely bothered to resist. Consequently, her friends all thought we were the sweetest girls, but only because they couldn't hear what I was thinking.

"Did they tell you they found the man of your dreams?" I teased.

"She didn't find me. I had already told her I was going to Eden's, so I was stealthier about my exit than usual. I feel bad, but…" said Jade.

"Don't feel bad. She is having fun and will have your wedding all planned by the time we get home," I laughed as she sideways nudged me.

"I confess I am curious to meet the new family. I'd just rather it not be a big spectacle," Jade said, looking over her shoulder one last time.

"Me, too. I have always wanted to meet her grandkids. Mrs. B was so nice," I said.

"Yeah, she was great," said Jade lowering her voice to a whisper, "and don't tell mom, but if her grandson was also sweet, and not horrid looking, I wouldn't mind going out with him," Jade giggled at her admission.

"I know, I hope he is a hottie who is perfect for you and he brings a mazillion cute friends to the neighborhood and we spend the entire summer, going to balls and dances..."

"You are ridiculous. This isn't one of your books, and you can't dance."

"Minor detail," I laughed. "I don't remember if it's just one boy or two, and I think there is a sister... all I know is one will be your soul mate. Maybe we can show them our summer traditions, like the meteor shower or county fair?"

Jade and I had grown up in this small town and so had most of our friends. It was the kind of place that would show up on the Internet in lists of 'the quaintest small towns of the midwest' or in 'small-town life' articles. Picture spreads always featured our lush town park and the town square with the cute shops and restaurants built around the county courthouse with the clock on top. I just knew it as home.

We could hear the pinging of a basketball being dribbled before we got to old Mrs. Bingley's house. I remembered the year my dad put the basketball goal up on her garage for her grandkids, though they didn't visit often. She had been the nicest of the neighbors. She always had a smile and a wave for us, even last winter before she was bedridden. When we were little, she allowed us to cut the corner on our bikes using her semi-circle driveway. She became a legend for having the best candy at Halloween. Her house was set further back than most on the street so at night, the full oak trees in the front yard cloaked the long sidewalk to her front door making it extra spooky, but we all agreed the full-sized snicker bars were worth it. I always covered my neck from a zombie attack with one hand and kept a death grip on my candy bag with the other and ran for it.

Jade was talking about a party we'd all been invited to later in the summer, but I was not listening. We came around the tall hedges and saw two good-looking young men. One blond and bright, the other dark and inscrutable, shooting the basketball and rebounding for each other in relative silence. A pretty teen girl sauntered out with bottles of Gatorade. This must be the grandchildren, and these boys must be what all my mother's shrieking had been about. They were pretty shriek worthy.

I wanted to say hi and tell them I was sorry about your grandmother, but before I could get the words out, the dark-haired one looked right at me and sneered. The sheer arrogance of his look froze me on the spot. I could never quite picture what it meant when I'd read "Professor Snape sneered" in the Harry Potter books, but the tall, brown-haired boy just did that, and to me!

He quickly passed the ball to his unaware friend and said not-so-quietly to the girl, "These must be the neighbors sent to show us this 'charming' town."

"Dressed like that? Good luck," laughed the arrogant, fashionably dressed girl.

All the heat rushed to my face and all the comebacks I might have said were strangling my throat. The other boy, looking up, saw us and shook his blond head.

"Don't tease them. Hi! I'm Finn Bingley and this is my friend, who isn't always a jerk, Owen, and my sister, Brooklyn.

19

This was our grandma's house, and we just moved in for at least the summer. What are your names?"

Finn flashed us the warmest smile, with maybe the whitest teeth I had ever seen, and I could see all the kindness of his grandma in that smile. He paused on Jade's face for an extra moment, like most guys did, as I tried to rein in the anger pounding in my head.

"Hi, my name is Jade, and this is my sister, Ellie. I was so sorry to hear about your grandma. Not sure if you knew she was the favorite in this neighborhood… we all loved her."

Owen was staring at me with the same knowing smirk, as if he thought Jade's heartfelt words were just a ploy to talk to the cute boys. I was so surprised by his outward rudeness I didn't hear what Finn was saying to Jade. I just caught "… here for the summer for the regional basketball invitational at your high school. So maybe we will see you guys a lot this summer."

I tried to focus on Finn's friendly face, but with Brooklyn looking me up and down, and that other creep just staring, all I could see was my lame overalls and old worn-out Converse. I guess I just walked away, because Jade said, "Ummm, okay, I guess we are leaving. It was nice meeting you," as she jogged to catch up with me.

"How. Dare. He. How rude. What a creep. Who does he think he is? I'd like to tell him exactly what I think of his stupid, smug face. He is not so cute. Not nearly as cute as he thinks he is, and honestly, I was just walking down my street," I muttered, clenching and unclenching both my fists and my jaw.

"Ellie, whoa, do you mean Owen? What did he say? I didn't hear him say anything?" Jade asked.

"You didn't hear him say we were the desperate girls our mom wanted to fix up? He mocked us like we were nothing. And that sister, she thinks she is better than us."

"Maybe you are just taking it wrong? They are new to the area… maybe that's normal for where they come from," said Jade.

"Jade, come on… even you can't make that much rudeness okay," I said.

"Why can't I think of the perfect comeback when I need it?! And seriously, there aren't enough mean girls at school? I don't need this at home, too!" I yelled as we wound down the wooded path to Emerson Park.

"Don't worry, you will think of the perfect thing to say. In like twenty minutes. You always do eventually," Jade smiled and tried to soothe.

"You know who would have shredded him immediately?" my eyes lit up with the answer. "Elizabeth Bennet! This is why I brought my trusty guidebook book today… and I'm going to scour it for the perfect comeback. Mr. Smug Face will get it next time… not that I will EVER speak to him. Just saying. Hang on," I said as I searched my pockets for my phone.

Jade always smiled at me as I ranted. She was so even-tempered. I think watching me in this mood was like me watching monkeys in the zoo. She looked both amused and a little wary of the potential poo fling.

Group Msg: The Invisibles

Ellie: Srsly you will not believe what just happened angry face emoji cursing emoji
        I just met Mr. Smug Face. Project "make him pay" is forming!

Marni: Oh no, does this involve hair dye again?
        Puke emoji

Marni: Wait, who is Mr. Smug Face?

Catt: Lol, can't wait!

Ava: Smug Face? Crying laughing emoji

Catt: Dancing emoji snack emoji Mani-Pedi emoji
Emma: Is this about the cute boys?
Ellie: Not cute!!!!!!!!!!!! Puke emoji times 10,
          soooooo rude.

4

"El, you okay? You haven't said a word in the last ten minutes," asked Jade as we started up the Norlands' driveway.

"I am fine, really," I said, taking a deep breath and smiling at Jade's worried eyes. "Besides, we are here, and I'm about to eat snacks and plot revenge... my favorite things!"

Jade laughed and unlatched the Norlands' side gate. The white wooden gate offered its usual welcoming creak, which weirdly made me calmer. For as long as I could remember, this house had held my second family and many of my best childhood memories. Even creepy staring people couldn't make me feel bad here.

"Happy summer ladies!!" I said as I bounded into the game room.

I knew it made me appear irrational to go from furious to happy, but my friends have always had that effect on me. They made me feel like I was not alone, and not a weirdo who couldn't dress and needed to be leered at. I also knew when I told them about Mr. Smug Face, they would hate him with me, and plan mean girl revenge on him. So, for the moment, I was happy.

The game room had dark wood paneling, a pool table at one end and a bar and couches on the other. It always smelled slightly like Sniffles the dog, old leather couches, nail polish, lemon iced tea, and sub-sandwiches. These were the smells of my summer.

"Hi everyone, congrats on making it through freshman year. Is Eden in her room?" Jade asked Marni as she headed toward the front of the house.

"She is in the kitchen with mom," smiled Marni.

"Two years older, and a thousand times sweeter," Marni and I have often said of our sisters.

The Norlands were such a nice family and let us invade them every summer. Mr. Norland liked to complain about girls overtaking his former man-cave. He would mumble that any day now he would get some friends and take it back. Until then, he said we owed him rent, which we paid in sandwiches and sweets. We knew he secretly liked us and has been using us as an excuse to eat the junk food Mrs. Norland wouldn't buy for him.

Mrs. Norland made us a pitcher of her amazing iced tea for our every visit. Why it tasted so different from ours at home, I didn't know, since it was simply tea bags in water, steeped in the sun. She must have put extra sugar or magic in it because it was deeee-licious.

"The Stephensons are already partying," I said, seeing a dozen teenagers jumping in and hanging around the neighbor's large pool.

"They won't even notice us, as usual," Marni said, thinking I was feeling self-conscious. "They have all the 'it' crowd over today."

"They are a grade above us and on a whole other planet," Catt Moore yelled from the floor where she sat across from Emma Hartfield.

"Aren't you guys tired of being invisible?" I asked, my breath fogging up a small circle on the glass.

I felt like I had been blotchy red my entire freshman year; either from some sitcom-like embarrassment or from holding in what I wasn't brave enough to say out loud. The one good thing was that I got to go through all of it with my four best friends, The Invisibles. In seventh grade, we named ourselves The Invisibles because we weren't the jocks, the drama kids, the popular crowd, the band kids, the bad kids, or even the nerds. We were good girls who made good grades and didn't make waves. Therefore, invisible, except to each other. And lately, I wanted more.

"It matters now," I muttered.

"I would be invisible with you any day," Marni said as she squeezed me from the side waking me from my ruminations.

I smiled at Marni and turned to look as Ava Wentworth walked in carrying several bags and her signature bright smile. "Let the summer begin," she said as she unpacked sandwiches, and put them next to the bags of chips on the bar counter.

Everyone started talking excitedly about new bathing suits, making summer plans, and grabbing handfuls of chips and M&M's.

Marni looked at me and yelled, "Okay, it's not hot enough yet to go to the pool, so spill it. Your horoscope said you would make life-changing decisions this week, so what is it we need to plan? And…" Marni started to ask.

"Who is Mr. Smug Face?" interrupted Emma.

Catt and Emma were on the floor painting each other's toes with a bright neon orange polish. Catt was a cute mousy everything, from her light brown hair and pale pink skin, to her tiny turned-up nose. You could almost imagine she would squeak. While Emma was her opposite; tall with long dark brown hair and warm beige skin. But they had the same love of adventure and romance, a dislike of reality, a clear love of all things neon, and they had been family friends since they were born.

"This is the plan." Out of my backpack, I drew out my pink leather copy of *Pride and Prejudice* and set it up on the bar. I also pulled out Soniah Kamal's *Pride and Prejudice in Pakistan - Unmarriageable,* Jo Baker's *Longbourn,* Amanda Grange's *Mr. Darcy, Vampyre,* P.D. James's *Death Comes to Pemberley,* and Tirzah Price's *Pride and Premeditation.*

"Ta-da!" I wildly gestured like Amber the meteorite at the array of books.

"They are books…" said Marni looking unimpressed.

"Yes! Jane Austen's best novel," I enthused. "I know that is debate-able, but…"

"Yeah, I'd vote for *Sense and Sensibility*," chimed in Marni.

"I've read all of her books!" said Catt.

"Me too," said Ava.

"I've seen a couple of her movies," said Emma with a smirk.

"Dude… no," said Marni to Emma.

"And these," I continued, "are all the adaptations I have read. As you know, Ms. Lemon gave us all the homework of fixing me this summer. These will help me have the right words to say when someone comes at me, or…" I said.

"Someone came for you?" Emma growled.

"No, not exactly. I'm not explaining well… let me start at the beginning.".

I told them the story of my mom being too loud and obvious about the new cute boys and those guys overhearing, and the stupid Owen guy sneering.

"Oh, Mr. Smug Face!!!" several yelled at once.

"Yes, and the other guy's sister, Brooklyn, total puke emoji, who looked me up and down like I was trash," I said.

"She's dumb. You look so great. I was going to tell you I

thought this whole look was super cute," said Catt.

"Thank you," I smiled. "My point is, I froze, as always, and I am sick of it. As you know, Ms. Lemon told me to channel my heros, the women in Jane Austen's books. They stood up for themselves, they could speak their minds, and in the end, they got the cute guy."

"You could have Collin. He is trying really hard there, El," Emma teased.

"Shut your face," I said, trying to look vicious.

"Oh, yeah, Ava, didn't she try to set you up with Collin last year?" said Marni pointing accusingly at Emma.

"Yes, she did. Poor Collin," said Ava.

"Poor Collin? He has asked out each one of us at some point," I said.

"He has a lot of love to give," said Catt.

"Someone will be quite happy with him. He is not bad; he just wasn't for me," said Ava wistfully, and I knew she had someone else on her mind.

"You are right, he's just not our Mr. Darcy," I laughed. "Speaking of which, I brought these books thinking if we all study what it means to be Elizabeth Bennet, we could figure out how to make me into her. What do you think?" I asked.

"Oh, I like this idea," said Ava, picking up the PD James book. "Jane Austen wrote strong women in a time when femininity with strength was not the norm. Her books were a commentary on the rigid social constructs of the day," said Ava.

"Translation?" asked Marni, looking baffled at what Ava had said.

"She hated the rules," I said.

"Oh, me too. Thank you," smiled Marni, blowing a kiss to Ava.

"If I were Elizabeth Bennet, I would have confidently said,

'There is a stubbornness about me that never can bear to be frightened at the will of others. My courage always rises at every attempt to intimidate me.'" I read from the marked page of my original *Pride and Prejudice*.

"What would that translate to today?" Marni asked.

"You don't scare me, Mr. Smug Face!" said Ava, cracking up along with everyone at her rare joke.

"But wait, how exactly do we turn Ellie into Elizabeth Bennet and get her that internship?" asked Emma.

"Let's do a makeover!" said Catt, continuing to focus on her pedicure.

"Dude, no, the outer Ellie is fine. The inner beast needs to be released," said Marni.

"Inner beast?" I asked, slightly horrified.

"Hey," I yelled as I didn't quite duck the pillow Emma meant for Marni.

"Okay, agreed, that was lame," Marni laughed, "but you know what I mean. She needs to get some inner strength, I mean, she is a Pisces."

"Wait! Pause the convo! Look how cute my toes look! This neon looks awesome. I wonder if it glows in the dark?" said Catt, standing to show her toes to each of us.

"You are aggressively orange, Kitty Catt," smiled Ava.

Ava, the most practical and mature of us all, was curled up in the corner of the sofa. She had a bright smile and soulful eyes and was described by one of the sophomore boys as "curvy-licious," right before Coach Carlson made him apologize and run ten laps. Ava was the first of us to have a boyfriend. They were together for a year until he moved away at the end of seventh grade. I think she still missed him.

"I love it on you," I said.

"Meow," said Catt. "Okay, so unpause. How are we going to unstick Ellie's throat? She's always been this way."

"Not all the time," I said, furrowing my brow.

"Not all the time, just when you get upset or embarrassed, or mad," listed Marni.

"Or nervous," added Emma.

"Okay, okay, I'm a mess. I think if we all study how Elizabeth handled things like rude people, then I can practice," I said. "But first, I need to eat this sandwich! Thanks, Ava, it's awesome."

"You are welcome. I've read the original *P&P*, so I'll take this 'Death Comes to Pemberley' for inspiration," said Ava.

"I will read *Pride, Prejudice and Zombies*, again," said Emma. "I have it at home. You can't beat zombie killing for unleashing your inner beast!"

Emma was our most confident and outspoken friend. She was fun and endlessly courageous. We decided she must have been a warrior in a former life. If I ever had to go into battle, I'd go with Emma. Maybe just slightly behind her.

"I don't want to read those, I want to binge-watch all the movie adaptations, starting with the one where they make out in a gazebo! 'You have bewitched me, body and soul,'" quoted Catt in a terrible British accent with a dreamy look on her face.

"I think this *Unmarriageable* looks good," said Marni, taking the paperback book from the bar, "I can tell it is going to be funny."

"AND, we have plenty of people to practice on. Do you guys remember this summer is when the basketball invitational is hosted by MHS?" asked Emma.

"Yay, a whole county of cute tall boys will converge on us for three weeks!" clapped Catt.

"Nice, we can all practice our flirting and Ellie can work on her confidence at all the summer events, The Big Three... oh this year, it will be the big four with the gala," said Marni.

"Can we not mention the gala for another few weeks? I don't

want to die of a heart attack before I get stronger!" I said.

"Yes, I agree. Sorry I said the 'g-word'," said Marni, "I propose we all read our books and pass on E.B. inspo as we find it. Then, you give a speech every time we meet. Like once a week. Maybe we invite our parents, or better yet, the Stephenson boys, over as you get more confident."

"Ellie doesn't always freak out over boys, that's not the biggest problem," said Catt.

"Yeah, just the ones she likes," Emma agreed.

"Oh, so maybe Mr. Smug…" started Ava, a knowing look dawning on her face.

"Well friends," I said, cutting off that train of thought. Lifting my iced tea I said, "thank you for your help. I propose a toast to having the most amazing summer of our lives! To quote our guru, Jane Austen, 'There is nothing I would not do for those who are my friends.' I think that is from her book *Persuasion*, but whatever, it works. Thank you for helping fix me!"

"To friends," said Ava.

"Here here…" said Emma, toasting back with a rice crispy treat.

"To unleashing our inner beasts!" yelled Catt.

"As Jane would say 'Let's goeth to the pooleth!'" laughed Marni.

5

I was fresh out of the shower and dressed in cut-off jeans and my favorite tie-dye t-shirt. It was the colors of rainbow sherbet. In my bedroom mirror, the lime green at the top made me look extra tan. My hair was drying in curls around my face and I braided the still-damp locks loosely to one side. I noticed the word "hope" backward in the mirror, standing out in bright white across the pink background on my chest. It was perfect for how I was feeling after a day of fun with my friends; hopeful and ready to practice my new attitude. I was brave and fearless. I was undauntable. Unable to be daunted? As I jumped the last two steps, I wondered, "is that a word?" I was about to Google it when the doorbell rang and I jumped again. This time nearly out of my skin because the doorbell was right by my ear.

"So much for bravery," I laughed as I flung the front door open and saw Finn's smiling face right in front of me… and Owen's scowling one, off to the side.

"Oh, um, hi?"

"Uh, hi Ellie, I'm Finn, this is Owen. Um, we met earlier?"

"Oh, I remember," I said, lifting my chin as I side-glared at

Owen, and then, to prove my new undauntablity, I smiled my biggest smile at Finn only. "Yes, hi. Nice to see you again."

"Is Jade home?" asked Finn as he wrung his hands.

My mother came into the hallway and yelled a little too loudly, "Ellie, invite those boys in already, don't be rude."

"Come on in, I'll go get Jade," I said to Finn before I ran up the stairs, leaving both him and Owen in our front hall looking uncomfortable.

"Do you boys want some lemonade?" I heard mom ask as I knocked on Jade's door and went in.

"Didn't you hear the front door?" I asked Jade, then noticed she had headphones on as she was cleaning out her closet.

"What's going on?"

"Finn is here. He stopped by with Mr. Smug Face. He wants to see you."

"Seriously? What does he want?" Jade asked as she ran to her mirror and grabbed her hairbrush. "I mean, oh my goodness, who just stops by people's houses anymore?"

"Does he have your phone number?"

"No, we just met today."

"Exactly," I said.

"Do I look okay?" she asked as I rolled my eyes and handed her the lip gloss from her dresser.

"You look perfect. You just need this."

"Lip gloss is always your answer," Jade smiled.

"And lose the headphones."

"Okay, let's go," Jade said as she turned to me.

"I'm not going down. He asked for you. But, save them from mom, they looked trapped when I came up."

"I will, thanks El," said Jade. I could tell she was nervous and excited. She was a shy person who didn't show her emotions much, but I could tell she really liked Finn. Much like my t-shirt, I had great hope he would be who he seemed to be.

First impressions were usually right.

I went into my room and left the door open because I was dying to know what Finn would say, and why he dragged Owen over, but I refused to act interested.

Group Msg: The Invisibles

Ellie: Not even home an hour and guess who is in my house?!!

Ava: Mr. Smug Face??

Ellie: Yup! Eyes staring wide emoji

Marni: No way!!

Marni: Why? Wait, right there watching you text?

Ava: Perfect time to practice. You are Elizabeth Bennet. He is just a guy, no big deal.

Catt: Yeah, you are cute and smart, and Emma could totally kick his butt if needed.

Emma: I can be there in 5!

Ellie: Lol, I'm in my room, alone! He is here with Finn, downstairs to see Jade. BRB I hear someone coming.

"The guys want me to show them where to get good pizza. Do you want to go?" asked Jade from my doorway with a pleading look on her face.

"No, I don't want to go," I said with my pleading face, or at least I started to when a loud voice whisper-yelled from behind Jade "you are going with your sister, I am not letting her go alone with two boys I don't know."

Coming all the way into my room, mom continued her louder-than-a-yell whispering "They could be ax murderers. Ellie, you are going."

"So, if they are ax murderers, you are sending both of us? I'm not feeling the love, mom."

"Don't be funny, you know what I mean. Now get."

"Okay, lemme grab my phone," I said as I texted.

Group Msg: The Invisibles
Ellie: Now I have to go have pizza with him! scream emoji.
Ellie: More later! puke emoji.

It was awkward being the third wheel in any situation, but the third wheel is not nearly as horrible as being the fourth wheel when the third wheel is a tense, tall, snob who is sitting next to you in the back of his friend's Range Rover. Technically, there was plenty of space, but his long legs seemed to keep creeping to my side of the seat, which made me oddly aware of my hands. I've never thought about where to put my hands before, but suddenly everything I did seemed stupid; lap, too prim; at my sides, too robotty; and way too close to roaming legs. I landed on one on the armrest and one on my lap, hoping to look casual.

Finn and Jade looked so happy talking and even being quiet together in the front seats. Jade was smiling and laughing, and her arm placement looked perfectly normal.

"The pizza place is across town," I said to Mr. SF, trying to be polite and kill the awkward silence.

"It should be quick then, I mean, unless we're ax murdered," he muttered while continuing to look out the window as we turned right onto Main Street toward town.

"He was the proudest, most disagreeable man in the world… and everybody hoped he would never come there again." I smiled as I quoted from *Pride and Prejudice*, also looking out the window at the passing scenery. Two could play that game.

"I'm sorry, did you say something?" Owen asked.

"No, I was just quoting a book I'm rereading."

"You read then?" he asked with a smirk on his face.

I immediately wanted to lash out at his rudeness, but when I looked at his face, I could tell he was trying to tease me. I refrained from ripping his face off for the moment.

"Yes, I'm sure it is shocking to you fancy city slickers, but we small-town folk read the occasional book… and sometimes the big ones without pictures."

He said nothing back. He just studied my face, so I looked away again, but I thought I saw him smile as I did so.

"We are here," said Jade, "Randy's Pizza, our favorite. I hope you like it."

As we parked, I saw Finn leap out of the car to Jade's door to help her out. I, on the other hand, couldn't figure out how to unlatch the seatbelt and when I finally opened the back door, I flopped out onto the parking lot. No help in sight. I pretended nothing happened and hustled to meet the others at the door.

Randy's All-American Pizza was a small place with wooden benches and tables slathered in Americana. Flags and pictures of local servicemen covered all the walls. The smells of wood fire, hand-tossed dough, and oregano welcomed us in. My lab partner, Kim, quickly ushered us to a back booth.

"Enjoy your dinner," said Kim, looking at me with wide eyes and sharply nodding her head for me to come closer to her.

"Hey, how are you? I forgot you hosted here," I said.

"Your date is sooooo hot!" she said way louder than anyone should say anything, ever.

"Kim, shhhhhhh, no, he is not my date. My sister is getting to know the blond guy who just moved down the street. The other one is his friend, not mine."

"Too bad, because wowza. He is like a vampire movie guy, all broody and dark."

"Okay, Kim, gotta order, so bu-bye," I said as I pushed her back to the hostess station.

Of course, the only seat left open at the table was next to Owen. Do boys not sit together in a booth? Ugh, I sat with Owen and tried not to touch legs again.

"Was your friend okay?" Owen asked, trying not to smile.

"Apparently you are swoon-worthy, like a vampire," I said, hoping to shock him somewhat with directness.

"So now I'm a vampire?"

"You seem a little broody, but it is still daylight, so I'd guess not."

I am not sure it shocked him, but I surprised myself. Those words had come out of my mouth before I had a chance to over-think and worry. When I dared to look back his way, he didn't look shocked or surprised but maybe intrigued… or ill at ease, his face was hard to read.

"Why don't you two order since you know the place? Darcy and I will eat whatever you choose, except for anchovies," said Finn.

Jade started talking about pizza toppings, but I wasn't listening.

"Darcy? You are kidding me," I said, stunned.

"That's my last name. Is it funny?" asked Owen, studying my face again.

"Hilarious, actually. Darcy is a character in the book I was quoting earlier."

"Oh, I see."

"Ellie, is sausage and mushroom okay?" asked Jade, interrupting my thoughts.

"Yes, sure," I answered, stunned I was sitting next to Mr.

Darcy, still pretty smug, but literally, "Mr. Darcy." I wanted to message everyone I knew so badly right then.

Most of the conversation was Finn telling us stories of him and Owen growing up and about their fancy school in the city. We laughed a lot, and Jade and Finn seemed to complement each other perfectly. I have always envied my sister's quiet grace, but unfortunately, it wasn't something I possessed.

"So, Mr. Darcy, how long are you staying with Finn?" I asked.

"I'm only here because we have basketball camp here. It would be too far away to drive back and forth to the city every day," said Owen.

"I sense this is not exactly your scene," I asked with a warning raised eyebrow he did not seem to notice.

"Uh, no," he scoffed, looking around. "I'm much more city streets and high rises."

I could feel my throat tighten and my eyes flash at the insult. I looked away from the arrogant smug face to my sister whose eyes begged me not to say anything... and lucky for her, I couldn't. I took a deep breath to calm down and when my throat relaxed I looked at Jade and quoted "My good opinion, once lost, is lost forever." I almost started to laugh when I saw how worried Jade looked that I would snap. The one who should be worried sat there unapologetic and stone-faced.

"Play nice, Darcy. Owen has champagne taste, but I like this town. It's homey and looks perfect to me," said Finn while looking at Jade's lovely face.

I smiled at Finn and crossed my eyes at Jade. I was going to put up with this snobbery for my sister's sake, but I couldn't promise more than civility.

The pizza came and Kim made certain she brought it to the table herself, winking at Owen as she placed it in the middle of the table and served the first piece to him.

Group Msg: The Invisibles

Marni: So?????

Ellie: So much. I can't even.

Catt: Was the pizza bad? JK

Emma: I already heard from Jamie, who got a call from Kim about the hotty you were with.

Ellie: You hear everything! And I know, Kim almost jumped him.

Ellie: More in person, but he thinks the city is so much better. It's not like he lives in New York or Paris. And just when I started to not totally hate him, he is obnoxious again. So arrogant.

Ava: This sounds like the beginning of every good romance novel.

Ellie: Don't even… angry emoji face.

Ava: side kiss emoji face

Ellie: But Jade is so happy. Finn is perfect for her. The world needs more Finns.

Catt: fish emoji fish emoji fish emoji crying laughing emoji

Ellie: Good one Kitty cat! Xxo Going to crash, ttyl

Catt: cat face emoji xxo

Emma: bikini emoji pink hearts emoji xxoo

Marni: Love you guys! Happy moon face emoji stars emoji xxoooxxo

Avi: Nighty Night! xo

6

"Morning, sleepyhead," my mother said as I flopped into my chair at the kitchen table. Mom was humming as she made scrambled eggs to go with the bacon she had already fried. The toast was popping up and Jade was dutifully removing and buttering the slices to add to the small stack of sourdough toast cooling on the white platter.

Across the table, my father put down his iPad and said, "so what is my duty today, dear?"

"I put you in charge of the grill. We are just doing beef burgers and a few veggie burgers. No hot dogs this year. I don't want John Garcia anywhere near the grill. He SMASHED the burgers down last year, can you imagine? Those burgers tasted like hockey pucks," mother said.

"I take the compliment dear," my father, Ben, said, smiling over his glasses at me. "As a professor of English Literature, I am uniquely qualified to undertake the duty of 'Master of the Grill' and I will fight off John Garcia and all his ilk who even stroll near it!"

I poured myself some cranberry juice and took the egg platter from my mom and put it on the table. "How exactly did your English Lit education prepare you for grilling meat, Dad?" I asked, amused, as always, by my father's silly humor.

"Ah, I helped pay my way through school as a short-order cook in a diner. I make a mean patty melt, too," he said, as he bit into the extra crispy bacon.

"The Welcome Wagon members are meeting in the cul-de-sac at 4 p.m. Ben, dear, if you could start the coals then, they should be hot by the time we are ready to cook the patties. Girls, I volunteered you to help serve the food. You only have to stand behind the table and serve until everyone has gone through the line once. The last time we did it freestyle, the Peters family ate all the potato salad before anyone else even saw how pretty I made it. Can you imagine? But they are good neighbors, so the committee let it slide."

Jade looked up at me and we smiled, knowing "the committee" only let something slide once they all ran out of snide things to say about a person.

"Oh, and Jade, the cake says 'Welcome to the neighborhood.' Maybe you should be the one serving it? We won't cut it until the end, almost dark, but we want them to feel welcome," mother smiled and tried to waggle her eyebrows up and down.

I might have groaned at that, except I was still sleepy from spending all yesterday in the pool, getting the first sun of summer. My skin was slightly pink and warm and I felt contentedness in the normal pattern of my family. On Saturday mornings, we usually ate breakfast together. Jade sitting sideways next to me, burrowing her always cold feet between my leg and the chair. Mom shared the local gossip and made sure we were well fed. Dad and I usually spent the morning making faces and raising eyebrows at each other in companionable agreement to find humor in everything.

"El, are you going to be my partner in the water-balloon

toss?" my dad asked, knowing the answer.

"I am ready to crush those lame-os!!" I threw my arms up and roared in exaggerated wrestler fashion, except not as loud, since the sleepiness was still a thing.

The round wooden table, with mismatched cane back chairs, fit nicely in the bay window overlooking our backyard. The view was a yard with lush grass and curved flower beds backed up to a small forest. Well, we called it a forest. It was probably five thin trees deep, but in the summer it blocked our view of a field that was sometimes corn and sometimes soybeans. We had a deck dad built, on which sat a table and chair set. A large red flowery umbrella shaded the entire area, which could be lifesaving on a sunny and humid summer day.

Our yard wasn't large until we got asked to mow it. It might be the only thing Jade and I ever fought over until the miraculous day when dad bought a riding mower and decided we didn't have to do it anymore. Of course, it may have been fun using the riding mower, but I would not volunteer and steal his joy. Besides, he had developed this weird competition thing with the neighbor. We would sit down for breakfast on a Saturday, and if Mr. Peters started his lawnmower, my dad's ears would suddenly perk up and he would start eating faster and say "I better get the grass handled, it's looking a little long," even though he had mowed two nights ago. Mom says it's a "man thing, they are always competing about everything."

That was probably sexist, but it sure seemed to be true about my dad and Mr. Peters. We died laughing a few weeks ago when dad was out mowing, and we caught Mr. Peters practically jumping out of his car after work and onto his mower. I don't get what they win, but they seemed to be vying for something.

By 5 p.m., we had the long folding tables covered in white

plastic tablecloths in a long "L" shape at the end of the cul-de-sac. Mr. Peters had brought us two easy-up tents, so we were not directly in the sun as we served. Families had covered the tables with side dishes and salads and my father was at the grill diligently not smashing the burgers.

The grassy area behind us was being readied for games and the evening air was cooling. This is the time of year when everyone dusts off their lawn chairs and brings them out of storage. Traditionally, people brought enough for their family and a couple of extras, so everyone had a seat arrayed in the open lot under the big oak tree. The chairs were a colorful assortment of neon pinks, greens, and yellows to red, white, and blue plaid, sitting alongside our royal blue set. The chairs were as colorful and varied as the families who occupied them.

"Hi Troy, you are my first customer. How was 5th grade with Mrs. Stephenson?" I asked, filling his plate with deviled eggs and potato salad.

"She was great, I mean, except for the day she made me sit in the corner for letting the frog loose, but still. She was fun. Are you and your dad still going to be in the water-balloon toss?" asked Troy.

"You know it! We have a title to uphold," I said.

"Rats, I thought maybe this was my year," he said dejectedly.

"You can be champion of corn hole... the Lewises have nothing on you!" I whispered as he moved on, looking more hopeful.

"Ellie, why are you so dressed up?" Jade asked me quietly between greeting neighbors.

"Just get prepared to serve the bean salad," I said.

"You girls look beautiful," said Mrs. Norman. "I brought some Waldorf salad. Can I put it here by the potato skins?"

"Yes, ma'am," said Jade, "and thank you so much."

"You know what I mean," Jade looked at me, "you are in a white cotton dress and sandals when you usually wear a t-shirt and shorts. How are you going to play the games?" Jade asked.

"It's cool and breezy and can't a person not look so small town for a minute?"

"Ooooohhh," Jade nodded. "I see."

"You see nothing," I said, pricklier than I had intended. "Speaking of seeing, I see someone practically running this way, looking straight at you," I said to Jade out of the side of my mouth.

"Finn, welcome to the neighborhood. "

"Thank you, Ellie. The others are somewhere behind me, but I was too hungry to wait," he said.

I side-kicked Jade's calf as she stood there frozen, looking at Finn. To be fair, he was just as frozen looking at her, but I couldn't exactly kick him.

Jade jumped and said, "Oh, sorry, the line is getting long. Right, do you want bean salad or potato salad or food?"

"Food would be good," said Finn with a flash of his super white smile.

I was so proud of shy Jade. She blushed and smiled up at him so openly as she served him everything. How could he not be in love with her instantly?

My mother saw this too and elbowed my father so hard in the ribs he flipped a burger right onto the coals. I felt warmed by the look on Jade's face until, from somewhere in the line I heard a singsong "Where is the girl who thinks she has a chance with you?" followed by a deeper "Oh, come on, be nice, she's sort of cute, for a country girl. But can you seriously imagine me with someone from this uncultured small town? Not tempted, thank you very much."

"Even if they were, as you said, 'sort of cute?' teased Brooklyn.

"Oh, really? Uncultured? Country girl? What an arrogant…
" I thought as I saw Mr. Smug Face in the line behind the Garcia family with Brooklyn Bingley, in nearly the same white dress as mine.

I tried not to look at them, but I accidentally locked eyes with Mr. Pompous Smug Face. "No!" my brain screamed. I was so horrified. I did not want him to think I was looking at him. I mean I WAS looking at him, but not looking-looking. It stressed me out so much I missed Mrs. Garcia's plate and dropped the cornbread on the table, making little Natalie laugh and stick her tongue out at me, as usual.

Jade helpfully took charge of the next few plates while I stood there mute, furious, and breaking all of my Elizabeth Bennet rules. I tried to remember my "you can't intimidate me, Mr. Smug Face" quote, but I was feeling hot and blotchy.

"Nice dress," snarled Brooklyn. "I didn't know Walmart was doing a Yves Saint Laurent line this season."

At that exact moment, hyper, naughty, and wonderful little Natalie Garcia turned too quickly with her full paper plate and smacked right into Brooklyn Bingley, smashing a ketchup-loaded burger down the front of her YSL dress.

Natalie looked abashed and backed away slowly, silently mouthing the words, "I'm sorry."

Brooklyn stood like an aghast statue, and oddly, Mr. Smug Face tried to hide a smile while saying, "Come on Brook, it was an accident, go change and come back. Your parents are coming in a few minutes."

"I will NOT be back. This dress is ruined. Why did I ever agree to come to this nowhere town?" Brooklyn yelled.

"It's just a dress and an accident. Come on," Owen said.

With a glare at me, she stormed off.

"Ellie, dear, you are holding up the line," my mother yelled.

I was standing open-mouthed, watching it all like it was in

slow-motion. I wanted to laugh, but I was so angry. "Why did I get glared at?" I dropped the serving spoon I was holding and came to life, trying to shake off my annoyance. I finished serving Mr. Garcia as Mr. Smug Face came up to me in full sneer. Here we go, I thought, it's now or never, though *never* seemed much more appealing. I had a goal and needed to move forward, no more being intimidated.

"My courage always rises at every attempt to intimidate me," I quoted under my breath for courage.

"Pardon me?" Owen asked.

"You no longer intimidate me with your scowling face," I accidentally said out loud.

"I'm not scowling. This is just my face," he answered, somewhat confused.

"Well, you may want to have that looked at. Potato salad?" I said.

His sneer turned into a look of amusement when he said, "Thank you for the advice about my face and for the potato salad."

"You are welcome," I said primly.

Jade raised her eyebrows and looked from Owen to me like she was watching Wimbledon. I felt relieved I had gotten some words out and didn't die on the spot, and triumphant I had been able to use my voice for once. It was a small first step, but I think Elizabeth Bennet would have been proud.

The serving line wasn't nearly as exciting after that. We met Finn's parents, who were much more like him than Brooklyn. They were down-to-earth, sweet, and easy to talk to; I had no idea where their status-conscious snotty daughter came from.

Brooklyn was true to her word; she did not come back to the party, and I was relieved. I even felt like running home and changing into a t-shirt and jeans once dinner was winding down. It was almost time for games to begin, but Mrs. Norman and Magoo came up to chat and I was too busy laughing with them to care about my clothes. Mrs. Norman had a hilarious was of making fun of herself. If we had been girls at the same time she would have for sure been an Invisible and possibly a stand-up comic. Unfortunately, one of her observations about the mowing wars going on between my dad and Mr. Peters made me cackle-laugh, only slightly less embarrassing than the snort-laugh. I glanced around and saw Mr. Smug Face looking at me, but not with his usual sneer. I looked quickly back.

"You do notice that friend of the Bingleys' has his eye on you?" said Mr. Norman.

"He hates me. But he does like to scowl at me. These days I'm trying to be more like Elizabeth Bennet so he doesn't make me so nervous," I said.

"That was my favorite book when I was your age. As I remember, Elizabeth laughed in the face of Mr. Darcy's stuffiness and scowling face. How about you try that? I bet it is just his own social awkwardness. Maybe see his scowl as his defense mechanism?" said Mrs. Norman. "He looks over at you a lot, and trust me, he does not hate you. Good luck and laugh it up."

I could hear Mr. Clark calling for participants and explaining the first game as I kissed Magoo goodbye. It was time for his diabetes shot. Twice a day Mrs. Norman gave it to him, but she said it didn't hurt him at all. Mr. and Mrs. Clark were demonstrating the three-legged race. Jade and Finn were tying their legs together to run it.

Mr. Clark was getting the racers to their mark. My father and mother were nearly falling over already, not even able to stand with their legs wrapped, much less run. Jade and Finn looked to be strategizing. Both blushed heavily as they had to link arms. I loved seeing Jade so happy. It made me wistful for a perfect match like theirs, effortless, exciting and fun.

"Ready, set, go!" The racers all took off, except my parents, who fell immediately, wrestled around trying to get up, then gave up and laughed uproariously. Finn and Jade looked like they had done this together for years. They moved quickly and easily won the race, followed closely by Natalie and her dad.

"Congratulations to Finn and Jade, winner's choice from the trophy table," yelled Mr. Clark through his megaphone.

The "trophy table," as we called it, was a table with a basket of apples, boxes of candy bars, and a box of plastic toys like fake spider rings and even more fake-looking diamond, ruby, and emerald rings, and plastic wind-up cars. I don't know where the Clarks got the odd assortment, but it made it extra fun. I had a collection of the "precious" gemstone rings going.

The next game was starting. It was one for little kids, with the egg on the spoon. People were cheering as I made my way to Jade and Finn at the trophy table.

"Congrats you two," I said.

"That was so much fun!" Finn said.

"I've never won that game before. Never even finished," Jade said.

"Not finished?" Finn asked, amused.

"We've ended up looking like mom and dad before, rolling on the ground, unable to get up," I said. "We are not a nimble family." I laughed as I felt Mr. Smug Face walk up behind me.

"Ah, Owen, did you witness our triumph? You need to get out there mate so you too can have one of these wind-up mini coopers," said Finn as he chose a blue car from the box.

"Maybe I should," said Owen, as I turned to see him standing very close, looking intensely down at me. He was so close I could feel the warmth of him.

I felt the cold panic start to well up at his stare, and then… I snorted. Something about his serious face in the middle of all the levity made me crack up, and, basically, I laughed in his face. I felt bad, and a little loony, but I couldn't help it. Mrs. Norman was right. Elizabeth would have laughed, too. It was supposed to be a silly, fun picnic, not stuffy and serious, and the bewildered expression on his face made me laugh even harder.

"I'm sorry, I am not laughing at you," I said, doubled over, trying to get control of myself.

Jade shrugged her shoulders at Finn in answer to an unasked question, and they both looked at Owen's bemused face.

"Sorry, again, whoo," I said, taking a deep breath and feeling lighter.

"Grab your partners for the water balloon toss," yelled Mr. Clark.

"Welp, this is me," I said, looking across the field for my dad.

"You? I can't toss a balloon to you. I've seen you drop like ten things since I got here," Owen tried to joke, misunderstanding me. "But if you ask nicely, I will partner with…"

"Second daughter, the reigning champion. Where are you?" my dad sang across the lawn, cutting over Owen's attempt to ask me to be his partner.

I realized Owen's mistake, a second before he did, and I felt emboldened. I plucked up one of the super tacky emerald rings from the trophy table and handed it to Mr. Not-So-Smug Face.

"I will be choosing this one," I said, flashing him my most dazzling smile.

It was amazing how good a little confidence felt. "'My confidence DOES rise at every attempt to intimidate me.' Who knew?!" I thought.

As I walked away, I took one last look at Owen Darcy, standing there with a plastic emerald ring in one hand and a too-stunned-to-move expression on his face. I flung off my sandals and walked backward ten paces from my dad for the first toss.

7

Early mornings had always been my favorite time to walk and think. It could probably be considered my therapy, that along with my problematic buying of every hair tie on the planet, and, of course, laughing with my friends. I didn't have anything heavy on my mind, just the desire to enjoy the cool of twilight and to review the picnic and my first step toward becoming like Elizabeth Bennet. Confidence, even temporary, had felt good. Winning the balloon toss with dad again, was great. Plucking the ring from Owen Darcy's hand and leaving him speechless, was even better.

The humidity hovered above the ground like a misty blanket as I entered the wooded trails of Emerson Park behind our subdivision. The muffled quiet of my footsteps on the well-traveled path and the bird song in the branches above welcomed me. I wound my way downhill, getting closer to the playground section of the park. I could hear the babble of the creek in the distance. I smiled as imagined the fun and fear induced by crossing the suspension bridge over the creek and the all too familiar sound of one person begging the other to stop swinging the bridge as they both passed over.

"Stop it, you are making it swiiiiing?!" was a constant refrain and probably could be the town motto.

I was thinking about all the swinging bridge shenanigans as I rounded a hairpin turn, and crashed bodily into Owen Darcy.

"Hey! Ouch," I said, stumbling backward.

"Sorry! Are you okay?" asked Owen as he held onto my shoulders, grabbing me toward him as he balanced us both.

"I think so, but what are you doing?"

"I was running."

"I can see that, but from what?"

"A bear."

"Wait, what?" I asked, looking around alarmed. When I saw the amusement in his eyes, I smacked his chest and stepped back, realizing we were nearly nose to nose.

"Shut up," I said, trying not to smile. "Why do you need more exercise than you are getting at this big training camp?"

"Camp doesn't start until Monday, and I want to be ready," Owen said. "Are you hurt? I really slammed into you."

"I think I'm fine. I can still walk, so if the bear comes back…"

"Where are you headed? I'm a little concerned I am going the wrong way," he confessed.

"It is easy to get lost. I was just going to go down through the swing sets, across the bridge, and circle back up past the little league field. But if you want a quicker way to get back, you can take the road out of the park and to the left," I said.

"I'd kind of like to see the swing sets," he said, grinning.

"Okay," I smiled, and lead the way down the hill. We walked in the stillness for a while. The only sound was my heart, or maybe it was my stomach, skittering. I took a deep, cool breath to quiet my nerves.

"So, how long have you and Finn been friends?" I asked.

"Our parents knew each other in college, and we grew up

51

like family. We go to school together and play on the same basketball team. I guess he is more like my brother."

"And Brooklyn is your girlfriend?" I shocked myself by asking.

"Brook? No, I think when we were six, we had a short fling, but she broke up with me and decided she loved some guy on the Disney channel."

"That's not embarrassing."

"We are like brother and sister, though she is nothing like my actual sister."

"You have a sister?" I asked, and saw a genuine smile of pride spread across his face.

"Yes, Georgie just turned fifteen. She is sweet and smart. She has had some challenges recently, but I am so impressed with her strength for a…"

"If you are about to say 'girl' you might want to start running again."

"For a girl who lives with a couple of men who, what did you call it, 'sneer' a lot."

We smiled at each other as we walked side by side, companionably along the path, avoiding the occasional low branch.

"She sounds great."

"Yesterday was sort of fun. You have friendly neighbors."

"For what do we live, but to make sport for our neighbors, and laugh at them in our turn?" I quoted.

"Who are you quoting in that horrible accent?" he asked, laughing at me.

"I am imitating my father quoting Jane Austen's *Pride and Prejudice*, so it's his bad accent," I laughed, "how dare you mock my father."

"Does your family all quote Jane Austen?"

"I am going to make a very prejudiced assumption. As a guy

and a basketball player, you have never read *Pride and Prejudice.*"

"That is a ridiculous assumption. Just because I am a basketball player and a male, I haven't read it? I'll have you know I am very well read."

I couldn't help smiling when I asked, "But you haven't, have you?"

"Okay, so no," he admitted, which made us both laugh.

"Your name is *Darcy*, for pity's sake," I said.

To his blank stare, I said, "He is one of the main characters, second only to Elizabeth Bennet, who is my current muse." I would never admit he was her love interest. I hadn't forgotten that this Darcy was just as full of himself and I would not give him the satisfaction.

We were nearly at the playground now, an area with huge swings, maybe ten feet tall, with long chains where we spent many days trying hard to make the swing go higher and higher. There were slides of varying sizes, one high with rubber mats below it, one low, one a corkscrew. All metal slides needed the wax paper slicking treatment to make them fun. The wooden teeter-totters we loved to ride up and down when we were little, sat idle in the mist. These all surrounded a covered shelter where I had hidden during sudden rainstorms as a kid and where families sang happy birthday and ate cake before letting their children try the slides.

"This place looks fun," Owen said as he sat on a swing and walked back to get a good start.

I watched him lean forward, then back to get higher. It was strange how relaxed I felt around him. And even more odd that the person swinging joyfully like a young boy, was Mr. Smug Face.

I grabbed the swing next to him and tried to get as high as he was.

"Why do we stop doing these fun things?" asked Owen.

"Maybe because we are too mature now," I laughed as I lay back to gain speed, my ponytail nearly touching the ground.

He slowed down enough to twist his swing tight one way and spin back fast the other way.

"Wow," I laughed, "I can't do that! I'd puke for sure. No! You stay back," I said, giggling and dragging my feet to slow down. I jumped off my swing when I noticed his eyes light up with a plan to twist my swing and test my theory.

"Party pooper," he said.

I walked across a green teeter-totter balancing in the middle before I walked off the other end, and he did the same to the one next to me. The water of the creek was flowing and gurgling a little faster from the recent rain. There were many discussions had in town on whether it should be called a 'creek,' or a 'river,' but if the Mississippi is a river, then this twenty-foot wide body of flowing water is a creek.

"I think you will like this." With a flirty, bold, not-me move, I beckoned him to walk across the suspension bridge with me. He looked both interested and slightly flustered. I did not know I could fluster someone with a crook of my finger. It was very exciting.

"This is one of the most unique things about our town."

I walked backward across the bridge, facing Owen, so I could watch his reaction when the bridge bounced lightly. He grabbed the railing cables and looked up at me in surprise.

"This is so cool."

"Yes, it is. But there is a $5.00 fee for bouncing the bridge, Mr. Darcy, so don't you dare!"

A scared cry pierced through my giggling and we saw a little kid struggling to get out of the creek below us in some small rapids. It was hard to run with two sets of feet beating against the bouncing and flailing bridge, but we made it to the other side and down the embankment. Owen got there first and went straight into the water. A little boy was coughing and spluttering, trying to get up and out of the water, but was being knocked down again and again. He was getting tired and having trouble getting up. It looked as if he had tried to get his bike, which had since landed on a patch of large rocks midstream where it was stuck, tires spinning ineffectively.

Owen waded into the stream until it was past his knees by the time he reached the exhausted boy. He grabbed the boy and carried him to the bank. Owen handed him over to me so he could wade back in and get the bike. I pulled the soaking, coughing boy up onto the bank and sat next to him, patting his back, not knowing how to comfort him. The boy was still coughing and trying to not cry, as he seemed embarrassed to have to be saved. Owen made his way through the creek to get the bike and drag it out to safety as well. His added height and weight made the fast water safe to navigate, but it still pulled at him as he carried the bike back to the shore.

"Here you go bud, I think it's going to be just fine. Only a few scratches," said Owen whose white t-shirt was now soaking wet and clinging to his muscular shoulders and stomach.

"What is your name?" I asked, dragging my eyes reluctantly away from Owen.

"Ronnie. I'm okay, only scraped my hands on the rocks," he said between coughs.

"Do you live close by, Ronnie?" Owen asked.

"Yeah, just up there. Are you going to tell my mom?"

"What happened?" I asked.

"I wanted to go to the swings, but I didn't want to cross the bridge," Ronnie confessed.

"Oh, it's kinda scary?" I asked with agreement written on my face.

"Yeah," he said as he stood up and took stock of his clothes. "umm…thanks for saving me…my bike," Ronnie directed at Owen.

"Do you want to try something before we walk you home? How about you and I take your bike across the bridge and see if we can do it with zero swinging? You want to try?" asked Owen.

I smiled, impressed Owen was so thoughtful with this young boy and willing to help him overcome his fear.

The duo walked together as I watched. I didn't remember noticing before how tall Owen was, but next to the small child, he looked like a super hero. It was so sweet to see the look of hero worship on Ronnie's face as he gazed up at Owen and hung on his every word. I continued to watch them as together they walked gingerly, at first, across the bridge one way and then a little less so on the way back. It surprised me at how quickly Ronnie crossed the bridge by himself. All the while, Owen coached him. He even jumped once on his final, alone lap. The two of them laughed and joked about that jump move all the way past the little league field and up to Ronnie's house.

After getting a promise he would stay out of the creek, we said goodbye to Ronnie, leaving him to explain his wet clothes to his bemused mom.

"You did a great job with him," I said once we were alone. "I was impressed."

"It scared me, I hate to admit," he said, his face set in a worried, yet determined look. "Something I didn't tell you about my sister. We've always been close, but since our mother died, I have been worried about stuff like that. Like her drowning in a creek, or getting kidnapped, or anything happening to her and me not being there to help her."

We walked for a few minutes in silence, crossing behind the baseball field toward the back path to our subdivision. Before we entered the woods I stopped and looked at him. "Owen, your sister is really lucky to have you watching over her. I am sure your mom would be proud," I said watching pain and stress briefly cross his face.

He stepped closer to me. I was motionless, but falling into his sad hazel eyes. He tucked a loose strand of hair behind my ear and cupped my face so softly. He leaned down and kissed me. I felt his full lips press against mine and I accidentally let out a little sigh. Almost before my brain comprehended what had happened, it was over. He pulled away and kept walking.

I didn't know what to say. "Hey, thanks for the kiss. Unexpected, but nice?" I started walking, too, but I was hoping for a sign from him of what to think, but I got nothing. He seemed unphased as usual.

The sun was fully up, and the mist had disappeared as we walked in silence. The trails were less steep and, for the first time, seemed shorter than I remembered. We emerged behind the Abramses' house. We weren't supposed to cut through their yard, but we always did. If Mrs. Abrams was outside, she gave us the disapproving pursed-lip look that served her well for years as an elementary school teacher. Usually, Mr. Abrams was the one outside when I passed and he just said, "good morning Ellie," from under his car hood, in his usual jocular manner.

This morning was no exception. I was so glad he was there to prove I do this walk all the time. I hadn't been out walking, hoping to pass by certain people playing basketball, hoping for random out of the blue kisses from really soft lips.

Why does this guy make me so paranoid? He kissed me. So what? People do it all the time, Right? It's a friendly gesture. Like a handshake. No big deal.

"It's been an eventful morning," said Owen, breaking the silence. "I'd really like... "

"Owen! I have been looking for you," said a voice I had learned to dread. I hadn't realized we were at the Bingley house already.

"I better go…" I tried to say at the same time he said "Would you like to…"

But we were cut off by an insistent and rather whiny "Oweeeen, mommy has made us a big breakfast before we go into the city and you need to get showered, you are soaked," she said as she took his arm like a lady in an old-fashioned movie, smoothly walking him toward the door. "Thank you for driving me. It will be so fun," Brooklyn said to him while turning to look disdainfully back at me.

"Okay, I'll just head home now. No need to thank me for showing you the way back, no problem. Nice randomly kissing you, too. Bye." I mumbled to myself as I made my way home alternately, smiling and panicking.

I pulled out my phone intending to message everyone, but I put it back. I was more confused than ever and needed time to think.

"Did that really just happen?"

8

Group Msg: The Invisibles

Marni: Summer Market day! Woo hoo!
When are we meeting?

Ava: I saw them setting up this morning,
all our fav food trucks are there!!

Ellie: I'm going to eat my way around the square,
so meet close to lunch?

Emma: Perf, 1 p.m. at the Holey Ones? Donut Emoji
Dancing lady emoji

Ellie: Classic Emma! Donuts first! Donut Emoji

Catt: Yay! I want to find the jelly guy, I need that hot
pepper jelly, its yum-o!

Marni: El, you want to pick me up on your way?

Ellie: checkmark emoji sidekiss face emoji

While we were enjoying our warm donuts and ice-cold tea, our reflection in the window of the Quilting Emporium looked like a billboard featuring typical teenagers. I was standing, and Ava and Catt were sitting on the wooden bench seat. Emma and Marni perched one-cheeked on the bench arms. We were girls with messy buns and braids; wearing colorful shorts, overalls, and sun dresses; carrying market bags and backpacks, and wearing sneakers and flip-flops. All talking, eating and laughing. I took out my phone to capture the moment. The picture of our reflection looked distorted, but I loved it. It illustrated that we went together perfectly even with our individual styles.

I continued to wear several hair bands and bracelets on my left wrist though the trend went out awhile ago. I felt naked without them because my theory had always been if there were a zombie apocalypse, I would need to tie my hair back immediately. Keith, in my Chem. class, said my logic was stupid as there would be other things to worry about, like running for your life. He only thinks that because he has short hair. Long-haired people get it. You couldn't think of running or fighting or whatever if your hair keeps getting in your face. Anyway, I didn't hope for a zombie attack just to prove I was right, but the affirmation might have been nice.

"So, I have something to tell you guys," I blurted out, failing to sound as nonchalant as I had intended. I threw my napkin and teacup away to stall for a second. "It's not a thing, but I saw Owen yesterday at the park."

"Who is Owen?" asked Emma, rising to continue our walk around the town square.

"Mr. Smug Face," Ava said, also standing.

"Oh, it's '*Owen*' now? Tell us everything! Did you ask his birth sign?" demanded Marni.

"I thought we hated him," said Catt, puzzled.

"We do, for sure, but we hate him slightly less... and all because of Elizabeth Bennet... heretofore referred to as Lizzy, my champion," I said. "She is helping me stay calm and say what is on my mind."

"She is like your Sasha Fierce," said Emma.

"Who…" started Marni.

"Beyonce's alter ego," answered Ava and Emma at the same time. 'Jinx!" they each yelled.

"Oh, pause right there. Forget nothing. I want to hear every detail. But I love these candles. Can we stop here real quick?" Marni asked.

As we smelled every candle, even the froot loops cereal flavored one, and the bonfire and honey one, I noticed we were being watched by a group of guys at the next stand. They were fake looking at jars of jelly and jams. It made me smile. They thought they were so discreet. A wall of tall and cute joined us at the candle table.

"Oh hey, how is that cereal-flavored one? I'd like to get one for my mom," said the bravest of them to Marni.

"It's good, but I think a mom would like something less kid-like. What about this basil and lavender one?" she asked as she handed it to him and smiled brightly.

He smelled it and said, "my name is Denny, and these are my friends, Eric, Mike, and Kyle. We are from Adams. What are your names?"

Marni introduced everyone with an ease I admired. "Do you guys want to walk around the square with us? We are eating our way from one side to the other… next stop, Terror Tacos." And to me, she winked and whispered, "in my book, EB is bold and ladylike."

"Noted, I take the lesson," I smiled back.

"They are better than the name sounds," Emma smiled at Kyle as she seemed to walk with a bit more of a sway.

"Hey guys, I'll catch up. I see some hair bands I need to look at," I said as I spied some cute ones out of the corner of my eye. Everyone seemed to be absorbed in the newcomers. Ava looked at me and mouthed, "you want me to come?"

I shook my head "no" and waved her on with a smile, happy

to make a quick detour alone. The vendor was a young mom with her baby strapped to her front in one of those colorful cloth wraps. She had an earthy artist vibe about her and her products were all handmade and organic. She had made more of the wraps she was using for the baby, the headscarf she was wearing, as well as turbans, headbands, neck gaiters, and hair bands. I loved the feel of them and was having trouble choosing when I heard, "I think the blue one would go well with your eyes." The artist and I looked at each other, both smiling warily for a moment before I turned my head and saw it was Collin, from school, who had spoken.

"Hey Collin, thanks. Um, my eyes are brown, but blue is nice," I said.

"They are just so pretty, your eyes, I mean, they could be any color. And anything would look nice on," he gushed. "Can we ummm…"

"Thank you. I'll just finish with this so I am not holding her up," I said. I felt my stomach clench, knowing I would have to balance not encouraging Collin and also not hurting his feelings.

"Do you want to get a boba drink with me?" he blurted loudly, "and then, uh, we could just hang out?" Collin asked.

I handed the artist the money for the two bands I was buying and thanked her. She looked at me and asked with her eyes if I was fine. I nodded I was and smiled.

"Thank you, Collin, so much, but I am not alone, I am here with… "

"Me!" said a confident voice from the crowd. A very tall and extremely handsome boy put his arm around my shoulders. His beaming smile warmed me from head to toe, and I smiled back.

"There you are," I managed to ad-lib. "I go to school with Collin. We are old friends."

"Hi, Collin. My name is Declan Wickham. Thank you for watching over my girl here. Maybe we will catch you later," he said as he walked us away from poor Collin.

I felt bad for a second, but walking through the town square with a super cute guy was new for me and I liked it. I hoped everyone from school would see me, but I couldn't look away from this charming guy long enough to check. How did someone our age have so much swagger? It baffled and intrigued me.

"You are welcome for the save," he paused with a question in his eyes.

"Oh, it's Ellie," I said as I stopped walking to look up at Declan. "Thank you. He is harmless, but thank you. Are you in town for the basketball camp?"

"I'll have you know, this is not just a basketball camp, it is the best of the best. And in case you are wondering, you are looking at the actual best, my lady," Declan said, taking his arm from my shoulder to bow.

"No need to bow, sir, this damsel was not in all the much distress," I laughed, "but I apologize for not knowing the greatness of my rescuer. I'm a little more used to the Shrek kind," to which he laughed a deep, hearty laugh, making me blush in delight.

This guy is so outward and charming. Too bad all good-looking young men didn't take a lesson from Declan. This guy would never kiss you and walk away, leaving you confused.

"My friends were all heading to the taco truck. Shall I buy you a taco as a reward?" I asked.

"I would love to meet the ladies of Meryton. I assume you go to school there?" Declan asked.

"All of us since kindergarten," I answered.

"That's cool. I have moved around too much for a close group of friends. Not sure I'd like everyone knowing my business," Declan said quietly, then lit up with a smile, when Catt began waving at us from the empty table she was saving.

"Hi, I'm Catt, not like meow, like Catherine. We just ordered; do you guys want to eat with us?" Catt said in her usual exuberant jet-stream of words.

"Hi Catt, I'm Declan, and yes to tacos."

"Yay!" said Catt. "Oh, here they come."

"Hey everyone, this is Declan, and you met Ellie." Catt introduced him to everyone as they came back with their taco plates.

"Declan? Declan Wickham? You play for Belmont, right? Nice to meet you, man. You were up for All-State," said an impressed Kyle.

"Best jump shot in the state, ladies. This here is a stud," said Denny, shaking Declan's hand.

"I owe you your reward. So I can go order if you want to stay and talk to these guys," I said, though, in the back of my mind, I was not sure Lizzy would have approved. It felt like I shouldn't be offering, maybe because old me would have done it, but what is the harm in being nice?

"Sure, thanks. It all looks good. And a root beer," Declan said, fully engrossed in the discussion of basketball.

"Mine isn't ready yet. I'll come with you," said Ava.

Ava is the friend who knows when you need help or want to talk, even before you know it yourself. I could tell she was keen to hear how I happened to be walking up with the hottest guy on the square.

"Before you ask, literally out of nowhere," I answered.

"Haha, I assume that is the answer to 'Where did you meet THAT guy?'" said Ava.

"Yup, seriously I was buying these hair bands when Collin—"

"Oh Collin," she sighed.

"I know. Then Declan popped up like he was my boyfriend, put his arm around me, and we walked this way."

"Wow, your smile!"

"I know. I feel pathetic, one touch made me feel giggly and proud," I said, blushing. "Don't tell the others how lame I am. I don't want to hear it from Emma all summer."

"I won't, but I get it. It's fun AND we only just started our new pact. Maybe there is some strong Jane Austen mojo happening," Ava said.

"You just used the word mojo," I laughed.

"I know. I think Marni got me using it. Oh, so what was it you wanted to tell us earlier before we got sidetracked by boys? It was about Owen Darcy."

I had ordered a taco plate for Declan and a couple of chicken tacos for me and some root beer when Ava's fish tacos were finally done.

"Oh, yes, Mr. Smug Face… well… it's a long story, but… the version we have time for now is: I was on a walk at the park, he literally ran into me. We walked over the swinging bridge, a little boy almost drowned, Owen saved him, we walked the little boy home, Owen kissed me, then Brooklyn Bingley stared death daggers at me again, the end."

"Whoa. He kissed you?" asked a shocked Ava. "What happened after? Was it nice? Do you like him now? Are you going to date him? We need to analyze the heck out of this!"

"Okay, okay, I know. It is a lot, and we will. It mostly just confused me, but not now. First, eat and smile at boys. Later, stories of other boys," I laughed.

"Wow, all these men, what would Elizabeth Bennet say?" laughed Ava.

Using the worst British accent ever, I quoted Lizzy "I am excessively diverted."

9

Group Msg: The Invisibles

    Ava: Anyone here yet?

    Catt: In line buying ride tickets. Yay! I think I see you.

    Marni: Come this way when done. I'm in the middle
            by the Ferris wheel.

    Ellie: Almost there, Jade dropping me off. Meet you
          at FW in 5.

"Bye, love you," I said to my sister as I jumped out of Finn's Range Rover. "Finn, be nice to my sister, but don't let her eat all your popcorn!"

"Have fun, and promise you'll call us if you need a ride home!" said Jade.

"Will do, I promise, no worries. I see one of my friends getting out of his car now, and Marni said they are waiting by the Ferris Wheel. I'm good."

I waved them away with a smile, but I understood why Jade was being a worrywart. She felt about carnivals like I felt about clowns. I think it's normal to be creeped out by clowns, but not carnivals. Turning toward the bright lights, the waves of screaming and laughter, and the potent smell of bad culinary decisions, I smiled at the promise of fun and corn dogs.

"I hope that smile is for me," said Declan as he walked my way.

"Yeah, I saw you parking," I said, but couldn't bring myself to say, "and I was excited about corn dogs."

"You look cute," said Declan, looking at me a little more like a steak than I was used to, but it was flattering. "I like the daisy dukes."

"They are not that short. Let's head this way," I said, feeling giddy.

Declan was wearing jeans and an aqua t-shirt that hugged his chest and made his green eyes even more alluring. I was not comfortable thinking the word "alluring," it seemed like those "studious person" words Catt and Emma mocked me for using. Alluring... luring me to something like a predatory cat of the wild... "oh, sorry, what?" I said, coming back to earth.

"Was that Finn Bingley's car you got out of?" he repeated.

"Yes, he and my sister are going up to the Rat Hole to see a movie," I said. "You know him?"

"He is friends with an ex-friend of mine... wait, did you say, 'Rat Hole?'" he looked down at me in puzzlement.

"Oh, funny. I didn't even realize I said it. Rat Hole is what we all call the movie theater in town. The Royal Theater. It's a dump, but the popcorn is great," I rambled. "Let me text Marni and say we are here."

"Are you having fun at camp?"

"Yeah, and most of the guys are cool. It's keeping me in shape, which means I can't eat any of this," he said as he pointed to the stand serving fried Oreos.

"Oh, no! Gross food is the whole point of being here," I smiled as we found our group.

"Hey dudes! Finally. I'm having trouble restraining Catt. She is going to explode if she doesn't get on the tilt-o-whirly thing," said Marni.

"Hey Declan, what's up?" said Mike, "Hey, Ellie."

"Hey, guys!" I said, hugging my girls. "Where is Emma?

"Emma is coming. She said to start without her," said Marni.

"Where do we get tickets?" I asked.

"I got a bunch here, my buy this round, you can get the next. Here is one for everyone, let's goooooo!" Catt grabbed Mike by the hand and started running to the line. Marni followed with Ava, Eric, Denny, and Kyle.

"Your friend is feisty," laughed Declan.

"Oh yeah, she is tiny and mighty. All my friends are fairly feisty, at least about food and carnival rides."

"So how does your sister know Finn?"

"He just moved to our neighborhood. Do you know his sister?" I asked.

"Whose sister?" he asked defensively.

"Finn's sister, Brooklyn. I met her too. She is not nice like he is," I said as we sat in an empty car and Declan pulled down the lap bar.

"And we met his friend, Owen Darcy. I am not sure about him yet. I can't figure him out."

"Whoa, ahhhhhhhhhhh!" I screamed as the ride jerked to life and launched me bodily into Declan.

This was not the flirting style I had been going for. Our car was spinning so fast I couldn't pull myself off of him. My face was smooshed into his very well-developed bicep, covered by a very soft aqua t-shirt. I was ugly-laughing and going to drool down his arm any minute if I couldn't catch my breath and peel my face off of his arm. Please don't let anyone be filming us. I was going to have to kill Catt. I hated this ride. At least Declan was laughing too and seemed equally paralyzed. Then we spun up a hill, down a hill, and finally, we spun the other way. I was relieved to be upright in the seat, but I was holding on with all my strength so I could stay that way. Glimpses of Ava and Marni spun past, and I could hear Catt. Everyone seemed equally out of control and giggly as the ride slowed.

"Oh my goodness, I can barely breathe. Sorry, it plastered me against your arm."

"You can be plastered against me anytime," Declan said with a grin as cheesy as that line.

"Shut up," I said, laughing. I turned my face away, looking over at my friends, so I didn't have to look up into his face. His interest in me was flattering and overwhelming. Something about him didn't feel genuine, but he was so cute and confident I just assumed it was me being nervous.

"I can help clear up the mystery of Owen Darcy. He is spiteful and jealous, and it cost me a lot," said Declan as the ride now stopped and the lap bar released us.

"Really? I'm sorry, what happened?" I asked.

"Long story short, my father used to work for Mr. Darcy and when dad died unexpectedly, Mr. Darcy honored him by starting a scholarship program to send a student through private high school and on to the university of their choice. I was the first recipient of his scholarship.".

"Oh, wow, I want to hear the rest of this," I said as we got off the ride. "Should we take a walk, or do you want to tell me on the next ride?"

"So much fun!" said Ava smiling and breathless, "I was flinging everywhere!"

"I know, me too," I said, still a little embarrassed about the arm smoosh.

"Ferris wheel next," yelled Catt, "I still have tickets! Let's gooooooo!"

"Mike, do you need saving?" Ava asked.

"No, she's fine. If she gets too much, I will just pick her up," he said and allowed himself to be dragged.

We joked and laughed and pointed out all the games and rides we would do next as we made our way through the midway.

"Emma is missing it all, but she is coming after she helps Phillip, so we can ride again with her," said Catt.

"Is Phillip her boyfriend?" asked a suddenly forlorn-looking Kyle.

"No, ewwww, he is old, and he is my brother," answered Catt.

"He is not old, he is in college, but they have been friends since they were little, family friends," Ava answered.

Kyle looked happier at that response.

"Catt you are ridiculous, and I am telling Phillip you called him old," I said, looking up at the Ferris wheel that suddenly looked scary and too tall.

As we got in line and I heard the grating voice of Amber Raine, and her gaggle of friends piling off the ride. Amber sashayed our way, eyes locked on Declan, but speaking to me.

"Little miss nervous Nellie, going on the big kid ride?

I wanted to snap back, but with the whole group looking at me, words froze in my throat. My finger nails dug into my hands trying to pry open my voice. I squeaked, "move on Amber."

But she had locked her cobra stare on Declan, and my voice floated into nothing. I heard her purr "come play with the big girls when you get bored here," as Amber sashayed and into the midway.

"Dibs on the green car… it's my favorite color. Who is with me?" Marni asked trying to break the spell.

"I am," said Denny.

"Ava, will you and Kyle go first in the yellow one, please, behind Catt and Mike? It matches your outfit, and your undertones," begged Marni.

Before jumping into the green car with Denny, Marni whispered in my ear, "ignore her, she was just jealous that you were with a cute boy and she had no power over you, typical Scorpio, seriously, let it go."

Declan watched Amber walk away and nearly got the smirk off of his face by the time he looked back at me and we could load into a bright blue car.

I was sort of hoping Declan would say something about Amber's rudeness. Hoping he would say he hated girls like that, that she was gross and he couldn't imagine being with someone like her (perfect, confident, and not even slightly awkward), but he said nothing and just smiled at me as our cart jerked us upward.

"You explained you got the scholarship. And that Owen is spiteful," I said, starting where we left off.

"Yes, he is."

He seemed to look for the right words, or maybe more like he lost his place in a speech, but then he turned his mesmerizing green eyes on me and continued the story.

"Owen Darcy can't handle anyone being better than he is at anything. He has all his daddy's money and his father does whatever he can to cover for his son's weaknesses. So, since he could not match me on the court, his dad took away my scholarship to Pemberley so I couldn't play basketball there and had to go to Ben Davis. He also made up lies about me and suddenly my college scholarship is gone, too," Declan said.

"No way, that is horrible," I said. "He sneers a lot."

"Yes, he does. It's just because he thinks he is too good for other people. He must hate this small town, not a bunch of rich people, and not under his father's control," he said with disgust and I felt proud that he felt he could tell me his story.

"Helloooo Ellie and Declaaaannn," yelled Marni from the top of the circle as the ride slowed and our car gently swayed with the motion of our waves. We were in the front heading backward to the top and I finally took a moment to look out over the lights of the carnival and further beyond to the fairgrounds where 4-Hers were setting up the animal pens for next week's county fair. The light breeze was warm and up here smelled less like fried food and the Ferris wheel motor, and more like fresh grass and the sweet lambs being tucked in their pens for the night. I had never lived around farm animals, so seeing them each year at the fair, especially the lambs, was my favorite part of the summer.

"Hellllllooooooo Ava and Eric," I yelled down at them when we were on the top. "Helllloooo world," I added and said, "yell with me," to Declan, and he did "Helllooooo World! Woo hoo!"

It was dumb, but exhilarating. I felt the elation of good friends and cute boys and the possibilities for the best summer ever. I was ignoring the confusion over Mr. Smug Face making me think he was nice for a second. It made little sense. He had seemed full of himself, but the way he had treated the little boy, Ronnie, was so genuine. They say your first impressions are right, don't they? Anyway, corn dogs and cotton candy, and Declan's green eyes were reason enough to be excited. I had no room for smug-faced people in my brain.

The boys all went to play the basketball game, and I finally got the corn dog I had been craving. I had no idea why I loved having a corn dog at the fair. I loved the tang of the mustard and the gritty texture of the corn batter, but the challenge of eating it without getting clothes-ruining mustard on me made it must-do fun. Marni making me laugh while biting into the most mustardy part added to the challenge, but my Malibu t-shirt remained baby pink, not a yellow spot in sight. After corn dogs, we walked to the merry-go-round and chose the prettiest horses to ride.

"So Catt, you and Mike look like you are having fun," I said.

"He seems nice, and he really likes you," Ava said.

"Emma threatened his life, so I know he is, at least, brave," Catt laughed. "But he is nice to me and fun. I just do not want a boyfriend in high school. Emma and I agreed "no boyfriends until college."

"Really?" asked Marni. "But what about all the gazebos and romance you always talk about? Don't you want that now?"

"In my mind it is fun, but it isn't very real. Teenage boys don't say those things irl," said Catt.

"Except maybe Declan. He is Mr. Smooth, eh?" said Ava. "How do you like him, Ellie Bean?"

"He is sooooooo cute. He is almost too perfect looking," said Catt.

"I wonder if he is a Cancer? I can't get a read on him yet," said Marni.

"He is cute, right? And he is fun. He said some things about Owen, Mr. Smug Face. I should have trusted my first impression," I said.

"What things?" asked Marni.

"These rides are never long enough," I said as the ride slowed down and people got off their horses. "Remind me on our pool day, and we can obsess about it. I need to think about it some more."

"We are getting quite a list pushed to discuss later," said Ava shooting a quizzical look at me.

"There is Emma!" Marni yelled.

"Let's take her back on the Tilt O' Whirl and smash her!" yelled Catt excitedly.

10

"Hey lovelies, check out this patriotism," said Emma as she flashed us her new red, white, and blue bikini. "Uncle Sam never looked so good."

"I think it is safe to say you're right," I answered, smiling at Emma's antics. She was the most confident of us all. She was always driven and smart and clear on her path in life.

"That looks so cute on you. And you are almost covered," teased Marni.

"My dad only let me buy it because I promised I was only going to wear it here with you guys," said Emma.

"Who is he kidding? Your dad lets you do anything," said Marni, "I had my back tooth filled with him a few weeks ago, and he is still telling everyone you are coming into the practice with him and Phillip. You could probably ask for a car right now and he would give it to you."

"Yeah, Phillip is always "blah blah when Emma comes to work with us. We can provide a much broader range of patient care. Blech, what does that even mean?" Catt said. "He isn't even in dental school, but he tries to act like he is a real dentist already."

"Your brother and my dad may be excited, but it is going to be a long time from now. I still have all of college and dental school and then residency... this is like an eleven-year plan, though I am going to get it done in nine. Meanwhile, you are all still dry," said Emma as she cannonballed from the decking into the pool, soaking everyone.

"Emma Marie, my magazine!" yelled Catt. Now I will never know who my perfect love match is!"

"I think his name rhymes with Shmike," I teased from under my big Panama hat as I floated in the old pontoon chair in the middle of the pool, riding the wake of Emma's cannonball.

"But now I will never know for sure. I asked him. He is a Taurus. I am not sure if they are a good match with Gemini. He doesn't seem too stubborn," Catt mumbled sleepily in the afternoon sun.

"Gemini and Taurus are a good match, but not your greatest match. You need an Aries man for that," said Marni, our guru.

"Hi guys, are any of you awake?" asked Ava as she entered the backyard with a young girl wearing a bright purple and white polka dot bathing suit. "This is my cousin, Fallon. She is staying with me this summer and is excited to hang out with us, right, Fallon?"

Fallon looked like she was anything but excited. She looked like she might start crying and run away any second. But she bravely looked around and caught my eye, peeking out from under my hat.

"Hey Fallon, I'm Ellie. How old are you?"

She looked toward Ava who nodded encouragement, "I'm eight and a half."

"Perfect, I am the boss of the floaties. And eight and a half is old enough to use one. You want the big flamingo?"

"Not fair," teased Catt. "You never let me use the flamingo."

"Because you are not well behaved," I said, teasing the

truth. "That's Emma, she is sorta the boss of all of us. She will help you get on it," I said pointing to Emma who was treading water, though she could easily stand and touch the bottom.

Fallon looked shyly at the imposing Emma, who warmed her with a genuine smile. Emma was tough, but not on underdogs, and Fallon seemed to be just that.

Ava mouthed "thank you" and I smiled and gave her a thumbs up.

"So, Fallon, do you like gummy worms?" said Marni, offering the candy bag. "In a bit, we can have lunch. Turkey and cheese sandwiches, Cheetos, and iced tea. Does that sound good?"

"Yes, thank you," said Fallon, biting the next color section on the gummy worm.

"Don't say lunch," I groaned.

"Since when are you not ready for lunch?" asked Ava as she put her towel on the wooden deck between Catt and Marni.

"She is pouting because I told her after lunch she will give us her first speech of the summer," Marnie said. "It is impromptu, so you don't even have to prep."

"But first, forgive me, Fallon, I am going to corrupt you with boy talk. I have to ask my friend there a question about a cute boy. Are you ready to see if she blushes? Look at Ellie's face and see," said Marni.

"You are so dramatic, don't corrupt people," I said as I flung water with the back of my hand toward her.

"Denny said most of the guys are going home after camp today for the long holiday weekend, but he said it sounded like Declan was going to stay for the '*fireworks,*' and yes he said it all air-quotey, like that," said Marni pointedly to Ellie.

"You know we aren't a couple," I said, glaring at Marni and checking to see if Fallon was listening. The big pink flamingo glided past with a still nervous, but smiling Fallon sitting atop and a water-treading Emma piloting below.

"We just talk easily. Usually about him."

"Well, he seems to think it's moving forward," said Marni.

"Oh, I totally forgot!" I yelled and scared everyone awake, including myself. "I never told you what Declan said about Mr. Smug Face!"

I launched into the entire story about Owen's jealousy and how he got his dad to stop giving Declan the scholarship named in honor of Declan's father.

"Can you believe it? Isn't that so petty?" I asked.

"Mike says Declan is really good," said Catt.

"Denny said Finn and Owen are good, too, just not showy like Declan, no offense," said Marni. "He is rather impressed with himself."

"Can we be sure Owen did it? It doesn't seem to fit, even for someone we are currently hating," asked Emma.

"I don't know why he would lie, though. He has nothing to gain, really," I said. "And besides, just because someone is maybe a little cute and seemed normal for a second, doesn't make them normal," I said to puzzled faces.

"Did you just call Owen Darcy 'maybe a little cute?'" asked Ava with her knowing smirk.

"No, ewwww, you have a wild imagination, Ava."

"Oh, you guys. Finn is so cute with Jade. He bought her a big stuffed bear and gave it to her last night. I guess she had said she liked his cologne so sprayed one of his T-shirts with his cologne and put it on the bear... for her to snuggle," I said.

"Nice change of subject, you," smirked Ava, "but that is sweet. Is she crazy about him?"

"You know how shy she is, but I can tell she is a smitten kitten," I said.

"Meow," said Catt from behind her wet magazine.

Fallon surprised herself and accidentally laughed out loud

at Catt.

I smiled and said, "she meow's a lot."

"Okay, so we haven't talked about Kyle," I said, looking at Emma.

"He nearly came unglued when Catt said you were with Phillip," laughed Marni, turning over on her towel.

"You what?" growled Emma.

"I said you were with my brother helping him and I said 'Ewwww he was old' and that seemed to make him smile again," explained Catt.

"He likes you, clearly, but what do you think of him?" asked Ava.

"Which one, Phillip or Kyle?" I laughed and then realized my mistake as Emma lurched toward me to tip me off my floating chair.

"So much for keeping my hair dry," I said as I emerged from the bottom of the pool and put my now-soaked hat on the pool deck.

"Is this violence what you are learning from your studies of *Pride and Prejudice and Zombies*?" teased Ava.

"I was going to bring it today to read. Glad I didn't since, for some reason, we are all soaking wet," said Emma.

"The book is brilliant. I had forgotten how bad-ass, sorry Fallon, the zombie hunting and training were and how well Seth Grahame-Smith stays with Austen's same themes. Female roles are being challenged by society and by their love relationships."

"My takeaway is this particular Elizabeth is fearless and goes after what she wants. She trains really hard, so in the end, fighting comes easy. So, Ellie, I think you should just go after your internship full force, and visualize cutting off the head of your anxiety like it is a zombie," said Emma.

"Gross," mumbled Catt.

"I love it. I will definitely practice visualizing zombies," I said, wringing out my hair. "Now what about Ava's question, Miss Evasive?"

"Takes one to know one," said smiled Ava.

"Kyle, is nice and fun to hang out with right now. And he is tall and very good looking, but I still don't want a serious relationship until college, or maybe dental school. I don't need the distraction. I won't dignify your implications about Phillip, with an answer, Miss Funny Pants. He and Catt have been family forever. We are friends and we have a lot in common, and he is easy to talk to," said Emma.

"Yup, Emma and Phillip talk smart people stuff all the time, blech. And we agree, no serious boyfriends until college, just lots of dates and kisses!" said Catt.

Again, Fallon giggled at Catt.

"Sorry, Fallon, no smooching boys for you until you are at least twenty-five!!" said Ava.

Fallon was wide-eyed at the idea she would ever be part of a conversation about smooching.

"At the risk of getting closer to my terror, is anyone else dying of starvation? My mom sent your favorite no-bake chocolate cookies," I sang.

"Shut up!!!" yelled Catt and Marni together as they scrambled off their towels and down the stairs. Marni's lime tankini streaked past me in a flash. Emma handed Fallon out of the pool to Ava, and I peeled my legs off the decking, leaving funny wood stripes down the backs of my legs.

"Well, that was fast," Ava laughed.

"Chocolate cookies work every time!" I said.

Before going inside, I opened my backpack on the patio with my dry towel and lunch t-shirt. I dried myself off and pulled on my t-shirt and wrapped the towel around my head like a turban. I grabbed my phone and looked to see a few missed messages from Declan.

Declan: hey babe
Declan: you with friends at the pool?
Declan: starting practice could use some motivation. Winky face
Declan: send pics.
Declan: come on. one bikini shot u know I think u r hot.

I frowned at the phone and felt weird. "Hey, Ava, can you come here a sec?"

Ava showed Fallon into the game room and I could hear Emma helping her get lunch when Ava came back looking concerned.

"What do you think about this?" I asked as I handed her my phone open to Declan's message stream.

"Really?" she said out loud. "Just out of the blue? You guys haven't messaged like that before, right?" asked Ava.

"No, not even slightly. I'm surprised he called me 'babe.' I feel like I'm being a baby for not wanting to send him something. Is that dumb?" I asked.

"No way. It is not babyish. You never have to do stuff you don't want to do. You aren't even dating. And even then, you don't ever have to. Would Elizabeth Bennet?" she asked.

"Don't make fun of me," I sighed.

"I am not at all! I'm serious. You wanted to change into someone like Lizzy who didn't get pushed into anything by anyone. Not rude people, not mean girls, and certainly not a guy you have known for a few weeks. Either don't respond or send him something funny. He'll get the message," said Ava. "And if he doesn't, good riddance."

"Okay, go on in. I need to think of something," I said. "And, Ava, thank you!"

I hugged Ava, my confidante, and sage warrior sister. "I want to be you when I grow up," I said in her wet hair.

I wracked my brain for a moment, deciding if I wanted to even respond and I finally decided, pushed send, and went into lunch.

Ellie: Gif of cat dancing in a bikini

After lunch, Marni placed me at the end of the room in front of the couches, where everyone sat in anticipation. It wasn't so terrible facing these people I had known all my life and I knew were rooting for me, but I still fidgeted with my braid.

"Ladies and gentleman… we have gathered here…" Marni started.

"Sniffles, what a good boy gentleman," said Catt in a baby voice, squishing poor Sniffles.

"Ladies, Sniffles, and mom, I gather us here today to witness our friend confront her fear of public speaking. She has been practicing the confidence of one Elizabeth Bennet and is ready to take on today's challenge."

"Come on already, you are stressing her out," said Emma.

"In this hat, I have four impromptu speech topics ranging from boys to *Pride and Prejudice*, the community center, and the dangers of microplastics. When I say go, you are going to choose one. You will read it out loud to us, then you will have one minute to think about the topic and then three minutes to speak."

"Only four minutes of torture," said Emma.

"Okay, ahhhhhhh, wait, so okay," I said, bouncing from foot to foot and sounding incoherent.

"Deep breath," said Marni.

"You've got this, Ellie," said Mrs. Norland.

"Bark," said Catt for Sniffles.

"Go!" said Marni, shoving the hat at my eye level and shaking it wildly.

I took a deep breath and chose a slip of paper and read aloud, "Finish telling us the story about running into Owen Darcy at the park."

I immediately looked up and saw Ava's wide eyes. She shook her head, letting me know she hadn't told anyone about the kiss. I was glad I hadn't had the chance. It was too embarrassing to admit I hadn't seen him since. I assumed it was just a joke to him, the silly small-town girl falling for him.

"Oh, wow, you drew the easy one. Good job!" said Marni.

"You are right. I should choose something else. In fact, I insist," I said as I grabbed the hat.

"Wait a second, something happened," said Emma jumping out of her seat and pointing at me. "You are red and blotchy. You didn't just walk with him, did you?"

"Woo woo, Ellie, did you go to a gazebo and declare your undying love?" asked Catt.

"You have got to stop watching that movie," said Emma.

"Spill it, sister. Emma is right, I can tell. Time starts now," Marni directed as she began the timer on her phone.

"Okay, fine. So I got to the trails early and Owen ran into me, coming up the other way. He said he was running from a bear, which was kind of funny. He thought maybe he was lost and asked if he could walk back with me. We stopped at the playground and played on the swings and the teeter-totters before we crossed the bridge. It was nice. We talked like normal people. He was different. Less grrrr. Anyway, I was excited for him to cross the swinging bridge and he thought it was cool. Then we heard a scream, and he saved a not-quite drowning boy and a bike. He was muscle-y and soaked from the river. And he was so great to the little boy, Ronnie. He taught him not to be afraid of the bridge. It impressed me that he could be so thoughtful. We walked the boy home. He lived up by the community center, behind the pool. So, umm, then, we talked about his sister and his fears, and well… he kissed me."

The room exploded in screams.

"But that isn't the end of the story," I began again when they quieted. "He kissed me and yes, it was really nice, and his lips were really soft, but then he just walked away like nothing happened. I felt so awkward. I just kept walking in silence, showing him the way up behind the houses. He was going to say something. He started to, but then we heard Brooklyn's whiny voice and he clammed up. And that's it."

"And that's time," said Marni dodging a pillow launched from Emma.

"She just poured her heart out and you call time?"

"I know, I know. We can unpack it all in a minute, but this was your first speech, and you did well. The audience was certainly engaged."

Standing up, Mrs. Norland said, "Ellie you did very well. I'll let you girls obsess about the smooching, but if you ask me, boys can feel awkward and uncertain, too. Make of that what you will. Good work on projecting confidence."

"Thank you," I said, wondering if she was right about Owen feeling awkward. He was so arrogant most of the time, I couldn't imagine it.

11

Loudspeaker: "Ladies and gentlemen, on behalf of the Tri-County Regional Basketball Invitational, we welcome you to friends and family night. The proceeds from tonight's exhibition go to the local Community Center. Please join all the players and coaches after the final buzzer for refreshments in the lobby. Enjoy the game!"

We climbed the bleachers as the last of the games started to whistles and cheers. The bleachers were filled with noisy families applauding their favorite player's every dribble. Marni led us up the clanging metal stairs about twenty rows up to the section mid-court where there was a space. The hard, wooden seats were not comfortable, but I still did not want to be like the older people who all brought their own bleacher cushions. Yes, my butt would hurt, but I still judged them.

"Why in the world did you bring binoculars? Are you trying to see their nose hair?" asked Emma.

"I told Mike I would watch him play," said Catt.

"Mmmmkay," Emma said, shaking her head.

"You *can* see every nose hair, cool," murmured Catt

"My parents are taking Fallon to the carnival tonight. Things are not good with her parents, so it looks like she may stay with us a while," said Ava to me.

"The carnival will be fun for her."

"So, what did Declan have to say after yesterday?" Ava asked.

I looked around the bleachers not knowing whose friends and family were sitting around us, so I whispered.

"He said little, just messaged 'lol' and that's it. I'm honestly so confused. 'D' says 'O' is a petty jealous creep. I can't respect that kind of person," I continued to whisper in code.

"Respect is everything, but do you believe Dec… I mean 'D'? I'm not sure we know him well enough to know if he is honest," said Ava.

"He is honestly cute," I laughed, and Ava smiled at me indulgently.

"There he is. He just got put in," said Marni, pointing to Declan.

"So, Mike and Denny are on the blue team and Declan is playing with Kyle… and Finn on the white team," I said.

"Where? I don't see Finn," said Catt, swinging her head wildly with her binoculars glued to her eyes.

Emma grabbed Catt's head, removed the binoculars, and aimed her face toward the basketball court. "Look with your eyes, he's right there… number twelve."

"Oh, yeah, that is much easier," said Catt. "I want to meet him, and Mr. Smug Face. Is he here?"

I leaned down the row and whisper-yelled to Catt. "Yes, he is here, blue team, number…" and I mouthed "five" while showing five fingers. I didn't see Brooklyn or anyone near us that looked like they were listening, but I would die if Owen knew we were talking about him. His ego was big enough.

We cheered for both sides, not choosing one team over the

other. Everyone got a little show-off time. Mike made a shot from almost half-court, then pointed up at Catt, who lost her mind cheering. Owen and Denny had a pass and layup combo that got a lot of cheers, too, and Declan even dunked the ball to wild applause. I could sense aggression between Declan and Owen, but I didn't know enough about basketball to know if it was normal. Judging by the way the other players looked at Declan, it seemed he was being unusually confrontational. By the end of the game, Declan had fouled out and walked off the court without joining his team for the "good game" hand slaps.

The players waved at us as they left for the locker rooms, like rock stars running off stage. We made our way with the rest of the crowd to the lobby to grab a cookie or three and wait for the players to come out of the locker rooms.

"Ellie, I want to meet Finn and you-know-who," said Catt.

"It looks like Finn came out and is over there with Jade and Eden, do you see? Head that way and I will introduce you," I said.

"Hey Finn, you were great. I'd like you to meet my friends. This is Catt, this is Eden's sister Marni, this is Ava, and this is Emma."

"Nice to meet you all," said Finn.

"Ellie has told us all about you moving in. Welcome to Meryton," said Ava.

"Thank you, I like it here. Everyone is so friendly," he said, smiling at Jade.

"Well Finn, I can always find you in the middle of the fun," said Owen Darcy, fresh from the shower and smelling faintly like lemon and spice. He was talking to Finn, but looking at me with warmth in his eyes, and for a second, I forgot I was disgusted with him.

"Hi, are you going to introduce me to your friends?"

"Hi, ummm, sure, everyone this is, Mr. SmOwen Darcy.

This is Marni, Ava, Emma, and Catt," I rattled quickly.

Mike came up and hugged Catt, and Ava started talking to Owen as I scanned the room for Declan. I saw Denny, who motioned me over.

"Hi, Denny, good job tonight. Is Declan still in the locker room?"

"Thanks. No, he asked me to give you a message. I didn't want to say it in front of…," nodding his head toward Owen. "He said to tell you he didn't want to run into Owen's father, Mr. Darcy. He said you would understand why, and then, well, he left with a friend."

"Oh," I said, looking disappointed as I saw all the people around me greeting girlfriends and family. "Thank you for telling me, Denny."

"Ellie, I know we haven't known each other long, but I'm not sure about that guy."

"You mean Owen?"

"No, Darcy is a good dude, I mean Declan. You and your friends are great, nice girls, and he is, well, he has a reputation. That's what I have heard from the guys from other schools, anyway. You do realize I broke the bro-code telling you," he said, smiling.

"Thank you, I'll keep it in mind," I smiled back and then mimed locking my lips and throwing away the key.

Once Denny walked away, I sighed. I no longer knew what to think about anything. It was all so confusing. I intended to walk back to my friends when I was overtaken by a tsunami of excited chatter sweeping me out to the parking lot.

"The big kids are driving us to Pizza Hut," explained Catt as we ended up outside.

Almost out of my earshot, Finn said to an uptight looking Owen, "relax, going out for pizza is not what the coach banned us from doing. This isn't a party and there won't be drinking.

We are not getting kicked off the team for pepperoni! You drive some people. I've got this group. See you there!"

"I love that you have traditions for everything. Pizza after a ballgame works for me," Finn said to Jade as Jade, Denny, and Eden loaded in his car.

I looked at Marni with my eyebrow raised, "yeah, so that happened," she said laughing at my surprised expression, "and it's perfectly okay. I introduced Denny to Eden, and they get along great. I never kissed him, so it's not super weird. He is her age and he is so nice."

I saw Mike picking Catt up to get her in his raised truck where Emma, Ava, and Kyle were already adjusting the radio.

Owen appeared at my side, "you two want a ride?"

"Yes, thank you," said Marni, grabbing my arm and dragging me into the car.

"How do you know he is not going to murder us?" I loud whispered to her.

"Owen, will you be murdering us?" Marni asked him.

"No," he said, a little smugly, I thought.

"See?" Marni said.

"That is exactly what a murderer would say," I said.

"Shut up and get in," Marni said climbing in the back seat, "I want a booth, which means we need to beat those guys!"

I jumped in the passenger seat and fastened my belt. I kept my face pointed out my window, feeling uncomfortable this close to warm, clean-smelling Owen Darcy.

"Owen, step on it," Marni commanded, and he did.

Marni said, "did your family come tonight?"

"No, my dad had to work late this week. We are heading out of town for the Fourth of July weekend, so I will see them then."

"Them?" asked Marni, while I feigned interest in everything out my window.

"Yeah, I have a younger sister, Georgiana. She is a year behind you guys in school. You'd like her, she is fun," said Owen. "What about you?"

"Am I fun? Why yes I am, and so is this," Marni mades circle gestures indicating all of me, "in spite of what is being projected right now."

Owen looked at me warily but continued talking to Marni and I continued to be fascinated by the passing houses.

"I meant, tell me about you," said Owen.

"I am an artist, I was born on the Aquarius/Pisces cusp, I work at the community center tutoring after school with Ellie, and I am focused on Jane Austening her before the big gala fundraiser for the center."

"Is this like your *Pride and Prejudice* thing again?" Owen asked me.

"Yup," I said without looking at him.

"Ellie just lacks a little confidence in certain situations," said Marni.

"I have all the confidence I need to murder you right here," I interrupted and out of my peripheral vision I saw Owen try not to smile.

"Marni, do you have brothers and sisters?"

"Yes. My sister, Eden is Jade's best friend. Turn left here! We are winning!" screamed Marni to a startled Owen, who executed the turn safely regardless.

"Oh, hey whatever happened to Declan?" asked Marni as Owen and I both whipped our shocked faces toward her.

"Denny told me he left with a friend," I said making my "shut up" face as best I could without Owen seeing me.

"You two know Declan Wickham?" Owen asked.

"Yeah, we have hung out with him a few times," said Marni, finally getting the hint.

"Yes," I said, feeling irritated and guilty at the same time.

"He said you used to be friends."

"I wouldn't call it friends, exactly," Owen said.

"Okay, park up there, we totally won, I am going to jump out and grab us a booth," Marni said as she did just that.

When Marni was out of hearing range, Owen said, "last time I saw you we were walking through the woods. I wanted thank you for helping me find my way back, and... I was hoping... "

"You are welcome," I said fumbling to undo the seatbelt. I unlatched it and jumped out so fast I didn't hear the last thing Owen said.

"Hey everyone, let's eat pizza."

12

My dad dropped me off at the fairgrounds near the large white metal conference center. I smiled at him thinking of all the times he had dropped me and my latest not-so-award-winning creation at this very building for judging. I had been in 4-H for years, with the dedication many people had for Girl and Boy Scouts. It was supposed to teach you life skills and leadership. I don't know if it either of those, but I did have fun memories. I started with photography when I was seven, but my dog Sammy wasn't the world's most photogenic beast and we both quickly lost interest. Later, I tried my hand at cake decorating because I loved eating the icing. I didn't know beautiful cakes used a heartier frosting than my mom's butter cream. So my entry that started out as a white two-tiered cake with big pink and white roses when dad dropped me off, ended up looking like Frosty the Snowman on the first day of spring when we came back to see the display. My last year, I entered in gift-wrapping. It was the strangest category, but I decided to try it because it seemed easy to do and easy to transport. No ribbons were won, but I was proud I could make even cheap gifts look amazing.

"Call me if you need a ride. Your mom wants to stay home with Jade. We will probably watch from the deck. Have fun honey, oooo and ahhhh enough for all of us," said my father.

"Thanks, dad, I'll make you proud," I said grabbing my bag and shutting the door.

I felt disloyal to my sister to be out having fun when she was so sad, but she made me go. I don't really understand what happened. Two nights ago we were all together having pizza. They seemed happy. The next day, it all fell apart. Finn had gone to the Darcy lake house and Jade was convinced he wasn't coming back anytime soon. No one belonged together more than Jade and Finn. It had to be a misunderstanding. He would definitely be back.

The fairgrounds were filling up with families hauling picnic baskets and coolers, chairs, and blankets. We always use blankets because the chair people have to sit at the very back and don't get to be as close to the fireworks display. July 4 was probably the biggest town event. It marked the midpoint of summer and the end of the county fair. And it was a great night for summer couples to share a blanket under the stars. I couldn't wait to be one of them.

"Hey Elliebee, why are you carrying 400 blankets?" asked Ava.

"Hey Ava. Hi, Fallon, good to see you. For your information, there are only two. I just wanted to have space, in case," I said.

"In case Declan came to sit with you?" asked Ava.

"Well, I told him not to pick me up, since I didn't want to give any false impressions, if you know what I mean," I said and made a stealthy nod toward Fallon. "But he did say he would see me here," I said. "It is odd, there are no signs of the carnival, right?"

"Yeah, they pack up and leave without a trace, except the grass is smashed flat," I noted. "Fallon, I heard you got to go to the carnival the other night."

"Uh-huh, Aunt Mandy and Uncle Michael took me on the swing ride and I rode a horse... his name was Peanut and he let me kiss his nose."

"Did you go on the ferris wheel?"

"No, too scary," said Fallon, shaking her head.

"It looks scarier than it is, but one day, when it looks like you would have fun, you can go... but only if you want to, not because other people make you. No judgment," I said.

"Okay, Miss Life Lesson, she gets it. This isn't about a ferris wheel at all is it?" Ava smirked.

"Don't psychoanalyze me," I smiled. "Where is everyone?" I asked.

"Today was the last day of camp so the out-of-towners all went home. We may see them at the Jake's party in a few weeks. The rest are coming," said Ava.

"I know Marni said her parents would give me a ride home, I guess they went into the city for a fancy birthday dinner for Mrs. Norland before coming here. They went to one of those crepe places, I think it's called Le Crepe. Marni kept trying to say it with a French accent and was saying "le crap" instead. We are eating at Le Crap, so hilarious," I said with an even worse French accent than my British one.

Fallon and I laughed at that. "Oh, stop with your adult face," I said to Ava, "it's funny, give me five Fallon," I said as I offered a high five to my humor twin.

We spread our blankets near the front, three wide, and left our bags and sweatshirts holding down the corners. It had been hotter than usual, but I was always hoping for a night cool enough to wear my hoodie.

"Should we go get some snacks? Not le crap... still funny,"

I said winking at Fallon.

"You know, this holiday always reminds me of Freddy," said Ava, as we walked to the food trucks and got kettle corn and snow-cones. "It's his birthday. He used to joke that the whole town came out to celebrate it."

"Oh, wow, I didn't remember that," I said shocked she had brought up his name. It had been a few years since he moved, and she was never interested in talking about their breakup. She had always been the queen of avoidance of all things Freddy related. "Are you going to call him and wish him…"

"Hey Collin… and Charlie, happy fourth of July! This is my cousin Fallon," said Ava, the Queen of Avoidance.

"Hi Fallon!" said Charlie cheerfully.

"Charlie is the captain of the girls' soccer team and she was my lab partner in Mr. Cassady's ninth grade biology," said Ava to Fallon. "She proves you can be both smart and good at sports."

"Who is giving life lessons now?" I muttered to Ava and smiled at Charlie.

"Good to see you both, happy fourth," I said.

"I promised this beautiful woman cotton candy before the fireworks, so if you will excuse us, Charlotte, shall we?" Collin said as he took Charlie's hand and she smiled at him warmly.

"Did you hear him? He called her 'Charlotte,'" said Ava.

"That's her real name," I said.

"He called her 'Charlotte.' Not 'Charlie,' because unlike the rest of us, he sees the whole girl, not just the awesome soccer stud the rest of us see," said Ava."People forget you can be both."

"It's romantic when you say it like that," I said.

"I told you he just needed the right girl," Ava said.

"I am happy for them," I said as we with snow-cones and bags of kettle corn. "It feels lonelier tonight, not as raucous as usual."

"Well... not everyone is lonely. Don't look now, but slowly glance to your right at the truck parking under the light," whispered Ava out of one side of her mouth.

"Don't look, but look?" I started to laugh.

"Ellie," Ava said in a tone I had rarely heard. It was the "shut up and focus" tone, "danger is ahead" and I did what she said immediately.

"Le crap, are you serious? Are you kidding me? Declan brought *Amber Raine?*"

"Girl, straighten out your face now, here they come," Ava sternly whispered.

I took a deep breath and plastered on a fake smile at Ava and laughed like she had said the funniest thing, "Oh, hi Declan, hi Amber, happy fourth," I said a little too happily and kept walking.

"Yeah, we hung out a little," I heard Declan say behind my retreating back.

"Hmm, I can't see it. She is too boring for you, you need someone a little more my speed," purred the meanest girl at school.

"Oh, really? And exactly what speed is that?" said Declan lecherously.

I hurried past the sea of chairs and families to our blanket island. My heart was racing, and my face felt so hot. I sat quickly and hid my face in my hair and tried to deep breathe my way through the threatening tears.

"I am so sorry you had to hear that. It was so gross. You know she can't hold a candle to you," Ava said.

"Well, she obviously can. And she is willing to let him *drive her home* after knowing him for ten minutes... unlike me. More what he was looking for I think."

"You can ride home with us, Ellie," soothed sweet Fallon,

thankfully, missing the subtext.

I fist-bumped her for her solidarity.

"Are you okay?"

"It's just embarrassing, and with AR," I said under my breath as if anyone was listening to our conversation. "Puke emoji."

"Amen to that," said Ava cheers-ing me with her cherry-red snow cone.

"You know, Denny warned me about him after the basketball game," I said thinking back.

"He did?" Ava said.

"Oh, of course. I'm so dumb! Denny told me, he-who-shall-not-be-named left with a 'friend' after the game because he didn't want to run into O and O's father. I will give you one guess who the 'friend' probably was."

"She is so scandalous," said Ava. "I heard she was furious because 'Ken' and his friends left right after graduation to go backpacking across Europe. This must be her revenge."

Both of our phones lit up with texts from Emma, Marni, and Catt who had all arrived and were searching for us. We told them to watch for the waving cell phone lights in the middle of the front and we made Fallon hold both phones like she was landing a jet fighter on an aircraft carrier. Sadly, it wasn't quite dark enough, nor was she tall enough for it to be more than a show just for us, but it was cute, nonetheless.

"Hey guys, is that Declan over there with his face stuck to Amber?" asked Emma.

"Yup, you missed all the fun," I said.

"Dang, that's nasty," Emma said.

"I thought he was supposed to be meeting you here. I'll go kick him, what a jerk!" Marni said as she started toward him.

"Whoa killer," I said grabbing her arm, "it's fine. I'm not devastated. My pride is not thrilled to be tossed over for the mean queen, but honestly... I'm fine."

I interrupted Catt and Fallon who were exchanging friendship bracelets they had made each other. Catt still had eight year old girl energy, so they looked like two besties hiding under a fort blanket, trading secret treasures. "Catt, did Mike go home?"

"Yeah, he wanted to stay longer, but his parents were all packed and ready to head to the lake. I guess they spend a couple of weeks there every summer. He promised to take me to the fund-raiser though, so I hope you are all coming, too."

"Not only is it Ellie's debut as EB, but my parents are on the board of the community center and the event sounds beyond! The park will look so pretty," said Marni.

"And it is a good excuse to dress up," pointed out Ava.

"I will not be wearing high heels though, I draw the line and those torture devices," proclaimed Marni.

"I will be racing Emma for the hoochiest shoes. I love high heels," I said.

I looked over at Emma who gave me a pro-high-heel bro nod as she ate my kettle corn.

"Do we use that word anymore?" asked Ava. "Is it slut-shaming?"

"Good point, I dunno, but I will be wearing some shoes of ill-repute, not that I judge, and no disrespect to the shoes," I said.

"You know it!" said Emma with a high five to me.

Looking around us at the sea of blankets and families and couples, I felt a little melancholy at how quickly the summer seemed to be going. We had met a few new boys and they were mostly nice, but it felt like the opportunity to make this an epic summer was slipping away. I could see Collin and Charlie snuggled up on a blanket looking so happy and I could guess how Collin felt. Finally, he was the one with a date, he was a couple. I wanted that feeling. I had felt it for two minutes with Declan at the farmer's market. But I wanted it for real, with someone I could trust with my feelings. A guy who wouldn't make me feel stupid and was honest about his own feelings.

"I wanted this to be an epic summer for all of us... of self improvement for me," I sighed.

"And meeting boys," said Emma.

"And saying yes to fun," said Marni.

"And not being invisible," I said.

"The summer is not half empty, it's half full," said Catt cheerfully.

"And just because you-know-who is doing you-know-what with the other you-know-who, doesn't mean you aren't meeting your goals. YOU did what you were comfortable with, right? The old you might have given in to the pressure of the hot guy right?" said Ava.

"You're right, as always. Seriously, I would have hated myself. Thank you, Jane Austen!" I laughed.

"When are the fireworks starting? Sheesh, I think it's dark enough now," whined Catt whose positivity was beginning to wane.

"Eden told me what happened to Jade," Marni said quietly.

"Oh yeah, this is terrible," I said to the five expectant faces around me. It started yesterday. Brooklyn Bingley walked over to our house allegedly to say 'goodbye.' She said they were all going to the Darcy's big lake house for the holiday. It's some family tradition. She said she and Owen were going to have so much fun boating with Finn and Georgie, Owen's sister. She was trying so hard to annoy us, implying Finn had moved on. I just kept my mouth shut and smiled. I think I even said, "Oh goody for you."

"I see your comebacks haven't evolved much," smirked Emma.

"Jade called Finn and wished him a good holiday and said she hoped to see him when they got back. I guess there was a long pause and he blurted out that he wasn't coming back. He has to move in with Owen, so he doesn't mess up his eligibility to play basketball his senior year. His coach told him he can't live in our town and play for the private school in the city."

"But they don't have to break up over it," said Ava.

"Yeah, they are perfect together," Marni said

"Well, Jade said she hoped to see him when he visited his parents and he didn't say anything. By the time she told me, I could tell she had been crying. But you know Jade, she said, they weren't a committed relationship, just dating, so if he wants to break up she is not going to beg him to stay. It sounded like he didn't want to do the long-distance thing or more likely his sister poisoned his mind," I said.

"So wait, we are now calling thirty minutes, long-distance? They both have their driver's licenses for pity sakes," said Emma.

"At least he said it in person, instead of messaging," said Marni.

"But she had to call him," Emma pointed out.

"I am so disappointed. Finn had given me hope there were good guys still out there," I said.

"There are, somewhere," said Ava.

"Eden told us at dinner that Jade is pretty devastated, but she never shows it. Both of our sisters hide their feelings, whereas when I am crushed, I crush right back!" said Marni as she rolled from her spot, lying on her stomach, and rolled on top of Emma then Catt causing giggles and yelps from below.

The dark sky lit up with a loud cannon boom and the first fireworks of the night, three all-white flower bursts rained down with a whistle, followed closely by five pink flower blossoms that lingered above.

"Awwww, pretty. That's us," said Catt.

The sparkling, booming sky illuminated our faces as we each grew introspective, "oooooo-ing and ahhhhh-ing" along with the joyful crowd.

13

Marni: 811!

Ellie: 811? What is that?

Marni: Not a full 911 emergency, but close!

Ellie: Weirdo. What up?

Marni: Can you help me cover classes at the Center at 10:45 a.m.? It will be good practice for your internship!

Ellie: Oh, yeah, it will look good to the Board and Ms. Lemon!

Ellie: Wait, it's not horticulture or bug catching or something gross is it?

Marni: No. eyeroll emoji.

Ellie: See you in an hour!

"Mom, can't you just drive me? I feel so bad for Jade, but she is sort of a bummer right now." I whispered, not wanting my sister, who I dearly loved, to hear me. But honestly, her play list of every sad song in the universe was killing me. I could hear her Spotify switching from mournful and heart-wrenching to throw-him-against-the-wall-and-yell-at-him songs. I didn't know which was worse.

"No, honey, I can't. I'm finishing this brisket for dinner and making a lemon meringue pie, plus it will be good for her to get out of the house even for ten minutes."

"I am so mad at Finn. I was hoping he was different," I said, drinking down some orange juice.

"I am sure this is all just a misunderstanding. He will realize you can't find beauty and sweetness like Jade's anywhere else, and then he will crawl back. And when he does, I hope he leaves that sour-faced boy in the city."

"Agreed," I said to my mom, but I didn't fully agree with her. I still couldn't stand that 'sour-faced boy,' of course, but I missed being annoyed by him. I guess I felt a little abandoned, too.

"Your day will come, and it will be your turn to mope around here, so be nice and patient with her," my mom said with a warm smile.

"I'll meet you in the car, El," Jade yelled before the front door shut.

"Oh, boy, I hope you are right. I've never seen a heartbroken Jade. It's awful."

"But honey, love is worth it. The ups and downs are a grand adventure."

"Love you, mom," I said, kissing her cheek, not sure the adventure sounded so grand.

I jumped in the car and turned mom's radio on. An oldies station blared "Ain't No Sunshine when she's gone." I scrambled to flip to the next station, which was playing "Wrecking Ball," by Miley Cyrus. The next station had Adele. I think it was "Someone like you," so I just turned it off and looked sideways to see if Jade noticed.

She looked a little pained as we drove past the Bingley

house. It looked pained, too, and lifeless even though they had only been gone 48 hours. Apparently, Mr. and Mrs. Bingley had a business trip to Switzerland, so Brooklyn and Finn would stay at the Darcys' house when they got back from their "lake house."

"It must be confusing having so many homes," I said, though I knew Jade was not hearing me. I tried to think of something to say to be supportive and not make her sadder. I couldn't think of anything good so I just dove in. "Jade, I'm sorry you are sad. I am sure he didn't…"

"Ellie, thank you," she said firmly. "I don't want to talk about him. I know you are worried about me. I will be fine. I promise. I just need to be sad for a while."

The drive was a quick one, out of our subdivision and into the park over the speed bumps, up and down, then up and down again, past the pool, and finally to the community center.

The Center was a cement block building formerly used to be a public utility building and now was in the middle of a large renovation. They were adding a gym with basketball and volleyball courts and a larger kitchen.

Jade stopped the car and turned toward me. "I will be fine."

"You will listen to happy music again?"

"Someday, I will listen to happy music again," she reluctantly smiled.

"Thanks for driving me," I said as I jumped out of the car. "Love your face!"

"Love yours, too."

It was muggy outside, and the sky was grey and gloomy. It was mid-morning, but the low fog still covered the ground. I already felt sticky and gross, though I had been out of the shower less than an hour.

"Oh good Ellie, so glad you could come on such short

notice," said Mrs. Norland opening the front door for me.

"You're welcome. I wasn't doing anything."

"We had two teachers call in because they had car trouble. They are married, so coming in the same car. Anyway, I think Marni is around here somewhere with the instructions. I am so excited. I just finished a preliminary phone interview with a potential youth counselor. She can do part-time and her specialty is in childhood trauma."

"Is that something you need here?"

"Oh, you would be surprised. We have a lot of young people here struggling with their mental health and unpleasant family situations. Oh, there is Marni. Hey sweetie, I was just telling Ellie I think the counselor I mentioned will work out. The gym project is slightly under budget, so we can swing it."

"That's great, mom," said Marni turning her phone on to see the time.

"You girls are all set for class? You start in about 10 minutes. Then they have summer lunch and everyone goes home. Let me know if you need anything."

"Okay, you pick. Do you want the Mommy and me class or the grade school group?" asked Marni.

"Please, not the little ones. Those guys are sticky! I can play games with grade schoolers. No problem," I said.

"They are all boys today. Ten of them."

"Yipes, okay, well, it will be a workout, but I can do this."

"Okay, first you get another chance to practice your public speaking," said Marni, handing me a piece of paper.

"Wait, where?"

"Everyone gathers in the common area and 'we,' meaning 'you,'will make these basic announcements before everyone takes off for class," instructed Marni. She was way too good at bossing me.

"Sounds easy enough." I took the list and read it, noting the words 'summer lunch,' again. "What is the deal with lunch here? Why don't they just go home and eat? I mean, not to be rude, but…"

"Well, some of these kids get most of their food for the day at school and when summer comes, their parents have a hard time affording the food. Some of them are from single-parent families who are working during the week and aren't home, so at least with us they get one good meal and have people to hang out with," pointed out Marni.

"I had no idea. I guess I need to check my privilege."

"Oh, definitely. We both have privileges we don't realize. I didn't understand it until my mom and dad started bringing me with them when they volunteered. Just having food in our fridge is a luxury some of these kids don't have. Actually, the internship you WILL be getting will reach out to families who could use our help."

"Wow, it's so important," I said, finally understanding.

"Let's go, it's almost time. I can tell because it's getting loud."

"Lead the way, boss," I said.

"Okay, get their attention and go for it, really loud," said Marni.

"Hey everyone," I said.

"I can't hear you and I am next to you," said Marni.

"Woo hoo, everyone?" I said, waving the scrap of paper above my head as people milled about.

"Pathetic," Marni rolled her eyes.

"YO! YO!" I yelled so forcefully that I ended up on tiptoes. The room fell silent, and all eyes turned toward me.

"Ummm, hi everyone, my name is Ellie. I have a few announcements. Here on this folded paper. Wait, um, okay, ready?

Construction continues on the east side of the building.

Please don't play on the scaffolding.

Mommy and Me class will take place on the mats in the back with Miss Marni, and I will take the grade school class."

Cheers went up from the group of boys currently horsing around in the back of the group.

Pointing to the noise, I continued, "We will meet by the ping-pong table.

Summer lunch today will be cheesy ziti pasta, cucumber and tomato salad, milk or water, and a warm chocolate chip cookie." Loud cheers went up for the cookie.

Clean up after lunch, is everyone, so don't take off until you are dismissed.

That is all. Enjoy your class!"

"Wow, you did it. You got loud as needed and you didn't freak out at all. Elizabeth Bennet has nothing on you!"

"It was a small group, and no one was giving me stink-face."

"Next practice, we need stink-face giving hecklers," Marni proclaimed.

I met the group of ten boys and saw someone familiar. "Hey Ronnie, I know you. How are you?" He looked momentarily panicked that I might tell his friends how we met, but I didn't and he visibly relaxed.

"How is that tall guy? He was pretty cool."

"Oh, umm, I think he is fine," trying to shake the visual of Owen and his wet t-shirt helping Ronnie out of the creek.

"What are we going to do today? We can't all play ping-pong," a large boy named Edgar asked.

"Wanna bet? I know a super fun game we can all play at the same time. It's called round robin," I said, picking up one paddle and pointing to the other.

"Grab that paddle. I have the ball, so half of you line up behind me, half behind Edgar. I am going to serve the ball, then put the paddle down and then hurry to the end of the line right there behind Edgar. So Edgar is going to return my serve, then put his paddle down. The next person picks up the paddle and plays, and it just keeps going until someone messes up. When you do, you are out. Eventually, we get to two people playing in the final. It's tricky, but instead of running to the other side, they just spin around and grab the paddle up and try to play the ball. Make sense? It will if we just try it and I'll explain as we go. Ready?"

During the first game, I noticed the smallest boy, Danny, was watching the bigger boys with their show-off moves. They tried to hit the ball hard at everyone instead of just hitting it on the table and moving along. He looked stressed and got out pretty quickly. When I got out, I went and stood by him.

"Hey Danny, you don't look like you are having fun."

"It's okay, they are just better at hitting it."

"You know, the real trick is to just calmly hit it and move around the table. Hitting it hard isn't an advantage. Being fast is, though. Watch as we get toward the end and you'll see what I mean."

Just then, one of the show-offs, Edgar, tried to make a big slam, and the returned ball missed the table.

When it was down to just four people left, each player had to hit it carefully and run.

"See what I mean? You are fast, so you will have an advantage." I could tell he understood as I watched the smile grow on his face.

After three games, the last one won by a very proud Danny, we had a break at the water fountain and headed outside to play freeze tag for a few minutes then class time was over and everyone ran inside to get ready for lunch. Their energy was still on high, but their parents totally owed me. These boys were going to sleep early tonight. I knew I would.

The sky was heavy and looked like it would rain soon. I

hoped it would cool us down.

"Payment by cookie always works for me," I told Mrs. Norland when she offered me one from the basket. "Those boys wore me out."

"I can tell they had fun. They are still talking about the ping-pong game. Why don't you stay for lunch and I will drive you home right after? Like, thirty minutes? It looks like it could rain any second."

"Thank you, but I'll just walk. It is muggy out. I wouldn't mind getting rained on."

"Bye, Marni," I said and waved to her as she finished helping the last mom put her baby in the car seat and leave. "Text me later. I'm going to head home."

"Kisses," she said.

I headed across the baseball field and passed the spot where Owen kissed me. I wonder if I should find another route so I didn't have to think about him every time I passed this way.

The wind picked up as I headed into the trees and up the hill. It was getting darker, which I assumed was because of the thick canopy of trees, until I heard large raindrops hitting the leaves above me. But because I didn't hear thunder and lightning, I didn't feel unsafe. The air felt heavy, and I was dripping in sweat by the time I reached the top of the hill and the back of the Abramses' house. The rain was coming harder and faster now and was blowing in sheets. I began to jog. I could feel my phone buzzing, but I didn't want to get it wet, so I just went faster. It was probably Jade worrying about me in this weather.

I was nearly at the Bingleys when I heard the ice cream truck come around the corner and drive up next to me. "Jump in!" Mr. Evans said out his side window, I'm taking Miss Natalie home. Hurry it's getting bad. Radio just said there is a tornado watch for Hendricks county.

I jumped in and saw Natalie and her pink bike sitting next to Danny from the Community Center.

"Hi Danny, oh! Is this your dad?"

"Yeah, he's my boy. I just picked him up."

"Natalie, there is your mom. She's looking for you." Mr. Evans honked and waved as we pulled into Natalie's driveway and I helped Natalie get down and then handed her mom her bike.

Lightning flashed and Natalie and her mom screamed as they ran inside and yelled, "thank you."

"I'll run from here," I said, and I was about to when suddenly the rain stopped and everything went eerily silent.

Mr. Evans backed the bright yellow truck out of the Garcia's driveway and was in front of my house when I yelled, "wait!"

My heart raced. I knew the signs. "Wait, Mr. Evans, it's coming!" And then I heard the siren. The tornado sirens emitted a haunting moan throughout town indicating a tornado had been sighted. It was no longer a warning that conditions were perfect for a tornado to form. One had been seen within the city limits.

I ran to the ice cream truck as the wind picked up and the rain started in earnest. Mr. Evans seemed reluctant to leave the truck, his livelihood, unprotected.

"You and Danny need to come to my house. Leave the truck."

We ran across our lawn. The lightening streaked angrily across the sky. The wind was so strong it blew Danny and I backward. Mr. Evans pulled us both onto the front porch as grape-sized hail bounced all over the grass. My front door flung open and there was my dad with his keys in his hand.

"Oh, thank goodness. Everyone inside."

I lead the way through our front hallway and dining room to the basement stairs. It was surreal watching our patio furniture blow past the French doors and continue toward the Garcia's house.

Our basement was carpeted and furnished with overstuffed couches, a big screen tv, and a large sturdy farm table we used to play board games. We grabbed blankets and cushions from the couches and got under the table right as the power went out. I grabbed for Jade's hand and she and I held on to the same table leg hugging it and each other.

My mother turned on a lantern and I could see she had an armful of flashlights. I would bet a million dollars she had snacks with us in the basement as well. I was so grateful my whole family was together. I started thinking about Mrs. Norman across the street and hoped she was snuggled safely with Magoo.

"Mr. Evans, was everyone gone from the center when you picked up Danny?" I asked.

"Yes, the Norlands were waiting with him because I was a little late. I saw them get in their car."

"Oh, good. I don't think the Center has a basement, but the Norlands do at home."

The roar of the wind could be heard even down here and I could see a sliver of grey light coming in from the top of the stairs under the basement door.

"Are your ears popping?" Jade said and we all could feel it.

"I think a tornado is going over us right now," said my father.

"I think you are right," said Mr. Evans.

Everyone was frozen in place, scared to move and ready to brace ourselves if the worst happened.

We could hear glass breaking and the continuous wail of the tornado siren far away. I expected to hear the freight train sound everyone always talked about, but all I heard was a groaning in the wind. It felt like the table was shaking, but I think all of us clinging to the legs was making it shudder.

Danny said softly "Daddy, I'm scared."

"I'm a little scared too son, but it's is almost over and it will be just fine. Thankfully, we had friends to help us."

Danny looked over at me and I smiled. "I'm glad you guys stopped and picked me up."

"Me, too," said Danny.

"I think it has passed," said my father taking a flashlight and heading toward the stairs.

"Mr. Evans…"

"Walter, please."

"Walter, would you like to join me and see if it is safe for everyone to come out?"

Danny was reluctant to let go of his father and stay with these near strangers. He watched his father accept a flashlight from my mom and follow my dad upstairs.

"Danny, are you hungry? I have some home made cookies right here. Do you like chocolate chip?"

"I wonder why I eat when I am nervous?" I smiled at Jade and rolled my eyes.

14

"You can all come up," my father said from the top of the basement stairs. "The house is still intact. We are going outside to check Walter's truck and see about the neighbors," my dad called down.

At the top of the basement stairs, I had a view of our whole backyard through the double French doors of the dining room. It looked like Fall with the number of leaves and branches on the ground.

Danny ran past me and out the front door, where his dad was examining his truck. I had been worried because I knew the ice cream truck was important to their family and I had been the one to encourage him to abandon it. I was so relieved. It appeared to be fine. There were leaves stuck on the windows and blobs of sod on the side, but no damage I could see.

"Oh no," I heard Mr. Evans say, and my heart dropped. "Clarence, the Clown is gone."

"I don't see it anywhere," my father said, looking down the street.

"You mean the creepy-faced thing on top? Oh, good… " I said.

"Ellie!" Jade said.

"I mean, I'm sorry, it's the stress of the storm," I said, feeling guilty.

Mr. Evans turned and looked at me... and laughed.

Then I laughed loud and hard, too. All of us began laughing and kept laughing for several minutes. The stress of the storm was released by Clarence, the creepy-faced clown... may he rest in peace.

"My wife is always telling me the clown scared the children. She will be so happy. Speaking of which, my cell phone is still not working. Would you mind if I take Danny home and check on the rest of the family?"

"Absolutely Walter. A pleasure to shelter with you, sir," said my father, shaking his hand.

"Thank you so much for taking us in!"

"Thank you for teaching me round robin today, Ellie," said Danny.

"You are so welcome, Danny. Tell your dad about your big win when things settle down."

"Dad, I'm going to check on Mrs. Norman." I yelled, moving someone's plastic kiddie pool from her front door.

"Mrs. Norman? Magoo? It's Ellie. Are you guys okay?"

I heard a muffled bark and an "okay, Magoo, it's alright."

"Hi young lady, are you guys all okay?"

"Yes, and you?"

"Yes, we have a spot all set up for emergencies and we got there in plenty of time. I think this one was close."

"I agree. It was so loud."

They both came out on the porch with me and we looked around. Limbs of all sizes covered her lawn. We watched with some amusement as my dad and Jade carried our patio chairs back from alongside the Garcia's fence.

"Good thing the fence caught them or they'd be all the way

to Indianapolis by now," said Mrs. Norman.

"Speaking of which, you have someone's pool in front of your garage."

"I am sure someone will come to get it."

"Oop, there is the power, that was fast," she said as the television, ceiling fan and the central air all came to life. "Oh good. I won't have to throw out everything in my frig."

"Do you need help with anything? Want me to check the backyard?" I asked.

"Thank you, but I already did. Everything is fine. I may go gather sticks later, but right now I want to catch the news and see what all happened."

"Call if you need anything. Oh, well, when the phones come back on," I smiled.

"Bye, dear."

I found my dad in the garage, grabbing supplies and putting them in the trunk of his car.

"Ellie, do you want to go with me? I want to drive around town and see if anyone needs help."

"I wouldn't normally get in the car with a man who just put rope, duct tape, tarps, and a chainsaw in the trunk, but why not, YOLO!"

"I don't know what YOLO means, but yes, YOLO to you, too!"

"Can we make sure Marni and those guys are fine? Maybe check the center on the way?"

"Sure. We will do a big sweep through town, then Norlands, and through the park."

"WIBC News on the nines… a strong F1 tornado touched down in Meryton, Indiana this afternoon. It had sustained winds of 110 MPH. So far, no reports of injury, but several have reported extensive property damage. We will update you as reports come in."

"That's good, I guess. No injuries."

"Main Street isn't bad so far," my dad said, waving at the few cars we passed. Waving is normal in a small town, but I sensed it had more meaning after the tornado. Like the wave was saying, "I am glad to see you are okay, neighbor."

We drove around town and saw a man trying to move a tree as big around as a hula hoop that had fallen across his driveway. My dad jumped out and grabbed his chain saw. It took a long time, but they got it cut up into sections and stacked it all over on the side of the house.

I watched my dad from the passenger seat and thought, "not bad for a book nerd." I felt slightly proud as the man shook his hand and thanked him for the help.

I kept checking my phone and my texts were still not going through.

"The cellphones are still out! Dad! This is officially a disaster… a step too far tornado, a step too far," I muttered. "Don't you dare smile."

"What happened to YOLO?"

"Who wants to live more than once when you are cut off from the rest of the world?" I pouted.

My dad attempted not to smile at my sudden downturn in mood and headed back toward the Norlands and the park.

"Oh no, dad look. I think the roof is missing," I said as we drove the back way to the community center and saw Mr. Norland leaning a ladder against the back of the building.

"There's Tom, I better help him. You want to go look around?"

"I'll see what else they need."

The back of the community center had been covered in scaffolding and much of it had fallen down. The tornado had scattered wooden planks and pipes across the ground like a game of pixie sticks. Now I was closer, it didn't look like the entire roof was off. There was just a hole where a tree branch had fallen through to the common room I had been in just a few hours ago. My Dad and Mr. Norland were nailing plywood over the hole, so I walked around to the front to see what I could do.

The front door was wide open. I cautiously went inside, not sure how torn up it would be. I walked back to the common room. No one else was here. I could see the area where they were patching the roof, and I was relieved it didn't look worse. Maybe they could still use it for summer lunch if it had a good cleaning. I began dragging a tree branch out. It was only as big around as a light pole, and not as tall as me, but it was so heavy. I yanked and walked backward and yanked some more until I dragged it outside and to the side of the building. There were a few smaller limbs inside, and I dragged them all out. My pile was getting big, so I amused myself by making a sign from the craft bins and poster paper. I then took twine and branches to my poster until it looked like a realtor's sign. I hammered the sticks into the ground and looked at my less than artistic sign. "Don't '*leave*' without some Free Firewood."

I was sweeping the common room when Mrs. Norland and Marni walked in. I ran and hugged them both and we all started talking at the same time about the close call and how everyone was fine.

Mrs. Norland went to assess the damage outside.

"The phones are still out. Have you heard from anyone?"

"Eden saw Emma at the grocery store, and they are all fine. I guess they didn't even get hail. You got hail, right?"

"Yeah, hail after it had gone super quiet and then it all let loose. Oh, and the scary loud groaning sound."

"Oh I know, right? Wasn't that terrifying? We had barely gotten home. I was letting Sniffles out to pee and he took one look out and sort of sniffed the air. I swear he said 'nope' and he turned around and started whining. Then the siren went off."

"He saved your lives!"

"He was the first down the basement stairs. I don't think he was worried about anyone but himself. Anyway, it was creepy."

"So, should we clean more in here? I was thinking of gathering the sticks in the yard for my free firewood pile," I said.

"I saw your sign. Good idea."

"It looks good in here, so why don't you go do sticks and I will meet you there in fifteen-ish. I want to ask Mom what she wants us to do."

There were so many branches all over the front lawn. I dragged the larger ones across the lawn first, but all the little ones were taking forever. I wished dad had put a rake in his murder trunk.

A woman and a man hustled over to me from a van. The woman said something to the man, put something in her ear, and then shoved a microphone in my face. He put a big camera up to his eye and turned on a light, momentarily blinding me.

"Hi, Lynette from W.I.N.D. It looks like there was some tornado damage here. What is this building?"

"Hi, umm, yes, this is the Meryton Community Center. I don't know the extent of the damage, but I know I just dragged that big branch out from the common room inside."

"Oh, so it crashed through the roof. How terrifying. Was anyone inside at the time?"

"No, no one was here, but we had all just left for the day maybe thirty minutes before," I said, pulling at my sleeves. I consciously took a deep breath and tried to concentrate on being poised like Elizabeth Bennet. I tried to ignore the fact that this report might be seen by thousands of people tonight

117

on the news. And convince myself that it didn't matter that I was still wearing the same sweaty and disgusting clothes from this morning. I would act confident if it killed me.

"This place must be important to you if you came here to help with the clean-up?"

"Yes, well, I tutor here during the school year. Today I was playing games with grade school kids." I could tell she was getting bored with my answers and I thought I owed it to the Center to advertise while we had the chance, especially now with more repairs needed.

"But the important thing I learned today was that this place is a surrogate home for some kids. I didn't realize that some families struggle to feed their kids when school isn't in session, so the people here serve lunches six days a week. One boy told me he comes here because his mom works two jobs and he gets bored at home. This place is important and in a small town, people help each other. Sorry, if I said too many words, but that is why I came."

"I think you said just the right amount of words."

"No, I didn't," I laughed. "Sorry to interrupt, I almost forgot, the most important thing. There is a fundraiser gala on August 15. Now more than ever, we will need donations. Please buy tickets on our website and join us!"

"Well, this young person said it all, a community center for a small community who pitches in and helps their neighbors. This has been Lynette Romero for WIND."

"And out," said the cameraman as he switched off the blinding light.

"Great, thank you," said Ms. Romero absently.

"Ahhhhhh! You were amazing," yelled Marni. She tackled me from behind.

"You heard all that?"

"Yes, mom and I both did! When did you get brave enough

to talk on camera?"

"I honestly didn't notice the camera at first, and then I decided to just talk about the stuff you taught me today. And I mean it. I really learned today how important this place is. I get it now."

"Well, thanks to you, we are going to sell tons of tickets! Now we need to get our dresses!"

"And about that, I have a plan!"

"Oh, no."

15

By mid-July, when most of the town had finished clean-up from the storm, and Jade had still not heard from Finn, my mother contrived a plan. We girls should go spend a week with her youngest sister in the city. Mom was certain the change of scene would lift Jade's spirits and even offered to pay for our gala dresses if we found one in the boutique shops. Later, when asked, she pretended she didn't know Aunt Cassandra lived less than a mile from the Darcy home where Finn Bingley was currently living.

Aunt Cassie's swanky downtown condo building for the "discerning professional" had a doorman, a pool, a juice bar at the gym, and a rooftop restaurant overlooking the entire city. It was the perfect girl's getaway.

I stood in front of the the floor-to-ceiling windows taking in the explosion of color the setting sun left behind the skyline. The urban landscape was vibrant and serene in the fading light. "What are men to rocks and mountains?" I quoted as Aunt Cassie joined me.

"Pride and Prejudice?" asked Aunt Cassie.

I laughed, "I was quoting Elizabeth Bennet when she was in

Derbyshire with her aunt and uncle. She was saying she cared more about the surrounding beauty than stupid boys."

"But don't forget she said that before she saw Pemberley and suddenly Mr. Darcy was better looking than rocks and mountains," laughed Aunt Cassie.

Jade was curled up on the charcoal gray velvet sofa in front of the fireplace texting away, not listening to either of us. Aunt Cassie looked over at Jade and then back at me and asked, "Your mom says this has been going on for awhile?"

"It has only been two weeks since 'certain people' left without saying goodbye. She says she is fine, just needs some time," I said whispering the "certain people" part out of the side of my mouth.

"We will make it fun while you are both here," said Aunt Cassie, trying to imitate the side of the mouth whisper and failing.

"Jade, you girls want to go to dinner and plan our attack on the week?"

"Sure," said Jade, "sounds good. I was just texting Brooklyn Bingley to say we were in town this week. I thought maybe we could get together sometime."

"Brooklyn, is 'certain people's' horrible sister," I side whispered again.

"Great. You can certainly invite her here anytime, unless we starve to death. How about the bistro on the corner, the one with the big outdoor patio? We can walk there and don't need a reservation."

"Let's roll," I said, grabbing my denim jacket and cross-body bag. "I get to push the button in the elevator," I yelled like I used to when we were little.

"Really?" said Jade with a reluctant smile.

"Still fun," I smiled.

"What are you girls planning for this week? Your mom told

me you need to go shopping for dresses?" Aunt Cassie prompted.

"Yes, my friends are coming to do that with me," I said.

"And Eden is coming to go with me, probably on different days, maybe the same. We have some things to discuss," said Jade.

"Like how you are going to get Finn back? I hope you two are planning on driving by his house."

"Ellie!" Jade glared at me.

"You know mom probably already told her anyway. She might as well know the entire story," I said, pleading my case.

"Fine. A boy I like is staying near here at his friend's house for a while, maybe forever. Who knows? I was hoping to run in to him. I didn't even get to say goodbye," said Jade.

"And you are hoping this Brooklyn will give you some information about him?" asked Aunt Cassie.

"I know Ellie doesn't like her, but she has been nice to me. She reached out after the tornado on behalf of all of them to ask if we were okay. I guess she saw you on the news, El."

"On behalf of all of them? Right!" I said, rolling my eyes, but dropped the subject when I saw Jade's face fall. "Sorry, that was nice of them to ask."

"Three, table on the patio, please," Aunt Cassie said to the host.

The patio had low bean-shaped couches in dark teal, and funky orange sculptural chairs interspersed with traditional tables and chairs and small fire pits.

"Maybe you have it right, Aunt Cassie," said Jade. "Stay single and live a cool life in the city. It seems less complicated."

"Ha, yeah, it seems less complicated, but it isn't always. I have had a lot of love in my life. I almost got married a few times. Did you know that?"

"No," I said, intrigued.

"But right now, with my career being so busy, I am happy with the choices I have made. If something extraordinary comes along, I am open to it, but not pining for it. I want that for both of you… open to extraordinary, not settling for 'meh.'"

"To being open to extraordinary," I cheers-ed Aunt Cassie. Jade ignored me and looked down at her vibrating phone.

"You guys, I just got a text from Brooklyn. She wants to come over tomorrow. "

******

"Welcome, Brooklyn. This is my Aunt Cassie, and you know Ellie," Jade said opening the door with a warmer smile than I thought necessary.

"Hello, Jade. So nice to see you, don't you look cute in this dress."

Brooklyn walked in room like she was appraising the place. She took in the eclectic decor with its mix of modern art and 1920's architecture. She looked past me like I was invisible, then turned a wide fake smile on Aunt Cassie.

"Nice to meet you, Aunt Cassie. Your home is lovely."

"Thank you, you can just call me Cassie. You ladies make Brooklyn at home. I have work to do. It's going to be a long night."

Aunt Cassie caught my eye and winked. I knew she saw what I saw, and didn't like it. She looked more like a trial lawyer as she summed up Brooklyn. The Cheshire cat smile and fashionable clothes did not fool her.

"Night, Auntie C, I said winking back. Brooklyn, so happy you are here." I said with the most fake smile I have ever smiled. Would you like a drink? Water, tea, soda?"

"Yes, thank you. Hot tea would be great," she said. Brooklyn continued her appraisal of the wall of windows overlooking the city, and then the rest of the room. "I have always wanted to see inside this building. Not bad," she proclaimed.

"How is your family?" Jade asked from the kitchen.

"Mom and dad are in Switzerland. They keep sending us pictures of tiny storybook villages surrounded by snowcapped mountains, saying "wish you were here." I, for one, have had enough of quaint towns. I'd prefer Paris, but Daddy has a big client in Zurich and they want to 'get to know him.'" So Finn and I are staying with the Darcys," she said.

"They don't trust you to stay home by yourself?" I asked.

"Ellie, I am sure they don't want them to get bored in the house by themselves," said Jade, as I passed out the fragile teacups of steaming Earl Grey.

"True. In your small town, in my grandma's house, there is nothing to do," Brooklyn said, taking the tea. "It's fine though, we love being with Georgiana and Owen. Our parents have talked of us four being together for as long as I can remember."

"I think, Jade, you maybe harbored hopes of yourself with Finn in the beginning, but you should see him with Georgie," Brooklyn said while I shot flames at her through my eyes.

"Well, yes, I mean, I thought he liked me, too, and I mean... " stammered Jade, as Brooklyn sat there looking pleased with herself.

"There is just something about private education that makes a person special. Georgiana has always gone to the finest schools and it shows. She is refined and accomplished and, of course, pretty. Finn is so relaxed with her, and you know Owen is like a brother to Finn."

"So you want to date your almost brother?" I said, wondering if I could shove this whole teacup down her throat.

"Ellie!" said a shocked Jade, and for a minute, I worried I had said the teacup part out loud.

"You know, Ellie, I was talking to Heather Parkinson the

other day. She spent middle school in Meryton and transferred to Pemberley for high school. A fun and accomplished person, she has fit in well. She was in your grade, in fact, but she has no memory of you at all. It is like you didn't exist in your own school."

"Interesting. I also met someone this summer that used to go to school with you. He had some pretty strong accusations against your friend Owen. Maybe not everyone in private school is perfect," I said.

"I can't imagine anyone having something against Owen," Brooklyn said.

"Declan Wickham does," I said.

"The boy whose father worked for Darcy International? The one on a scholarship? He is no good. I'd steer clear of him if I were you. I don't know what happened, exactly, but Owen won't speak his name," Brooklyn said.

"Oh, I see. So his claims are irrelevant because he was on scholarship?" I asked.

"Look, I am just telling you what I heard. I was just trying to help," Brooklyn said.

"I am sure there was just some sort of misunderstanding between them," Jade said. "So, did Finn get to water ski at the lake? I know he was looking forward to it?"

"Yes, he did very well. He and Georgie did a double skier trick. I am much happier inside the boat. I can work on my tan and not get my hair wet unless Owen teases me and drives over a wave and I get splashed."

"What a character he is," I said, rolling my eyes back in my skull. "You two are perfect for each other."

"I'm glad you recognize it, too. We have a history and he gets me, certainly more than my family does. The plan has been in place forever. Finn marries Georgiana, and I marry Owen and our families stay close forever," Brooklyn said, staring into the fire. "Thank your aunt for the dinner offer, but I should go. Georgiana and I are making dinner and then we are having a movie night, boys' choice. Probably some action movie, I am sure. Owen loves my chocolate malts, so I will probably make those for dessert."

"Sounds fun," said Jade with zero fun in her voice."Well, um… tell them we said hi and happy summer and good job water skiing."

"Sure. I will. Thank you for the tea, Jade. Oh, and I was wondering if you'd like to come to a summer BBQ tomorrow afternoon, much like the charming one in your neighborhood, but with a lot of our old high school friends."

Brooklyn deigned to look over at me and gave me what I think was meant to be a smile, or maybe it was a muscle spasm, "It will be casual dress, there is even a pool, so… anyway, it is on the Circle at the Camden Club. I'll put you both on the guest list," Brooklyn said as she pranced out of the room and into the elevator, looking like a triumphant spider.

I looked at Jade, sitting on the couch, her feet curled under her. The firelight danced in the unshed tears clinging to her lashes before they slid down her cheek, one by one.

"I'm so sorry," I said, curling up in the corner facing Jade and burrowing my feet under her. "She is horrible."

"Maybe her brother asked her to let me down gently, so he didn't have to," Jade said. "It wasn't like he promised me anything."

"No way. She came here with an agenda. You and Finn are meant to be together. Anyone who was around you for five minutes could see that," I said. "His face lit up every time he looked at you."

"We didn't know each other very long. Maybe he is always like that with new girls," Jade said.

"I doubt it. He was very clear about his feelings for you," I

126

said.

"Something changed then."

"Or someone changed him. Could have been Brooklyn. Or even Owen, getting in his head."

Jade wiped her cheeks on her sleeve. "He was so sweet. He would talk about going to the same college. We both have Penn on our list. He wanted to go to football games together and tailgate with all of our friends and drive back home together to spend the holidays with our families."

"That all sounds nice," I said my heart breaking for my sister. I wanted to find Owen and punch his face.

"I wanted those things, too. And I said so, but I was so careful not to initiate talk about the future. Isn't that what everyone says? Don't scare guys by talking about the future, so they don't feel trapped. I was careful, but maybe I was too careful. Act like you like him, but not too much. Flirt, but don't be too flirty. It's ridiculous. I am going to be a senior in high school and I still don't know how you are supposed to act around a guy."

I almost couldn't hear her when she mumbled to the fire, "I feel so stupid. I believed he genuinely wanted those things... with me."

"I am sure he did, DOES want those things with you. Finn is a good guy. Brooklyn is a horrible creep. I am sure all her talk about Georgiana and Owen was a lie to make us give up. I mean make you give up."

"Ellie, Brooklyn was just being herself," Jade said and looked over at me. "You, however, were not acting like yourself. You were mean."

"Mean?" I said, shocked at the disappoint I heard in Jade's voice. "I was standing up for myself, and you! It's my new thing. I want to be more like Elizabeth Bennet. You heard what she said. Heather what's-her-face didn't remember me being in her class. I think we sat next to each other in English. I don't want to be invisible anymore and I don't want to stand by and let people get away with pushing us around."

"I know you want to stand up for yourself and me, and I love you for it, but you have to be careful," Jade said, "you don't want to become the jerks you hate and there are consequences for being too direct, you may do it to the wrong person and it could backfire."

"Let's go to her stupid BBQ and maybe Finn will be there. And I will show you I can behave around the likes of Brooklyn-stupid-face," I said.

"Ellie," Jade scolded, and laughed at the same time.

Group Msg: The Invisibles

Ellie: The Wicked Witch of the West visited us tonight

Catt: witch emoji puke emoji

Ellie: We are going to a BBQ/pool party at the Camden Club tomorrow, hope we see Finn.
Jade's sad face emoji.

Marni: I was hoping you would have seen him by now.

Ava: BBQ at a club?

Emma: Be careful, I've been to the Camden, it has a pretty strict dress code, no shorts or jeans, no flip flops

Ellie: Really? That's a thing?

Marni: She is probably hoping you will dress too casual… look up the website.

Ellie: Grrrr… just looked, you are right, thank you!!!
Witch emoji puke emoji

16

I woke up determined to show Jade I could be around Brooklyn and not blast her with my newly found voice. More importantly, I knew if Finn and Jade could just see each other again, everything would go back to how it was supposed to be.

I met Aunt Cassie in the kitchen. She had a death grip on a coffee mug and looked like she had just woken up.

"Morning, want some eggs? I was going to make a spinach and feta omelet, want one?"

"Sounds amazing, but we are going to this lunch thing soon."

"I guess it is late for breakfast. I worked too late last night."

"May I pour some coffee, though?"

"Yes, though it weirds me out people your age drink coffee. Your grandma didn't let us drink it until we went away to college. She told me it would stunt my growth."

"That's funny, mom told me I could drink it if I never did it in front of grandma. Now I know why."

"What did you girls do when I went to bed?"

"I searched the Camden Club website and Googled "outfits for a fancy club lunch" because Brooklyn invited us to a BBQ there this afternoon. I don't have anything 'hoity' enough but decided to wear this linen dress I had brought for our dinner on the roof."

"You look great. Why are you so worried about what you wear?" asked Aunt Cassie.

"Always, or today?"

"I meant today, but let's start with always," she said.

"I think because I get embarrassed if I am dressed differently than everyone else, I mean *very* different like I am in shorts and they are in dresses. It's just one more thing to be made fun of."

"You have a nice circle of friends, it surprises me when you say you would get made fun of a lot."

"Maybe not a lot now. I used to be, by some mean girls at school, when I wasn't with my friends. I'm beginning to think it's because I never said anything to stop it."

"'You teach people how to treat you.' I believe that was a quote from Maya Angelou. Another strong woman to add to your Jane list."

"'You teach people how to treat you?' I like that… I am not sure how to do it, but I like it," I said.

"I'm not perfect at it, but as I have gotten older, I have realized some people will push you to see how far they can get. Those people need a clear message back. And I don't mean physical. Let's practice. What is something a mean girl would say to you?"

"Usually, stuff like making me do a whole project by myself, and then when the teacher came over she would act like the results were hers."

"So when the teacher comes over, you could say "well I'll let Meany explain our findings, she knows it best," and watch her flounder.

"No way, she would …" I started to explain.

"What? Talk about you to her friends? Was she nicer to you when you did her work?"

"It just seems easier to do it."

"It is easier. But the consequences are bad treatment. What about today, what if Ms. Brooklyn makes fun of your dress?"

"Why? Is it bad? Should I go shopping real fast?" I asked.

"Whoa, no, this is what I mean. We need to practice so you can be calm like you promised Jade," smiled Aunt Cassie shaking her head at my sudden paranoia. "I am not sure you should be aiming for speaking your mind. Maybe you should be aiming for calmly stating your needs. You speaking your mind is a little dangerous at this point."

"My quest to be like Elizabeth Bennet," I said.

"Remember, Elizabeth had to overcome her own stuff; her pride, her outspokenness, and learn to control her emotions. So maybe you have been emulating her... and need to get to the Lizzy at the end of the book, quickly," she teased.

"Okay, haha, so what do I say when she looks me up and down with disgust as she does."

"Nothing, you just tell yourself she is admiring your awesomeness," she said. "I am serious, say that in your head."

"But if she were to say, where did you find that old ugly thing?" I asked.

"Then you look at her and smile. Don't hurry anything. Take a calm breath so you sound unphased and say, 'thank you, I like it, too.'"

"But that doesn't make sense. She didn't say anything to be thanked for."

"It doesn't matter. She knows she didn't get to you. You win. Okay, try it. "Hey lady your outfit is ugly, and your hair looks like you got it cut by a blind man," Aunt Cassie yelled in a New York cabbie voice.

"Thank you, I like it too?" I tried.

"It will work, I promise, just try not to say it with a question mark at the end. I would then smile again and walk away. Well, I would strut, but that is another lesson for another day!" laughed Aunt Cassie.

"And then text my friends how much I hate that person!" I said.

"Yes, absolutely."

"Thank you for helping me, Aunt Cassie."

"Of course, kiddo, I grew up watching the Oprah show so I have plenty of good advice. Between Oprah and Jane Austen, you don't need anything else. You've got this."

"We ready to go?" asked Jade, walking in with her hair down in beachy waves, and a tiered dusty rose-colored dress with lightly puffed sleeves. She could make even this simple dress look elegant.

"That dress looks cute, Ellie," said Jade, "I love the mint green."

"Thank you, I like it too," I pointed to Aunt Cassie, making her laugh.

"You girls have fun, and I will see you later for movie night on the couch."

17

"They are having a BBQ… here?" I asked looking at Jade incredulously as we stepped out of our Uber and onto a red carpet. The club was situated in the beautiful old center of town with limestone buildings and brick roads, next to a very old Catholic Cathedral. It was awe-inspiring and screamed class and luxury.

We walked under the burgundy canopy covering the walkway and a doorman opened the heavy brass doors, welcoming us with a nod and a smile. The grand foyer was a large open room lined with dark wood-paneled walls contrasting the shiny white stone floor. Big bowls of fresh-cut lilacs greeted us from the dark wood entry table as we walked in and the aroma was sweet and inviting.

In the middle of the vast room were four red oriental rugs marking cozy conversation areas. Each section had two red leather high-backed chairs on either side of a gold tufted couch and a cherry wood coffee table. The ceiling was white with thick dark wood beams holding up four ornate, gold chandeliers. I noticed there was the same coat of arms in the stained glass windows as was on the large stone fireplace at the far end of the room. The fireplace reminded me of Aunt Cassie's, but much larger.

"This place looks like a castle," I whispered to Jade.

From a side room whose entrance was framed by a heavy gold drape, came a smiling woman in a navy pantsuit and cream-colored pumps that clicked on the floor as she walked toward us.

"Welcome to the Camden Club, are you here for a private party?" she asked politely.

"Yes," said Jade. "We are meeting Brooklyn Bingley. She mentioned she and her friends were having a BBQ here?" Just hearing the word BBQ in a place like this seemed wrong.

"Oh, I see," smiled the lady. "Let me get you checked in," she said as she motioned us behind the curtain to an equally opulent alcove with a reservation desk. "Here we go, Jade and Ellie Gardiner?"

"Yes," I said feeling relieved that Brooklyn had at least been sincere in putting us on the list.

"Your friend is at the pool for the 'Friends of Summer' luncheon. Please head down this hallway to the first set of double doors on your left. You will see the pool and your party on the south terrace."

We walked through a hallway with floor to ceiling windows on both sides showing small gardens with benches and fountains. The garden on the left gave way to a patio with white umbrella-covered tables. As Jade opened the double doors, we could see beyond the patio tables to a pool with deck chairs all around it and a wider patio on the right where girls our age stood around drinking something out of champagne flutes.

I felt fifty pairs of eyes on us at once and I took a deep breath to try to keep the blotchiness away.

I heard Jade say, "Hello Brooklyn, you look so pretty.

Doesn't she, Ellie?

"Oh, yes, you do. This orchid is your color," I said sincerely, reminding myself I was being 'not mean' for Jade's sake.

"Thank you," she said, looking us up and down. I noticed with pleasure her disappointment that we were not in cut-off jeans dressed for a BBQ.

"I notice this is all girls," I said. "I was hoping I would see Finn."

"Oh don't be silly, he is not here. Didn't I mention this would be an all-girls party? Oops. Here, have a mocktail, they are grapefruit and club soda," She said as she grabbed a few flutes from the waiter's tray.

"Like Fresca?" I said smiling at Jade.

We looked appropriate, but we were not well dressed compared to this crowd. I was not overly impressed by money just for money's sake, but this place and these girls were Instagram-ready. There was not a freckle in sight, everyone had a professional do their hair, and not one of these dresses was under $500. They were beautiful, poised, and almost looked happy in each other's company.

"I'd like to introduce you to Heather and Harlow, this is Jade and Ellie, they live in Meryton where my grandma's house is," said Brooklyn a little pointedly, I thought.

"Hello," said Harlow, "do you go to Meryton Academy?"

"Oh, no, actually, that is the name of a private school in another town, no, we go to Meryton Community High School, public school's finest." I laughed nervously.

"Oh, I see," said Heather as she smiled, not at us, but at Brooklyn.

"Thank you, I like it, too." I blurted out quickly and knew I sounded like I had lost my mind.

Brooklyn and Harlow walked away together giggling a little. Jade furrowed her brow at me and I tried to relax my fake smiling face.

Jade said, "so Heather, did you organize this gathering, it looks lovely."

"Thank you. Yes, I did. We like to have one last lunch together before the school term begins. We thought it would be fun to lean into the backyard BBQ theme, so rustic and fun," she giggled.

"So rustic," I nodded and looked around for what she considered relaxed or rustic, or even fun.

"Looks like they are serving the food, I better let everyone know. Notice the grilled shrimp on skewers, those were my idea. So fun!" said Heather excitedly as she bounded off.

I looked at Jade, my eyes imploring "can we just go?" when another perfect girl came up to us.

"Hello, I'm Monica. Did you just get 'Heathered?'"

"Yes," I laughed.

Jade furrowed her brow at me and said, "She was just telling us about the BBQ theme for lunch."

"They do like a theme here. I recommend you not flee the scene as the food is worth putting up with the people."

"So how do you fit into this group?" I asked, "Let me guess, you are the down-trodden cousin assigned to entertain the poor unfortunate outcasts from public school?" I joked as we joined the buffet line.

"Oh, no, my parents are nauseatingly rich," she teased as I choked slightly on my mocktail. "But," she said laughing at my reaction, "they are not normal rich folk. They are adventurers and raised me and my brother in Africa, mostly. I have lived on animal preserves tagging and monitoring the wildebeest migration and I spent time on archaeological digs in Egypt. So while I've had the privilege of money, I wasn't raised with this obsession with status," said Monica.

"You have lived such an interesting life, this must feel so

mundane," said Jade.

"It is not mundane to me. I didn't wear a dress until I was ten and I certainly have never contoured my face or had lash extensions… and I have zero social media presence. But we live here, at least for now, and they are not too bad once you figure out their 'whys,'" indicating the group of girls in front of us.

"What are their why's?" I asked eagerly.

"Nope, you have to tell me how you fit in this group first," said Monica.

At the buffet, I saw an array of food, in beautiful silver chafing dishes. All meant to be easily eaten in a ladylike fashion; bite-sized quiche and mini skewers of Caprese salad, and, like any proper backyard bbq, a man in a chef's hat hand-carving choice cuts of meat.

"We were invited by Brooklyn Bingley," said Jade. "The Bingleys moved into our neighborhood earlier this summer, they inherited their grandma's house."

"We only came because we thought her brother Finn would be here," I said.

"Ellie," scolded Jade.

"We can trust Monica, she is one of us," I said.

"I am honored if by 'one of us,' you mean, not one to take myself so seriously."

"Yes!" I said, exactly. "Do you know Finn? He is not at all like Brooklyn."

"I know the whole family. She is like her grandmother on the Father's side. The rest of them are nice. But, the grandmother knew the business and she guided her husband. It is said she was the reason they had such success, back in the day."

"Does their family history lead you to their 'why?'" I asked, taking a bite of the grilled shrimp.

"A bit. Once I realized why each of these ladies feels the need to put on airs, it made me understand them better and not be so annoyed with them. Some of them I still don't like to spend time with, but others you just see the pressure they are under," said Monica.

"Pressure?" I asked, thinking it looked like a pretty privileged life with very little pressure.

"I don't need to bore you with everyone's business, but I will explain a little bit about your tsala, Brooklyn. It might help you forgive her, or at least help you deal with her," said Monica in a lowered voice.

"Wait, tsala? What is that?" I asked.

"Oh, wow, I do that occasionally, I mix my Tswana language with English. Sorry. 'Tsala' means friend. I will explain a little about your friend, Brooklyn."

"Tsala," said Jade trying Monica's inflection on the word.

"Please," I said before Jade could make us feel bad for gossiping. I knew she would say "no thanks," out of big sister obligation.

"Well, since the grandma I mentioned was out of the picture and the son took over, the business has been in decline. Brooklyn's dad doesn't have the cutthroat approach to business and it's not doing well. I knew they sold their house and were moving out of the city to the house they inherited. I think they will still be able to finish at Pemberley and then go to college, but I think the lifestyle your friend Brooklyn loves is gone. I bet this is her last summer at this club. And honestly, if these other girls knew it, you would see some of them start to pull away from her. It's sad."

"Monica, what are you going to do after high school? Are you going to stay here?" Jade asked.

"No, I will probably head back to Africa and work with the animals again. I felt like I was making a difference working with animals orphaned from the poaching trade."

"No way, did you get to hug a baby elephant?" I asked.

"Yes," laughed Monica, "it is as wonderful as you imagine, except they are heavy! Like a heavy, messy puppy," she said, her eyes lighting up for the first time.

"That sounds like heaven," said Jade.

"Amazing, I'd love to do that. BTW… oh, that means 'by the way,' since you aren't on social media…this food IS amazing," I said.

"I text, so I know some things," laughed Monica.

"I should find Brooklyn and at least thank her for lunch," said Jade excusing herself from the table.

"Why did she invite us if she was just going to ignore us? Not that I mind. I just don't get the purpose," I said to Monica.

"I am sure she was hoping you would not fit in and she could feel better about herself. That happens here occasionally," she said.

"And she probably wants Jade to feel despondent about Finn. She keeps telling Jade he is meant for Georgiana Darcy… and she for Owen," I said, not meaning to spill that particular secret, but Monica didn't seem to catch it.

"Owen Darcy?! Now he is a catch. He's more like us than them," said Monica nodding her head toward the gaggle of girls. "I haven't seen either Finn or Owen in a while. Last I heard, Owen was patting himself on the back for saving Finn from a really bad relationship."

"He what? What relationship?" I choked on my Fresca mocktail.

"Fairly recently, but I don't know any details. Oh, brace yourself, here she comes," said Monica.

"I see you have found a friend," said Brooklyn as she waltzed over to our table with Jade in tow.

"Yes, I presume you know Monica?" I said.

"Of course, I do. Our families are old friends. I think our grandparents dined at this club together in the olden days. Quality people stick together. Isn't that right Monica?" said Brooklyn.

"Indeed, they do. Shall I give you girls a tour then?" Monica asked me and Jade with a smile.

"Absolutely, it is beautiful here," said Jade. "Thank you for inviting us today, Brooklyn."

"In case I don't see you before we leave, Brooklyn, please tell Finn we said hi. We'd love to see him while we are here this week," I said, because I knew Jade wouldn't.

"He is very busy, but I most certainly will," she said and pranced away.

"Monica, you have saved the day," I said sincerely, not blaming her for her bombshell about Owen's treachery. I knew I couldn't ask her more details in front of Jade, but my mind was reeling.

"It was so interesting speaking with you," said Jade. "I'd love to know about your next adventure."

"Let's keep in touch," Monica said, "I could use more quality people in my social circle."

"We can be tsala," I said proudly in my best Tswana accent.

"Yes, ditsala. Let's start the tour on the roof, its the one place I've never been. They play something called 'pickle-ball' up there. Another American game I know nothing about. Shall we?" asked Monica, leading the way.

Group Msg: The Invisibles

Ava: What time are we meeting tomorrow?

Catt: Dress emoji Dress emoji Dress emoji

Ellie: 12 p.m., 1 p.m. 2 p.m.??

Ellie: We still haven't seen Finn. Is Eden coming with?

Marni: IDK, lemme see. they could go stalk his house. lol

Emma: Got the credit card, ready to shop! I could bring eggs… and toilet paper!

Ellie: I'd love to egg them all, I haven't even told you the worst part of this day.

Ava: Oh no, what happened?

Ellie: A girl named Monica told me she heard Owen bragging about saving Finn from a bad relationship!!! angry face emoji I didn't want to believe he was all bad, but this is unforgivable. We are totally egging them!

18

My phone said it was 5:45 a.m. I could hear Jade stir as I grabbed my sweatshirt and sneakers and quietly shut the bedroom door.

Aunt Cassie was in the kitchen making coffee, with a half-eaten piece of toast hanging out of her mouth and her hair looking wilder than usual.

"Ummm, another all-nighter?" I asked.

"Mmmm hmmm," she said until her hands were free and she could finish the toast. "What are you doing up this late or early?" she asked.

"I'm going to take a walk."

"Ah, need to clear your head?" she asked. "Anything you want to talk about?"

"I'm fine, but thanks. Nothing big, just confusing people."

"And by 'people' you mean 'boys.'"

"Yeah, you know me too well."

"I do, and therefore I won't offer this mediocre coffee. Do you remember the flower shop down the block?"

"Yes, I love that place."

"Across the street is this excellent coffee shop named

Priscilla's. And the pastries are calorie-worthy! Let me give you some cash so you can pick up a selection for us on your way home."

"I've got money. Mom made sure," I said. "What is your favorite pastry?"

"I am going to lie down for a couple of hours, then shower and go into the office. If they have a cinnamon roll, I'll take it. If not, I'm good," she said, stifling a yawn. "Take the extra key in case no one is awake when you get back."

"I better leave a note, too, or Jade will get worried."

"Be safe. I'll leave my phone next to me. Call if you get nervous, but it's a safe area. Love you kiddo," she said as she kissed my cheek.

"Love you too. Good sleep."

Even at this early hour, the city wasn't quiet. The elevator chimed and dinged my arrival on the ground floor. The classical music in the lobby put a little pep in my step and made me feel hopeful for the day to come. I stepped out onto the city streets into a bustling world. Streetlights were still on and most storefronts were closed, but delivery vans stopped with dollies full of crates to unload, and the early birds hustled to be first in the office.

I was reluctant to disturb the peace with words. I smiled at an older man, sweeping the stoop of his greengrocery, whose "open" sign lights were slowly blinking to life. A couple of women jogged down the street, nodding a silent, but friendly "good morning." I breathed in the crisp, humid air. The city smelled like rubber with a tang of metal and the distant aroma of baking bread. The honeysuckle that climbed the alley gate next to the grocer housed busy twittering birds among its leaves. I was an urban Snow White with all the little woodland creatures. Maybe not, but it was a beautiful morning.

My mind kept replaying the visit with Brooklyn. She had

been so delighted to tell us how cute Georgiana was with Finn. I could see Jade trying to keep her face a mask, but her eyes showed the hurt. I had kept my mouth shut by imagining grabbing her by her strawberry blond bob and throwing her out onto the curb. And then the bombshell that Monica dropped on me. Could that be real? Owen was bragging about saving Finn from a terrible relationship with Jade? He was arrogant, but was he that manipulative? I think Declan would say yes. How could Owen think that of Jade? Why would he cause so much hurt?

The smell of the flower shop was growing stronger, easing the negative energy that was swirling in my brain. The shop was less than half a block up and I could see the owner setting out pails of fresh-cut flowers in every shape and hue.

"Good morning, young lady," said the shop owner, whose twinkling eyes shone out of her round dimpled cheeks. She looked like the summer sister of Mrs. Claus and I liked her immediately.

"Good morning, your shop smells so good," I said, sticking my nose into every bouquet. "I guess these aren't fragrant, but they are beautiful," I said, pointing to a flower with big pompoms of paper-thin petals in light pink and blue.

"Those are summer hydrangeas. You like the pink or the blue ones best?" she asked.

"I usually choose pink everything, but I think these baby blue ones are my favorite," I said. "Oh, and these… I forget the name, like yellow daisies maybe? My grandpa used to pick these for me when we would find them wild."

"I like those, too. They are Black-Eyed Susan. They look like yellow daisy petals, with a dark brown middle, or a black eye," she said, her own eyes twinkling, "but you can call them yellow daisies."

"I am staying with my aunt. I think I'd like to bring her some of these hydrangeas," I said on impulse. They made my morning, so it seemed only right to share them.

With a content smile on my face and an armful of soft blue flowers, I headed across the street for coffee and extreme yumminess. I pushed thoughts of Brooklyn and Owen to the back of my mind and enjoyed feeling like a sophisticated city girl on a morning stroll.

The sun was coming up and more commuters were bustling around, many craving caffeine and pastries. I opened the coffee shop door and was enveloped in the the the bitter, nutty scent of fresh coffee beans. My eyes feasted on the glass case filled with blueberry muffins, croissants with ham and cheese, and fist-sized cinnamon rolls with globs of icing dribbling down the sides. The businessman in front of me ordered a "dirty chai latte" which sounded funny, so I accidentally giggled out loud.

He looked at me and I stuttered out an apology, but he waved that away and said, "I know, I laughed too, but you have to try it, it's amazing. It is a spicy tea latte with a shot of espresso. It has a good caffeine kick."

"Sold," I cheered, and thanked the departing man as he lifted his cup in a salute. "I also need a mazillion pastries to go," I said to the girl behind the counter who was my age and whose name tag read Melly.

"Hey Melly, I'm Ellie," I sang, sounding like Catt, and together we filled the pink bakery box with the perfect treats.

I placed the hydrangeas and the box of pastries precariously in the crook of my left arm so my other hand was free to hold my new favorite hot drink… a dirty chai latte. The spicy smell tingled my nose and the mix of bitter espresso and the sweet milk was hot and smooth down the back of my throat. I was so overloaded I wasn't sure how I was going to open the door when I heard a voice say, "here allow me."

"Thank you," I said as I walked through the door and froze in place. Holding the door for me was Owen Darcy.

"Ellie, what a surprise. It's nice to see you."

"What are you doing here?" I asked, still too stunned to say much else.

"I live right over there and come here most mornings. How is your family and how are your friends?"

He asked with an unusually fond smile on his face. Something about the fact that he looked so happy to see me, like he hadn't been the source of so much sadness and awful music choices from my sister, made me furious. I was the kind of angry where you barely move a muscle, so it doesn't all come bursting out. I could feel my jaw clench and my eyes spark.

"Please, can I walk with you? Where are you headed? I'll carry some of this," he said as he tried to take the box and the flowers.

"Thank you, I've got it. I'm just going back to my aunt's," I said, surprised he wasn't afraid of the set of my jaw or the flames shooting out of my eyes.

"Look Ellie, I have been wanting to get a hold of you. I have so much I want to say. Can you stop for a minute?" he said, motioning to a park bench near a small grassy area between buildings.

He took a deep breath and paced back and forth, looking more nervous than I had ever seen him. He finally blurted, "I need to tell you that from the moment we met, I have not been able to stop thinking about you."

I was both furious and stunned, but unlike in the past, my throat did not close and I did not freeze in place. I looked directly into those intense hazel eyes and let loose the frustration I had been feeling for weeks.

"Please tell me, Mr. Darcy, to which magical moment you

146

are referring? The one where you and Brooklyn mocked my clothes, or perhaps the time you called me uncultured?"

"I'm sorry. I know. I have been such jerk."

"And I was just a nobody public-school girl from a small town."

"Well, yes, I mean, we are from very different backgrounds, obviously. In fact, my friends thought it was funny that I had to spend the summer where people detassel corn. You have to admit, this is not exactly where you'd find a petting zoo," he said, gesturing around the now noisy city street.

"A petting zoo? Do you mean the once-a-year county fair? Unbelievable. So now I'm a zookeeper." I said, having trouble staying in control of my growing temper.

"Look, I never intended to fall for someone who lives, well, who is not here, not heading to the ivy leagues, not…"

"Whoa, you don't know where I want to go to college. You know nothing about me and presume a lot because of where I live. Brooklyn is right. She is your perfect match, not me."

"I'm sorry. I am not saying it very well. I don't have your way with people. I shouldn't have mentioned my friends making fun of your town. And you are right, I don't know enough about you. The truth is, I can't get you out of my head and I was wondering if you would go out with me and we could get to know each other?" he asked, his eyes pleading.

"You misunderstand me," I snapped. "The way you asked is not why I would never, ever go out with you. Kindness and character matter to me. I knew you for less than a week when your true colors were revealed to me and I realized you were the last man in the world whom I could ever be prevailed upon… 'oh, holy cow, I am about to quote Elizabeth Bennet even now,'" I said out loud, laughing a little wildly.

He looked stunned by being called out, confused by my laughter, and a little terrified of the maniacal look in my eyes.

If I weren't so angry, I would have laughed at the expression I saw on his face.

"As I was saying, your friend Declan told me what your petty jealousy cost him. First, he lost his father, and then you can't even let him have the scholarship named for his dad? Because he is better than you at basketball? And today, I heard you saved Finn from Jade. You clearly told him Jade wasn't good enough for him, didn't you? Better not love a girl who lives near the fairgrounds… she could become a zookeeper, and then where would you be? Right? And you probably sent Brooklyn to tell us you and Finn could not possibly be interested in girls like us. Or didn't she tell you we were in town?"

Owen took a while to say anything, and when he finally spoke, he muttered, "Sent Brooklyn? I confess I told Finn I thought your sister didn't seem very into him."

"She is shy! She would never throw herself at a guy. Maybe that is what you are used to here in the big city, but in the boondocks, we don't act like that. Especially not Jade. You are a fool if you don't think they belong together."

"And this is what you think of me?" he breathed.

"You are acting comically like your name's sake. You really should read it sometime, *Mr. Darcy.* As Elizabeth would say, 'you spared me the concern I might have felt in refusing you, had you behaved in a more gentleman-like manner,'" I quoted and stomped away.

19

When I came back to the condo, I was still livid. I was ranting inside my head and sometimes I would startle myself by muttering out loud, "that guy has some nerve!" From the day I met him, I could tell he thought he was better than me and now he thinks he can just ask me out and all the past rudeness is forgiven. My first impressions had been right. He was an arrogant jerk who happened to look cute in a certain light. He also smelled good and saved drowning children. But it would be a cold day in…

"Ellie is that you?" asked Jade, sounding sleepy.

"Yeah, I brought pastries!" I chimed, sounding overly cheerful.

"How come you got up so early?" Jade asked, taking the box from me.

"Because you snore like a train," I teased. "One of the cinnamon rolls is for Aunt Cassie, and so are these flowers. Aren't they pretty?"

When I got no answer, I continued, "do you and Eden want to go dress shopping with us? They are coming at 2 p.m."

"No, I think Eden and I are going to hang out here while you guys go, maybe go out later. Not sure yet."

"You want to go sit on the balcony with these?" I said, indicating my coffee and ham and cheese croissant.

I couldn't decide if I should tell Jade about Owen. It felt selfish to tell her and make it about my argument when she was still hurting. I knew her. She would start taking care of me instead of herself. It also felt like she should know Owen's part in the whole thing.

I needed to wait and talk this through with my friends.

******

Group Msg: The Invisibles

Marni: Eden driving like an old lady. ETA 1:50 p.m.

Emma: Marni's just mad because she got banned from choosing music, pan flute again. eyeroll

Marni: It's relaxing, sue me.

Ava: We are excited to see you!

Catt: And shop!! Meow!

Catt: Oh and ask Emma about the cute construction boy she met. xoxoxoxox

Emma: Good news bad news situation. He's so fine, but… his name is Bert! I can't.

Ellie: Srsly? crying emoji crying emoji

Emma: I told him his name was now Xander.

Ava: Poor guy.

Ellie: I can't wait to hear more! See you soon.

I held open the door of Pixie, a trendy clothing store that was having an anniversary sale, or so the mazillion red and white signs showed.

"You guys, this is our rom-com scene," said a bouncy Catt.

"You mean where we try on increasingly ridiculous dresses, pose in stupid ways, and finally land on the perfect dress?" asked Emma.

"Dress montage, here we come!" said Marni.

Catt walked up to the sale rack, pulled an emerald green slip dress off the rack, and held it up. We all said, "that's it!" The color was perfect for her, but she would not be denied her montage, so she grabbed several others and headed to the dressing room.

Ava said, "only Catt could find something within ten seconds of walking into the store."

"Aye, she's but a wee slip of a girl…" I said, trying for an Irish accent, to the horror of those around me. "Okay, okay, I'm done with the accents… I promise," I laughed.

"So, Ellie…" Ava began in a confidential tone, even looking to see who else was close by. "You know, all this *Pride and Prejudice* talk sent me on a quest to reread all of Jane's novels. And, well, I am nearly done with *Persuasion*. I didn't think about it the first time I read it, but do you know why it is called that?"

I shook my head.

"It's because Anne was persuaded by others. Mostly their family friend, Lady Russell, who convinces Ann to break off her engagement to the poor sea captain. Anyway… it started me thinking about Freddy."

I was wide-eyed and excited. Since Freddy left, Ava hadn't wanted to talk about him. "And…"

"And… I cyber-stalked him," she said with both pride and a little guilt.

"No way, and…." I prompted.

"I found him."

"Ahhhhh," I quiet screamed and hugged Ava.

"I'm thinking red," said Emma, demanding our attention as she model walked out of the dressing room in a very vavoomy cherry red bandage dress.

"Well, the theme is "A Night Among the Stars," and you

look like a star, a movie star," I said.

"I mean, it works cosmically. Deep blood red is associated with Aries because it symbolizes passion," said Marni.

"But your dad will kill you dressing so… passionate," said Catt.

"It looks good though. It's just the bustier that looks so adult, and maybe the tightness," said Ava, "but you are fully covered, and it looks so pretty."

"The whole town will be there, and they will all notice you," I said.

"That's how it should be," laughed Emma.

I looked at Ava, and said "more later, I'm totally dying."

She smiled and nodded her head, heading to the dressing room. I watched her walk by with a few things over her arm. She looked so calm, but I know she was in turmoil. She had loved Freddy. No matter how young they were, I knew it was real and I have always hoped they would get back together somehow.

The sales clerks were surprisingly nice to us. Most often, salespeople see us as evil teenagers and follow us around like we are going to steal something. I was happy they let Catt do her montage in the dressing room area with no drama.

I felt most drawn to wearing something light-colored and flowy. I had a white dress at home, and though it wasn't YSL as someone had recently pointed out. it was pretty. But I wanted this to be more wow, like a cocktail dress. If it were Fall, I would go for a black dress with ballerina tulle I saw recently, but July in the mid-west is not the place for black or tulle. I chose a soft butter yellow dress with one flutter cap sleeve, strapless on the other side with a tea-length a-line skirt. I passed on a few pretty dresses with flower patterns. They felt too fussy and too casual at the same time. In the end, I grabbed a baby pink dress with longer flutter sleeves that dropped off

152

the shoulder. It was plain but was several layers of sheer pink wispy material. I was missing the montages, so I took these two dresses and headed to the dressing room.

I got to see Catt finally try on the green slip dress and it was as gorgeous as I thought it would be. The dark color made her pale skin shine and her eyes look luminous. She tried to model walk like Emma, but it didn't look as fierce as it did drunken, though she still looked cute.

They made me take Emma's dressing room, so I had to peek my head out from the curtain to see Marni start her show with an apricot-colored dress. It was pretty, but we agreed seemed too prom-like. She also tried a long chiffon multicolored dress that looked like an artists palette. I always loved to see what Marni was drawn to. She had such an artist's eye. She could put together what seemed mismatched to me and look amazing in it.

I tried on the yellow dress and walked out laughing. It was technically a cute dress, but they did not make it for someone my height.

"Emma, I think you need to try this on. It belongs on a leggy giant. Hang on, I'll hand it to you."

I went back into the dressing room and shed the yellow, handing it through the curtain. I turned back to my only other find and pulled it on over my head.

I looked at myself as I finished pulling down the skirt and smoothing everything into place. It was surprising how much better the dress looked on me than on the hanger. It cinched in at the waist and flared out toward the bottom. I swayed the skirt back and forth and loved the swish and flow. I turned to look over my shoulder at the back and loved the way it scooped low, but not too low so I could still wear a normal bra. I stuck my head out of the curtain when I heard some commotion, in the form of Catt chanting "Ava Ava Ava!"

"What are you doing to her, Kitty Catt? Leave poor Ava alone," I said.

"But I want to see," said Catt.

Ava dramatically flung open her curtain and posed provocatively against the dressing room door frame.

If Freddy had been here, he would have died right on the spot. Sweet, kind, conservative Ava looked like a bombshell. She wore a bright orange halter-top dress. It skimmed her body and hit her right at the knee. She looked like an orange dreamsicle, Marilyn Monroe.

"Yes, girl!" said Marni.

"Finally!" said Emma.

"Just wow!" I said.

And Catt clapped and yelled, "yay!!!"

We had had the place to ourselves until that moment when the bell over the door tinkled and Ava fled back into the dressing room, all confident posing gone. But I looked forward to seeing her confidence again when we finally got to wear these dresses.

Marni said, "Wait, Ellie, show us more than your head. Do you have the pink one on?"

'Yes," I did a less dramatic curtain fling, but I stood and spun. "I think I need some more sun, but what do you think?"

"It's a perfect water sign dress, romantic and flowy," said Marni.

"I love it," said the head of Ava from her curtains.

"And you already have those blush stack-heeled sandals," said Emma. "I think the color would match perfectly."

"Oh wow, that's true. Awesome. Catt, are you about to say 'yay?'" I asked, giving a final twirl, "I think this is the one."

"Marn, what did you pick?" I asked.

"I liked the ones I found. I just didn't fall in love. We have time, but I am getting hangry! Can we go find a coffee shop?"

"I have the place for you!" I said, just hoping Owen wouldn't go there twice in one day. "And I have a story to go with it."

No one wanted to walk the five blocks to the coffee shop because it was so rare we got to do things like take an Uber.

"If adventures will not befall a young lady in her own village, she must seek them abroad." I quoted from Northanger Abbey, Jane's fifth novel.

"Oh, I like that, did Elizabeth Bennet say that?" asked Catt.

"No, but I think you would love the book it is from. In fact, your love for adventure and whimsy… "

"Meow! I do love me some whimsy."

"Read Northanger Abbey. There might even be ghosts in it," I said.

The skeptical-looking driver pulled up. We felt very New York City cramming ourselves and our purchases into the silver Honda Accord. The driver was very patient, and I promised him I would be tipping. Marni sat next to the driver, Emma, Ava, and I sat in the back seat and Catt crawled onto Emma's lap and stretched out her legs with all the dresses covering her like a blankie.

"Catt, your butt is too bony. You need to eat a sandwich," complained Emma.

"Speaking of Jane novels, Ellie, how are you doing emulating Elizabeth Bennet? Are getting better at standing up for yourself?" asked Ava from under Catt's feet.

"Well, funny you should ask. I have definitely been confronting my issues head-on today. That's part of what I want to tell you guys. My Aunt Cassie says I need to find a balance, but so far, I'm full blast telling people what I think, or at least one person."

"I hope it was Brooklyn," said Emma. "She deserves a wake-up call."

"You've never met her," said Catt.

"We've all met her, at least her type, at some point," said Emma.

"Well, now we need to twist that confidence into speaking ability at the gala," said Ava.

"She's done well with her speech practices, but we need one more big one before you meet Ms. Lemon for gala rehearsal," said Marni.

"Ahhhh, I forgot. Yikes, it's soon. Like two weeks," I soft-screamed for the driver's sake.

"We are here," I said as the Honda pulled to the curb and Ava opened the door so we could start piling out. "Thank you, sir, for letting us all cram in. Have a good day." In the end, I don't think the driver was sad we were only going five blocks.

Inside the coffee shop, I showed everyone the menu, and I heard "back again, Ellie?"

"Melly! You are still working?"

"Yeah, I did a double shift. Someone didn't show up, but it's okay, all the closer to getting my new car!"

"Nice!"

"Since you are here, I kinda want to tell you something that is none of my business," said Melly.

"Okay? Sure, shoot." By this point, all of my friends had stopped looking at the menu and were watching Melly, but I was too curious about what she was going to say to stop and introduce them.

"You know the guy you were arguing with earlier?"

"You saw that? I thought we were further down the street," I said sheepishly.

"I mean, it wasn't a huge scene, but yeah, I noticed."

"What about it?"

"Well, I don't know what he did to you, but don't be too hard on him. He is, at least around here, a super good guy."

"Do you know him?"

"I know him as a customer who is always nice, tips well, and always does things like pay it forward. See the mug by the register? It is for people to buy a coffee for someone that comes in and can't afford a cup. He puts in every time. Some homeless people get breakfast every day because of him."

"That is nice," I said.

"And he isn't skeezy, you know what I mean? Girls our age are always getting gross comments, but not once ever. Always nice, never flirty," she said.

"Oh," I said, not knowing what to think.

"As I said, it's none of my business, but you guys looked good together and I thought 'Oh, good, he has a nice girl,' which is why I was looking at you guys when it went south," said Melly.

"Yeah, I was a little mad."

"He left with the longest face I have ever seen. I am not saying he didn't deserve it and I'm all for girls sticking together. I just want you to have all the info in case it matters."

"Thank you for letting me know. I'll think about what you said. In the meantime, let me introduce you to my friends who don't know that story yet, and now will kill me if I don't bring them up to speed."

"Melly, these are The Invisibles."

20

Sitting in the corner of Priscilla's with our hot chocolates and dirty chai lattes I related the conversation I had earlier with Owen and since Melly spilled the beans, they knew it was a lively one.

"I knew he liked you. I could tell at the basketball game!" said Ava.

"Is it disloyal to say I think he is cute and nice?" asked Marni.

"You guys are missing the point here... he has done some despicable things," I said.

"Not the least of which is mock our fair town," laughed Marni.

"We only have Declan's word for what Owen did to him. Could he have exaggerated?" mused Emma.

"But why? He has nothing to gain by lying," I said. "I mean, I am obviously over it, but I thought he was fun to be around."

"I am not sure that is true," said Ava. "He was fun, but I am not sure he had 'nothing to gain.' He gained your belief against Owen. And I noticed he doesn't seem to have any long-time friends."

"Not everyone has what we have," said Catt.

"You are right Kit-Catt. We are lucky," I said. "What do I do about Jade? That is the most important part. Do I tell her what Owen said to Finn? That she didn't act like she really liked him?"

"It sort of feels like victim blaming 'you didn't act how you should have so… he broke your heart,'" pointed out Emma.

"I know. It feels awkward," I said.

"And she is the sweetest person," said Ava, "but maybe it just means she marches over there and tells him she misses him."

I smiled at Ava, because I was sure she was not just talking about Jade.

******

It had been such a quick visit, but dress shopping had been a blast. We had hit a few more shops before Eden had to leave, taking a car of tired, shopped-out girls the forty-five minutes back to our hometown. I had shown Jade my dress and was wandering out of the bedroom for water when Aunt Cassie came in from work.

"Ellie, this letter came for you. The doorman gave it to me. A handwritten letter, how old-fashioned and romantic," she said, raising her eyebrows, much like my mother, and smiling.

"I was thinking I could take you girls out somewhere nice for dinner on your last night. What do you think?" asked Aunt Cassie.

"I'll ask Jade, but it might be more fun to order in," I said.

"How is Jade?"

"I think she was hoping Finn would find out she was here and come visit. Maybe that's what this is about," I said, waving the letter. "I'm going to go read."

"Of course, go. I'll find Jade and ask about dinner," Aunt Cassie said.

159

I took the letter out onto the balcony and settled in one of the cushioned chairs. I used my finger to pry open the flap and pulled out the five cream-colored pages written back to back in bold and careful handwriting. When I looked at the last page, I saw it was from Owen Darcy.

I was so surprised. What more could Owen have to say to me? I doubted he had more insults to pepper on top of the ones he had already shared. He had taken the time to handwrite a letter. It seems more important and more personal. My anger wasn't gone, but it had ebbed enough that I didn't fling the letter into the fire automatically.

Dear Ellie,

I am hoping you will read this letter and not throw it immediately in the fireplace, though from your perspective, I would deserve that. I have so many things to say, and I thought a letter might be the best way to organize those thoughts and express them to you.

When I am talking to you in person, I get my words twisted and say the absolutely wrong thing. I have never had a great way with people or words, but I swear I am worse around you than anyone. Maybe one day you will see that I am normal. You are probably right. I am a snob, but I think you have at least opened my eyes to that part of myself. It matters to me what you think of me, yet I know right now it is not much. I am sorry about that, but I have written today, not to ask you out again. You have made your position on that subject very plain.

I have written to be clear on two of the charges you made against me. To the first one, you are right. I was the person who told Finn I thought he was much more invested in Jade than she was in him. I don't want to betray my friend by saying too much, but he had recently broken up with a girl from school who cheated on him and strung him along for months. He believes people are who they say they are. He is so genuine that he cannot see falseness or manipulation in others. This girl was a classic narcissist who used him to boost her ego when she was bored, and it devastated him when she finally broke it off with him. He begged me to watch when he started liking someone again and see if what he saw was real. I could see him falling for your sister, more than any girl he has ever liked, and I was concerned. While I could tell she was a nice person, not a narcissist, I didn't think she was as crazy about him and I worried he would get heartbroken. I was especially concerned when our coach told him he had to live at my house to keep his eligibility his senior year. If she didn't like him, he would waste his whole senior year on a girl that was ambivalent about him. I didn't want him to miss out on homecoming dance, prom, everything on a broken heart.

You know your sister and I have no reason to doubt you. If you say your sister cares for Finn, I believe you and I feel bad about my interference. I am not sure I can fix my mistake, but I promise to think about how to make it right.

As to the accusation about Declan, 'my childhood friend,' and 'stealing his prospects out of jealousy,' I cannot let that accusation stand. He is a liar, and he is not nearly as good at basketball as he thinks he is. I would rather not have any of what I am about to tell you spread around. It is so far known only in my family, for Georgie's sake and at her request.

Declan is a predator disguised in charm and, I suppose, somewhat decent looks. He is 100% about his self-interest at every moment, with guys and girls alike. Sadly, none of us knew that until it was too late. The basics are that he 'dated' my sister, though my dad had forbidden her from being in a committed relationship since she was only fourteen and he was seventeen. Declan was a family friend. His father had just died a few years after our mom, so he hung out at our house and went on our family trips. We trusted him so much that we didn't see how far he had manipulated his way into Georgie's heart until I accidentally walked in on her one morning before she pulled on a jacket and I could see bruises all up and down her arms. At that moment, I knew it was rough grab marks, and I knew it was Declan. What I didn't know, and still don't know for sure, is how much more abuse she suffered than the physical she finally admitted to, nor how long it had been going on. She saw a therapist a few times, but refused to go anymore and didn't want to press charges because she thought it would be just her word against his and was too embarrassed. It takes everything in me not to punch his face every time I see him. I want to tell the world what a lowlife he is, but she begs me to let it go. My father took away his scholarship so he, at least, wasn't in the same school as Georgie, but the Declans of the world seem to worm their way through life hurting others and taking what they want. Please, for your sake and mine, stay away from Declan Wickham. You are far too good a person to be caught in his web of lies.

Thank you for reading this and giving me a shot at telling you my side of both stories. I am sorry I caused hurt to Jade, and you. I had fun learning about swinging bridges and your friendly town, and I guess it's time I read about my namesake. Maybe I will learn a thing or two.

Yours,

Owen Darcy

I sat still, staring at the pages. What he said about Declan shocked me and I felt the relief of the close call I had, grateful I had trusted my instincts when things felt not right. I was glad Owen felt he could tell me such a personal thing, but I wasn't sure what to do about it. He asked me not to mention it to anyone else and I would honor the part about his sister. But surely I should tell my friends Declan wasn't trustworthy, and maybe even that troll, Amber Raine. She made me want to scream, but I didn't wish anything super bad to happen to her. I mean, if spiders crawled all over her or she fell face-first into the mud, I would be fine with it.

I had accused him of being insensitive and prejudiced, but I had been the same. I had always prided myself on being able to read people. Now I felt shame at the way Declan had easily played me from the beginning. And for how I had mistrusted Owen based on lies. He was still rude sometimes, but maybe he wasn't a horrible smug face.

How embarrassing, I had laid into Owen in the middle of the city, on the word of a creep. I totally deserved to feel ashamed. "Till this moment I never knew myself," I said out loud with an ironic laugh. "I am exactly Elizabeth Bennet right now. Good thing I don't have a younger sister for Declan to run away with."

My thoughts were spinning. Elizabeth couldn't take any action in her time, but I could. One minute I thought I wanted to go apologize, then I thought I should just let it go. I was not sure. Should I tell Jade about Finn? I would want to know.

"We decided on Chinese. It will be here in 10 minutes," said Aunt Cassie, accessing my body language and becoming more curious. "Anything you want to talk about?"

"Nope, just more confusion. I'll tell you both over some fried rice," I said, as I sprang up and headed inside to wash up.

"May I say that when I die, if there is nothing else I can be proud of, my legacy to the world will be that I taught you two how to use chopsticks. You make me proud," said Aunt Cassie looking over at us both curled on the couch eating out of Chinese take-out boxes.

"I think there will be much more to your legacy," laughed Jade.

"But if not, this is enough. Oh, and I taught you guys

important grade school stuff like the use of cootie spray and how to do the MASH game on paper to figure out what house you will have and what boy you are going to marry, etcetera."

"Those were important things. Our parents were too busy with 'don't talk with your mouth full and do your homework,'" I said.

"At least someone had their priorities straight," Aunt Cassie said. "Okay, so I don't do subtle very well. Ellie, are you going to tell us what was in your letter or not?"

"It is probably better if I tell you what happened this morning, and then read this to you. I kinda need to hear it again, and out loud would help."

After I recounted the story of our morning encounter and got a mini-lecture from Jade on being too hard on Owen, I read the letter... skipping the part about Georgiana.

I had felt guilty about reading it to Jade. I hadn't wanted to sound like she was to blame for not being more demonstrative, but she actually looked buoyed by the news. Her eyes looked brighter than they had in days, and she sat up a little taller. I guess it was confirmation she hadn't been only a summer fling.

"Well, young ladies, you both have some decisions to make," said Aunt Cassie.

"You are right. But Jade, what are you going to do?" I said, not wanting the focus on me.

"I am not sure what to do, but I want to do something."

"Do you want to be bold and let him know clearly how you feel about him? Or do you want to wait to see if he contacts you on your own? You get to choose if a relationship with him is worth putting your whole heart on the line. Which pain do you prefer?" said Aunt Cassie.

"I need to think about how I want to handle it, but I prefer the pain of all cards on the table. The worst was no explanation and a lot of stories being made up in my head. All worse than the truth," said Jade. "But for tonight, I am happy knowing it was real."

I had my own feelings to sort out, but tonight I felt gratitude to Owen Darcy for giving us hopeful, happy Jade back.

21

While Jade gathered her courage to approach Finn about her feelings, I was reminded that my goal this summer had been primarily to be brave like Jade and Elizabeth Bennet.

If Elizabeth saw the error of her ways and could admit her faults, so could I. I pulled on my faded blue converse and headed out the door.

It was later than I had meant to head out. I had planned to get up early and ambush Owen at Priscilla's Coffee and Bakery, but I overslept and now wasn't sure what to do. I walked up the street Owen had pointed to when he said he lived "that way" and I tried to look like I was just strolling along. I fidgeted with the cuffs of my long-sleeved tie-dyed pink shirt a few times as I walked and tightened my high ponytail until it ached.

Each house set back from the road with a deep, well-manicured lawn and tall, lush trees. A few of the houses had imposing iron gates and one even had those lion statues guarding their driveway. I was thinking about those creepy lions watching me when the sprinklers near my feet sprang to life, startling me. A woman in a white bathrobe saw me jump as she picked up her newspaper and was kind enough not to laugh.

"Good morning," I smiled. While my internal dialogue kept rolling with my mantra. 'What would Elizabeth Bennet do? WWEBD?' She would stop fidgeting and talk to the gracious lady.

"Do you know which of these houses is the Darcy's? I was looking for Owen or Georgiana."

"Oh yes, dear, you just passed it. The one with the gate, not lions in front… with the circle drive."

"Thank you so much," I said as I waved and turned around.

I walked two houses past the sprinklers when in front of me I saw a house worthy of the Darcy name. It was a cream-colored stone building, in the Georgian style. It would thrill my father that his constant architectural tours were taking root. I remember him saying the Georgian style is rigidly symmetrical; a little like the people of that era. I didn't see it as rigid. I liked the warmth of the stone. The uncomplicated, even old fashion line of the house seemed inviting as well as grand. The landscaping was immaculate, and I loved the crunch of the stone driveway under my feet.

I felt under-dressed to be walking up this driveway to the dark blue door with a brass lion head door knocker. I was uncertain if people used the door-knocker or the doorbell. "Door-knocker or doorbell door-knocker doorbell" rang through my head. I was pulling at my sleeves again and tightening my poor ponytail when my hand darted out from my sleeve and rang the doorbell, seemingly on its own. I nearly fainted when I heard footsteps.

"Deep breath. WWEBD. You are brave and strong and not going to puke in this nice doorway," I chanted.

"Hello," said a pretty girl my age and height, with twinkling blue eyes and a shy smile.

167

"Uh, hi, umm… are you Georgiana?" I said.

"Yes, and you are? Wait, I know you. Are you Ellie Gardiner?" she asked, opening the door wider.

"Whoa, how did you know that?"

"Three different people have described you to me. Two of whom were right on," she said, giggling at her own joke.

"That's hilarious. I'm guessing the third was Brooklyn?"

Georgiana blushed and laughed along with me. "Yes, it was. I shouldn't have said it like that."

"Let's agree from this first moment of knowing each other we will be honest friends," I said.

"Great idea. I'm told I am a terrible liar anyway," she said.

"Come in, Owen isn't here. Were you looking for him?"

"No! Well, maybe, or Finn, but I also wanted to meet you. There is just so much swirling through my mind," I admitted.

"I think we need something to drink, maybe to eat, and let's talk. Inside or outside?"

"You pick. Where are you most comfortable? Wow, your house is beautiful," I said, stepping into a bright foyer with a winding staircase on my left, and a large formal dining room on my right.

"I think the back porch," she said, leading me through the foyer to the back of the house where French doors opened up to a sunny, exuberant backyard. "Unless you mind cats. Fitzy is sleeping on the couch and will probably curl up in your lap."

"I love kitties… and dogs. My mom won't let us have either because of her supposed 'allergies,'" I air-quoted.

"People selectively have those, don't they? Please make yourself comfortable," she said as she motioned to the overstuffed sectional with an equally overstuffed grey tabby curled right in the center. "I'll get some lemonade."

"Can I help?" I asked. "I feel weird inviting myself in, then waiting to be served. Since I promised to be honest… "

"No, thank you," she laughed at me. "Finn said you were funny. I'm fine."

The backyard felt homey. There was a basketball goal above the garage door that looked well used. And the garden beds on the far side of the bean-shaped pool were wild and colorful. The front lawn had been so precisely manicured, which made the backyard a warm and inviting compliment. I breathed in the English lavender and wet grass, and something indistinctly homey.

I was too antsy to sit. Owen wasn't there, but I felt his presence in this half stuffy, half relaxed home. I wandered to the outdoor dining table where someone had started a 1000-piece puzzle. The edge pieces were done and the rest of the pieces were turned up, ready to be placed. The picture on the box was of the United States and all the national parks. I found the next piece of Washington State and popped it in as Georgiana came out carrying a huge tray.

"Oh, you caught me! Here, let me," I said as I hurried to the teak coffee table and moved some books to make room for her tray.

"You are welcome to keep helping. We love puzzles. At least I do. I think Owen does them just to humor me. He is a good brother. I couldn't decide between iced tea or lemonade, so I brought both so we could make our own Arnold Palmer. You know what that is, right?"

"I really thought I invented it when I was little. I asked a waitress for half lemonade and half iced tea… I thought I was a culinary genius. When she put the glass down in front of me, she said 'Arnold Palmer' and left. I asked my dad why she called me Arnold. I was six, I think. Not the sharpest knife, as they say."

"I also brought these. But you don't have to try them if you don't want. I made them yesterday. They are my dad's favorite, snicker-doodles," Georgiana said.

"I love cookies. They are my favorite food group. Thank you!" I started to talk again, but had a big bite of cookie in my mouth, and just laughed at myself instead.

"So, earlier you said things are swirling through your mind?"

I was so glad I was still chewing, so I had time to think. I wasn't sure how honest to be now I was here. While I had a good feeling about Georgie, I hadn't had great luck with new people lately.

"These cookies are dangerously good, thank you. I need you to put them over there by you, though," I laughed. "I'm serious. Okay, Georgiana... "

"Georgie, please, since we are going to be friends."

"Okay, Georgie, since we are going to be friends, I'm going to lay it all out there. Here goes. Your brother said some really snobby things to me when we first met and agreed with the downright mean things Brooklyn said. I've been very angry with him, and didn't behave any better than he did. We got into a bit of a fight."

"I heard," she said.

"You did?"

"Not much, just go ahead," she encouraged.

"He sent me a letter defending himself from some things I said, and well, I feel somewhat bad and kind of want to apologize. But... then Brooklyn keeps sticking her nose in and I don't know what is true with Owen. Is he the great guy Melly at the coffee shop says, or is he the snob who thinks people who go to public school have no ambition and run petting zoos," I said, talking faster.

When she looked confused, I waved my hands as if to shoo the confusion away and took a deep breath.

"Never mind, I am rambling. I have to just come out and ask

you, are you and Finn dating?"

"No. No! Finn Bingley? Ewwww. I mean, he is wonderful, but he is like my second brother. Ewwww, no! Brooklyn?" she asked with a furrowed brow.

"Yes, she keeps throwing you in my sister's face," I said. "It's been hard to watch and not slap her face off."

We both looked at each other and laughed at the visual.

"Sorry, I don't mean to sound so violent. I forget you don't know that I'm all talk."

"She inspires violence, believe me, I get it," she smiled. "Brooklyn has talked about Finn and I being a couple all of our lives. Finn and I just ignore her. I think she is just projecting because she wishes my brother felt that way about her."

I almost missed the next thing she was saying because I was stuck on her confirmation. Owen didn't have feelings for Brooklyn.

"… It surprised me when Finn stopped calling your sister. He lit up when he talked about her," she continued.

"Sorry, yes," I said, shaking off an unexpected flutter in my heart. "That was really the biggest part of our fight. Owen told me he was the one who encouraged Finn to get over Jade. He didn't think Jade had serious feelings. But I told him she is just very shy. I was angry, and I said some pretty awful things." I paused to take a drink of my lemonade. "Some stuff I said was true. Like why is he so snobby about public school? And small towns?" I asked.

"You are not wrong. He is kind of a snob. It comes from our mom. Before she died, she was always pushing him to go to the Ivy League as if that was the answer to all the world's problems. She was great and loving and funny, but she cared a lot about the 'right' sort of education. Thankfully, my dad is not like that… because I want to go to the school of Design."

"So cool! My friend Marni is an artist, too. You two should

totally meet. I'd love to see your work. What do you do?" I got a text as she answered me, and I apologized. "My sister asking where I am, we leave for home soon."

"I work in watercolor. Next time you come, I'll show you my studio."

"I would love that. I'm sorry to eat and run," I laughed and stood up.

"And I'm sorry you didn't get to see Owen or Finn," said Georgie, standing up.

"Me too, but I'm so happy to have spent time with you. And thank you for telling me the truth about you and Finn. My sister would never tell him how she felt if she thought it would hurt another girl."

"She sounds really nice," said Georgie.

"She IS, like, actually nice. Not like me!"

"Here, put your info in my phone. I'll message you to set up our art studio tour," said Georgie.

"Please tell Owen I got his letter, and I came to apologize. Thanks for everything, Georgie. Bye!"

As she shut the door, I breathed a sigh of relief. This worked out perfectly. I could let him know I was sorry about my bad behavior through his sister, without actually having to face him. I was giddy knowing Brooklyn was wrong on all counts and I would get to tell Jade that Finn was 100 percent available if she chose to pursue their relationship. I headed down the gravel driveway… just as Owen Darcy drove in.

"Noooo! One minute earlier and I would have missed him," I thought very loudly. "Why didn't I run the minute Georgiana shut the stupid door?"

"Hi!" he said, surprised, but not annoyed.

"Hi," I said, feeling awkward and wanting so badly to tighten my ponytail again. "I stopped by. We're leaving town, and I met your sister, and I had wanted… I read your letter."

172

He looked toward the house and looked a little panicked.

"Oh, no, of course not," I said frowning, answering his unstated worry that I told her what he had written in the letter. "I met Georgie when I was looking for you, but I said nothing about what you wrote. Well, we talked a little about Jade and Finn, but give me some credit."

"Sorry, I just for a moment thought… sorry," he said, my awkwardness transferring to him. "You were saying you stopped by to see me."

"Yes," I said taking a deep calming breath and remembering I was as confident as any of the Lizzy Bennets. "I behaved badly. I am sorry for the things I falsely accused you of and the way I acted. That's what I wanted to say," I looked for anger or forgiveness in his eyes and saw his eyes crinkle in amusement instead.

"Well, we are leaving for home, we have a very exciting senior party to attend. I mean, I'm not a senior, but Jade is going to be, and… "

"I'm a senior, can I go?" he teased and stepped closer to me.

I couldn't look in his eyes when he was standing this close… so I looked at my feet and thought how much I love these beat up Converse. "It's at Jake Daniels 's house. I know you guys met at the basketball camp, I mean invitational. I am sure you are all invited. But didn't your coach ban you from hanging out with the country boys?" I rambled. I started to pull at my shirt sleeves again and thought I better get out of here before I said the inevitable stupid thing. "I better go."

"Want me to drive you?" he offered, though there was no way I could be that close to him right now. My mind was swirling.

"No, you know me, I like to walk," I said, over my shoulder as I started walking quickly, crunching the small stones of the driveway under my feet.

Owen Darcy smiled at me and my stomach did a somersault.

22

Group Msg: The Invisibles

Catt: What are you wearing? I don't want to look like a freshman.

Emma: What do freshmen look like?
crying laughing emoji

Emma: I'm wearing what you saw me in earlier, overalls and lime tube top. Minus the hat.

Ava: We are technically sophomores now. You always look great.

Marni: I am wearing cut-offs, white tank and mint boho cardigan thingy with daisies.

Ava: So cute, I'm wearing white shorts, light blue t-shirt with the tie waist

Ellie: Sorry, just got home. I think green ruffle tank with jean shorts. Catt, just bring some choices and we'll help you pick.

Ellie: Meet here at 7 p.m.? Leave at 8 p.m.?

Catt: Mkay, see you! Xxo kissy face emoji

Ellie: Ava, will you braid my hair, two loose piggies? You do it better.

Ava: Love to! Can I borrow your big blue
        butterfly earrings?
Ellie: Yes!! Umm, better go warn mom everyone is
        coming here first, lol… yikes face emoji
Emma: She loves us!

"I was hoping we could eat dinner together and you would model your dresses for your father and me? You've been gone for a week!"

"Tomorrow night, we'll do a whole thing. Dinner and dress modeling and family movie night. Please?? This is a senior party!"

"Oh, all right then, since your sister is taking you."

"Thanks, mom. And sorry everyone is invading at 7 p.m. to finish getting ready."

I ran upstairs to unpack and nearly ran over my dad coming out of his office.

"Hey dad, mom said I could go to the party with Jade, but fair warning, everyone is coming over here to finish getting ready."

"Ellie, you know I don't want you drinking," said my father, stopping to look straight at me.

"I don't think they will have drinks there," I stammered.

"They will, and I don't want you having any."

"Oh, okay, I wasn't planning on it, it's not my thing."

"But you know, if something ever did happen… "

"I know dad, I will call."

"No, don't wake me up. I was going to say, stay there and sleep it off!"

"No, you weren't!" I laughed at my dad as his eyes sparkled and he hugged me.

"Have fun, kiddo."

176

******

Unpacking had not been distracting enough. Every time I thought about Owen and the way he looked at me, my stomach flopped. I could still picture him in his driveway, watching me walk away. Wow, he was cute. But he was also confusing. It was double confusing that I both wanted to tell my friends, but also wanted to keep my feelings private for a little longer.

I had tried to listen to podcasts, watch YouTube videos about how to do fancy braids, and even tried to nap, but I still got tingly when I remembered him stepping closer to me. It was easier when I hated his guts.

Finally, the distraction I needed noisily piled out of Eden's orange Bronco and made its way up to my room. I was scream-excited to see them all, as always. It had been an entire week. Well, really only two days, but a lifetime of details had happened since then.

Catt told us she and Mike had been on an actual date since he got back from his family vacation. While she described the dinner and the coolness of having a boy come pick you up at your house, I looked at Ava. She smiled at me. I knew she had more to tell about Freddy, but she was not one to tell everyone her business. I would corner her at the party and get the details and possibly share my own.

"Mike was so nervous about meeting my parents. Emma was there, hanging out with Phillip, and Mike asked me later if they were boyfriend and girlfriend. I reminded him that Phillip was my older brother. Gross. He's so funny. I think he was still hoping his friend Kyle had a chance," said Catt while making weird "O," mouth faces as she put on mascara using my closet door mirror.

I saw Ava watch Emma and then look at me. Both Ava and I suspected Emma thought Phillip was a lot less gross than Catt realized. Maybe Emma didn't realize it herself yet. It was more fun watching other people in turmoil than feeling the butterflies yourself.

"Hey so, is Eden still seeing Denny?" I asked.

"Yeah, she is, but he couldn't come tonight, some family reunion he had to fly to. She was bummed, but that's probably the only reason she was okay with driving us," said Marni, who was sketching butterflies in the planner on my desk. I loved when she did them for me and I could later go in and fill them in with colored pencils. I was still in the coloring-book stage of my artistic ability.

"We look so cute," clapped Catt looking around the room. "Those senior boys are going to take one look at us and fall in love!"

"Do you want senior boy attention if you have Mike?" Ava asked, finishing my second braid. She made them look so effortless and loose. I could never get two braids to match.

"I always want attention, it doesn't mean I want more than that," said Catt. "Just fun."

"Have you ever noticed that when one boy notices you, it seems like suddenly they all do?" I asked.

"It's because when you feel excited, you act braver, you smile more. I think you cause the chain reaction," said Emma.

"I agree, Catt. I'd like just one senior boy to pay attention to me, too, and for me to not panic and run!" I said.

Marni threw her arm over my shoulder and said, "I would count that as your public speaking test for this week!"

"Alright! Bring it on! I'm ready to meet the challenge!" I said, feeling pumped up.

"Okay little sisters, let's get going," said Eden, opening my door. "While I have you here together," she said, coming in and shutting the door behind her. "Don't you guys dare embarrass us. Jade won't say it, but I will. Love you, but if you guys drink there, I will kill you dead. Got it?"

"We won't. Sheesh mom. We don't even like the stuff," said Marni.

"Okay, but these are my friends," said Eden, opening the door and giving us each older sister face. "In the car, five minutes."

I saw Jade leave her room and smile at us. She was definitely the good cop to Eden's bad cop. But we were very lucky they would take us to the party with them, and we all knew it.

"Okay," I said to the room, "let's go cause a chain reaction!"

23

Jake Daniels was the youngest in a long line of rowdy sons, so by the time he had come along, his parents let him and his friends, the Brew Crew, do whatever they wanted. As long as they did it at home, didn't drive and no one got hurt. They were known for throwing parties and pulling pranks, but they were all four kind at heart. Tonight they wanted to throw an epic party to welcome in their senior year. Their house was the perfect party house. It was a large, open ranch-style home with plenty of room to spread out. The back lawn sloped gently toward a fire pit and dock. The small lake was surrounded by woods making the place feel secluded, but not horror movie creepy.

"The Invisibles at a senior party, amazing!" I said, opening the side gate and heading to the noisy backyard.

"I know! I'm so excited and so nervous," said Catt, bouncing from foot to foot.

"Our sisters are the main reason, but I'm still glad," said Marni as we found the table with cups and all the buckets of ice and two-liter bottles. I could see a keg on the grass and more cups down there.

"Speak for yourself. I've been tutoring Jake in math for years. He owes me. Plus, I'm thinking we haven't been all that invisible lately," declared Emma, as she was eyed up and down by a few of the boys walking past.

"As she picked up one of the black sharpies and wrote her name, then drew small hearts all over the cup," Ava said, "This is a good idea; we need to do this on pool days. I am always grabbing the wrong tea."

"Ewwww cooties," Catt laughed.

"I love that Ava. What should I do?" I asked.

"And it's good for the environment, do yours like this," said Marni, making an oversized "E-L-L-I-E's" across the whole cup and then in small print "friend Marni" with the black marker.

"Okay, but when you end up drinking mine, don't come crying to me," I laughed and wrote a huge "MARNI's," then small "friend Ellie," and then added flowers all over mine.

Catt did her signature outline of a cat head with long whiskers and Emma put one thick capital 'E.' The art project helped calm our nerves and gave us a minute to look around without looking lost.

"You guys, did you see they have Mountain Dew??" asked Catt.

"Uh huh, no way. YOU cannot have all that sugar and caffeine… or you will bounce for three days. Stick to lemonade or Sprite," said Emma.

"Catt, do you need to be rescued from Emma's tyranny?" asked Ava.

"I'm not a tyrant, or at least not tonight," said Emma,

"She's right. I asked her to help me not do anything stupid," said Catt.

"So I am her designated 'right mind,'" said Emma.

"Right mind? Good one. Did you just make it up, or is that

a thing?" asked Ava.

"I just made it up right now, but it is good… more people should have a designated right mind. We all need someone around that has sense with alcohol or, more importantly… messaging boys!"

"That is kinda what girlfriends do," pointed out Marni, "we are each other's conscience… like when I said to Ellie 'you are wearing THAT?'"

"Shut up," I laughed. "This place is enormous. Let's walk toward all the sound and see what's happening."

Music and laughter were coming from a game room at the far end of the house with glass accordion doors that folded up so it was open to the outside. It had the biggest TV I had ever seen. In the middle of the floor were three girls and one guy standing on mats trying to follow the dance moves of their avatar on the screen. A girl I knew as Eden and Jade's friend, Dena, was winning. She could clearly dance and was being high-fived by her avatar.

We stayed and watched several groups play. My favorite were the football players because they were so big. It was fun to watch them try to stay on the small mats with their giant feet.

"Let's go down to the dock, you guys. I bet Jade is down there. Does anyone want to go?" I asked.

"I will," said Ava, and we proceeded down the lawn toward the lake.

We passed the back deck, the senior boys in full beer pong mode. It was much messier looking in person than it looked in movies. I could see some of the recent graduates from my Brit Lit class standing around the tables cheering. I was sure if they saw me they would most likely not remember me, and if they did, they would only remember my humiliation. Not going in there if I can help it. I was relieved I didn't see my final presentation partner, Amber, anywhere around. I was feeling braver these days, but still not ready to fight the mean-girl variety of dragon.

"There are like a million places to hide and make out if one chose. What? I'm just noticing, don't smile at me," said Ava in a rush as we passed a couple walking out from a path in the woods.

"Speaking of making out... whatever happened with Freddy. You said you found him. What does that mean?" I asked.

"I found his profile on Instagram. He doesn't post there much anymore, but it's definitely him."

"And... "

"And nothing. I just looked at the pictures and did nothing. I know, but what was I supposed to do? Slide into his DMs like in the olden days? I'm not eighty," said Ava miserably.

"Do you even know what you want to say?"

"He looked so cute," she said. "I still felt like I missed him, so it helped me know I want to reach out and apologize, but I am not quite ready to be that vulnerable. He could really crush me, and I probably deserve it," Ava said.

"He could surprise you and still be as crazy about you, too, just not reaching out for the same reason?" We approached a small group of people sitting in chairs around a fire with one guy playing the guitar. Jade was not there, but I heard her laugh behind me and I turned toward the dock.

A handful of people were lying on the dock, looking up at the stars.

"Hi Jade," I whispered to the bodies.

"Hey Ellie," said Jade as she flopped onto her stomach to look at me. Is that Marni with you?

"No, it's me, Ava."

"Hi Ava, Eden wants to go play Dance Dance and I don't

want to, so I was going to make her take Marni."

"Marni is up there, and she wants to play, too."

"Oh, cool," I heard another body say and jump up. "I'll go up." I saw the outline of Eden dust off her butt and head toward the house. "Be back in a bit," she yelled over her shoulder.

Jade laughed and said, "she has a gaming addiction, or more like a dancing addiction."

The guitar guy had gone and several chairs were open around the fire pit, so I motioned to them and we headed to sit around the fire.

"Can I have a drink of your drink?" asked Jade as she grabbed my cup.

"Sure. Are you testing to make sure it's not beer?" I asked.

"No, I am genuinely dying of thirst," she laughed. "Plus, I know you are scared of Eden."

Jade drained my glass in a very unladylike manner and said, "Save me a seat. I'll go get you more. Ava, do you want anything?"

It felt very peaceful around the fire. I could hear the loud music from the game room, different loud music from the deck, and the cheers of either when something exciting happened, all muted by the trees and the hypnotic dance of the crackling fire.

I knew Jade was still feeling a little melancholy and–while happy to be around all her classmates–she was subdued. She brought two full cups and sat next to us by the fire.

"Marni and Eden are kicking butt up there. I saw them do a super-fast hip-hop song. No way could my feet move so fast," said Jade, "and I am always surprised Eden can shake it like that. It's getting more crowded up there."

The three of us sat quietly, listening to the surrounding banter, each with something weighing on their mind, watching

184

the fire and other people come and go. As always, the only part of me wanting to move from this comfortable spot was my bladder.

"I'll be back guys. Want me to fill up drinks?" I asked as I jumped up and escorted my cup to the bathroom I had seen in the front hallway of the house.

I could hear the game room erupt in cheers and laughter and I heard a happy squeal that sounded like Catt was engaged in a flirty game of Catt and mouse near the woods.

I caught Jake Daniels's eye and smiled as I passed the beer pongers. "What's up, little Gardiner?" he said and waved his cup at me. I waved back and turned to head through the open door into the dark living room, and down the hallway.

As I left the restroom, the light fell on all the family pictures lining the walls and before I turned it off, I had seen the central one of all the boys giving a group hug to their poor mom, a tiny little woman in a house full of men. My eyes were adjusting when a voice came out of the dark living room to greet me.

"Well, hello," said the unmistakable Mr. Charming voice of Declan Wickham as he blocked my path. "Long time no see."

"Yeah, been awhile. Excuse me," I said as I tried to move around him.

"You look good, young lady."

"Declan, I am not interested in playing," I said, trying to remain brave, but feeling instinctively that something was very off. He looked twitchy and predatory as he came closer to me.

"Come on, you know me. We are old friends," he whispered, his eyes dancing and his hands reaching for me as I stepped slowly back. "I always thought we could be more than that. These other boys may not see you, but I do."

I looked toward the beer pongers. A dark room and a half

wall separated me from them and the music was so loud I don't think they could have heard me if I screamed. The old Ellie would have been scared and frozen in place by now. But I was sick of being lied to, of him making me say mean things to a guy who didn't deserve it, and done feeling like I could be silenced.

"You know what, Declan? I see you, too! I have learned a great deal about who you really are from our mutual friend, Owen Darcy. You forgot to tell me the part of the story where you attacked his under-aged sister, you freak!"

He snatched my upper arm so violently that I thought he pulled the biceps off of the bone. "You are a pathetic, scared little girl. All these people here and no one sees you."

"Let go of my arm," I said, mad that I could hear my voice quaver. He pulled tighter and got closer to my face. His aqua eyes looked nothing like they had when I thought them dreamy. They flashed with hatred.

Taking a deep breath, I yanked my arm back with all my might. I fell backward and scrambled up. I stomped his foot when he tried to catch me again and I yelled, "Stay away from me!"

The deep voice of Benji Wyman, formerly known as "That Creep Benji That Teases Me in Brit Lit." yelled, "Not cool dude, leave her alone. Little Gardiner, you okay?"

I was breathing heavily as I moved behind Benji, grateful he was big as a doorway. A few people walked into the room to see what the noise was about, but the music had drowned out most of it. My adrenaline was pumping, and it scared me to think that he could have done almost anything, and no one would have heard me.

"Stay out of this, man. This is between her and me. She is just being emotional. You know how young girls are," said Declan.

"Stop trying to manipulate me into feeling small, or naïve, or whatever, because unfortunately for you, I know exactly what kind of man you are… and you disgust me," I said popping out from behind Benji in a last burst of bravery

"Let's leave this loser. Come hang with us," said Benji offering me his arm like the knight in shining armor he was right now.

Declan looked around the room at all the witnesses and shrugged like it was some misunderstanding, but I saw the calculating look in his eyes and shook. I was so grateful for Benji and his gallant gesture I instantly forgave all his classroom teasing.

I turned back one last time as we walked away, but I didn't see Declan anywhere.

"Thank you so much. I think he was high or something. He freaked me out," I said.

"Well, why don't you stay here with us for awhile? Do you want to play beer pong?" He asked like he had offered me the greatest gift.

"No, thanks," I laughed. "I'm not allowed to drink tonight." He looked skeptically at my cup, oddly, still clutched in my hand. "I can drink liquid, just not alcohol. I'm sticking to lemonade."

"Hey little Gardiner," said Jake Daniels. "Perfect. Will you be our undrunk unbiased judge announcer person?"

"Sure?" I said, looking at Benji who knew what my public speaking talent entailed.

"I think you can handle this kind of talking," he said, as Jake plugged in an ancient karaoke machine and tested the microphone. "Everyone, take a five minute break, and then we go for the beer pong semi-finals!! What?! What?!"

"Sit up here so you can see," Benji said, and hefted me up onto the half wall. It was an amazing view. I could see down the deck to the game room crowd and I could see the tiny firelight of the fire pit by the lake. More importantly, to my host and to my hero, I could announce the final few rounds of the tournament.

Jake handed me the microphone and told me to test it out. I did so shyly at first. I was so stunned these guys who all ignored me last year wanted me to hang out with them, but I was breathing normally and I felt a lot better, especially when I looked back one more time and still didn't see any sign of Declan.

"Benji please, Benji… please report to the wall and tell me the rules," I said in the mic in what I thought was a scary, too close to the mic voice. He came over and I said, "it may surprise you to know I have zero idea of the rules and what is happening."

"The basics are there are four teams left, two people per team. The primary way people cheat is by having their wrist go over the back line of the table when they shoot their ball into the other team's cups. So watch for that."

"And a player is allowed to ask for the cups to be put back in place, but they cannot bounce the ball," said Jake, coming over. "Here are the team names. You could introduce them before each game. You good? I want you to call everyone in here in three minutes."

It was so funny to see this side of Jake. This game was serious business to these guys and their energy was contagious. I liked this new feeling of belonging in the party group. Not enough to drink gross beer with dirty ping-pong balls being tossed in it, but enough to cheer nonsensically from the sideline. I was enjoying trying different voices on the mic.

"Oh, HEY MARNI…GRAND MARNINO…YES, YOU. I SEE YOU WALKING BY… THE ANNOUNCER IS ASKING YOU TO COME IN HERE."

Marni did not want to join the chaos on the deck, so she visited me on the peaceful side of the pony wall. "Hello, friend, what's up?" I said, not in the microphone.

"You are taking to this master of ceremonies role very well. I will give you an A for this! That internship is yours for sure!"

"Yay! Now if the gala only has a ping-pong tournament, I'll do great," I laughed.

"And should we talk about the fact that you are talking with 'That Creep Benji That Teases You in Brit Lit?'"

"I know, but that is a whole story. Tell you later. I have two minutes until they get started and Jake is buzzing around here like it's the Super Bowl."

"Will you babysit my Ellie Cup while I hit the restroom?" Marni asked, setting it next to me and blowing me an exaggerated kiss.

I made a loud kiss on the microphone back. "Sure, and I want extra credit points for the flair with which I will announce these games!"

Jake gave me the look, and I settled on a faux wrestling announcer voice and said "Are you ready to beer poooooong?" and the entire room cheered. I was so surprised and elated. "In this corner, we have the two Steve-o's and in this corner, we have The Hot Shots."

The players vamped for the crowd and began playing. I said nonsense things, watched for wrists over the line and joined in the cheers on either side. "Steve-o! Steve-o! Steve-o!"

Having a microphone felt powerful, and I was so into it at one point I almost fell off of the wall and knocked cups over. It felt like this match took forever. I wasn't sure how long they normally lasted, but the Hot Shots took thirty minutes to take down the Steve-o's.

The crowd was wild throughout the entire King Pong vs Your Mommas game and it went a little faster. Your Mommas won and would play the Hot Shots for the big prize... which I found out was nothing but bragging rights.

I was announcing the teams to take their ends of the table with an extra dramatic flair when I saw a lot of movement in my periphery. The teams began, and the crowd was cheering as I looked to my left and saw Eden running with someone toward the front door. In the split second I saw her, I barely saw her face, but I could tell she looked terrified.

I whipped fully around and saw Owen Darcy framed in the porch light of the open front door, holding someone.

Our eyes locked. Did I see disappointment, or was that pain in his eyes? Eden caught up to him and they ran out the front door. My brain was processing in slow motion, but my body instinctively jumped into gear. I didn't yet know why, but I jumped down, dropped the microphone, and ran through the sea of Your Momma fans toward the front door.

"Oh, Ellie, there you are," said an uncharacteristically discomposed Emma.

"Was that? Why was?" I stammered.

Emma grabbed my shoulders and said, "something happened to Marni. Finn told Eden they were taking her to the hospital. Catt went with them and I came to find you guys."

"Owen was holding Marni? She was limp. But that doesn't make sense. I just saw her."

"Ellie, where is Jade? She can take us to the hospital," said Emma.

I could feel the rising heat of panic and fear starting to take over, but I didn't have the time to fall apart. I had to get moving. My friend was hurt or sick, I wasn't sure, and that thought got me moving quickly. I could figure out the details later. Emma and I ran down the path toward the fire pit, yelling for Jade and Ava.

24

We drove to the hospital in waves of silence and outbursts of questions to which no one had answers. Emma tried to text Catt, but found Catt's vibrating phone in her own front pocket, just then remembering her promise to "hold this for a second." Jade pulled into a parking space in front of the emergency room. The parking lot was eerily quiet, and my stomach was in knots. We ran through the entrance and saw our friends at the end of the long hallway in front of a room with glass walls. My heart was racing, looking for answers in those tear-stained faces as we hurried toward them. On the other side of the glass, Marni was in a hospital bed, propped up with pillows, an IV hooked up to her arm. She looked barely conscious, and a nurse was talking to her. She looked so pale and small; vulnerable in a way I had never seen her. Outside the room, talking to Eden and Catt was Finn.

I could feel the second Jade saw him. She stiffened as if to prepare for more hurt. I saw his face register awareness of her. It lit up in hope and relief. Then my reserved sister ran to him and flung her arms around him. Her unfiltered display released the emotion held tightly in us all and we all cried. I hugged Eden and Catt and barraged them with a dozen questions at once.

I heard Finn say softly to Jade, "I've been a fool."

"Wait, so Finn, why are you here? I mean, I am glad, but you found Eden?" Jade asked. Finally, letting go of him, she moved to comfort her best friend, Eden.

"I can tell you what I know," said Eden, putting on her big-sister face and looking at us, the little sisters. "Marni will be fine. Nothing happened to her that is permanent. No physical harm."

"You are scaring me. Just say it. Please Eden," I said.

"So, at the party, while it was my turn at Dance Dance, I saw Marni get up to leave. She seemed off, but I was too busy playing that stupid game," said Eden, her voice cracking.

"And..." I prompted Catt to finish the story.

"Finn and Owen came to the party through the front door. And in the living room, they saw Declan on top of a girl who was passed out on the couch. They threw Declan to the ground, and he ran off. Owen checked the girl's pulse and realized who it was. Finn came looking for any of us and thankfully found Eden. Owen carried her to his truck, and we all came here," finished Catt in a rush.

"And that girl was Marni?" I said, my brain and heart frozen in fear and anger. "So, he forced himself..."

"No! and yes. She still had her clothes on. They were in time. But it was obvious what he had planned," said Eden, the weight of what she had just said hit her. She leaned on the wall for support and sobbed. We all stood, taking in the implications of what could have happened. Finally, Eden could speak again and wiped her eyes and nose. "If they had been any later, who knows? Poor Marni, she didn't deserve any of this and it was my fault because I was too busy to watch out for my baby sister."

"No," I said quietly. "It was actually my fault. I thought he left. He tried to attack me earlier. I should have told everyone." I was feeling cold anger flow through my veins. They all looked at me and I explained a short version of what had occurred and how I hung out with the older guys rather than protecting my friends.

"It wasn't your fault. He is nuts," said Eden, wiping her eyes and continuing her story. "Finn came and found us in the game room and we all came here. They were worried she could have alcohol poisoning, but I knew she hadn't any alcohol. So it has to be that he slipped something into her drink, right? But the nurses don't really believe me. We are waiting for the blood test."

"Something in her drink?" I asked, my mind going somewhere else.

I heard Eden saying, "They want to talk to her by herself first, but then you can go in."

"Wait, you said he put something in her drink? In her red cup?"

"He might have. I just asked them to test because she was acting drunk, but didn't drink."

"Ellie, are you alright? What's the matter?"

"Her cup had my name on it. Ava, remember?"

"Oh yeah, it was sweet. It said 'Ellie's friend Marni'… with the 'Ellie' really big," Ava said, trailing off at the end, realizing what that meant.

"So wow, in so many ways, it really is because of me. I sat there with both our drinks while she went to the bathroom. I didn't notice anything except I was getting attention," I said, feeling my entire world had crashed around me.

"Ellie, it isn't your fault. You didn't make that creep a predator. I'd like to show him what being the prey feels like," said Emma, looking ready to go hunt Declan down.

193

"I think Owen is already hot on his trail," said Catt.

"Wait, Catt, what do you mean? Where is Owen?" I said.

"He dropped us off. He told the doctor what he saw, then he took off again. I think he went to find Declan."

"If one of you wants to go see her, you may do that now," said the nurse who had been with Marni.

Eden nodded I could go, so I ran into the room and hugged Marni, who was too weak to lift both arms, but I didn't care. "I'm so sorry. I shouldn't have left you alone. Girls go potty together! I shouldn't have been focused on the dumb seniors, totally my fault," I said in a rush.

"Dude… slow down, I'm okay, just tired and dizzy…"

"Okay, sorry, I'm just so sorry you got hurt. Do you remember what happened?"

"I remember your man, what's his face, carrying me in here," Marni said.

"Owen is not my man. I don't know why he was there, but I am so glad he was."

"Please, not now. Can I have some water? They kept asking me what I had to drink. I said, the only thing I had was Sprite. They don't believe me."

"Hi Mommy," said Marni in a soft, childlike voice, as Mr. and Mrs. Norland ran in and hugged Marni, who finally began to cry.

I left the room thinking about that ELLIE cup. With everything I now knew about Declan, I was sure he had drugged Marni. There is no way they cleaned up the house yet. I need to go get that cup. I texted my dad, and he agreed to come get me. He didn't exactly know what he had agreed to, but he knew I was determined. We had a mission.

"Look, you guys, I need to go do something. It is my fault Declan did this. I'm going over there to find her cup and whatever else I can think of as evidence against Declan."

"Maybe Owen will have found him," said Finn. "I'll text him."

******

I wasn't waiting around to hear what Owen had to say. I was determined to help, and I needed to be doing something. Otherwise, I would start crying again and might never stop. Besides, I didn't want to hear judgment from him about why I was acting all show-offy and loud while my friend was being attacked. I was throwing as much blame as I could handle on myself right now. I didn't need to see my guilt written on his face. My dad pulled up, and I jumped in the car. He had clearly been at least nearly asleep. He was in sweats and his Chicago Cubs baseball cap.

"Are you okay, kiddo? Your sister already texted me the basics."

"Don't be nice to me. I have to delay my freak-out. I need to see if I can get evidence."

"Evidence?"

"Dad, please. I will explain, but please just drive to the Daniels's house. I need to look something up."

"I will drive and not be nice. Got it."

As we drove, I Googled "what to do if you are roofied" and it said to get blood and urine tested and call the police to secure the security tapes if it happened in a public place like a bar.

"May I ask what we are going to do when we get there? It is 2 a.m.," asked my dad.

"I don't want you to go in there all judgey-parent," I said.

"But I am a dad whose daughter's best friend is in the hospital. I'm feeling a little judgey," he said honestly.

"Daaaad, the people still here are not the ones who did the bad thing. At worst, you will see drunk boys from a beer pong tournament. They will probably be asleep. Here it is. Turn in here," I said.

195

The lights were all on inside the house and there were a handful of cars around, but the music was down, and no one was walking around. When we arrived at the party earlier, we had walked in through the side gate, but that was closed now, so my dad and I went to the front door.

"Okay, dad, be cool," I said.

"I was born cool."

"Ugh," I sighed as I knocked on the door.

"No one could have heard that. Knock again," my dad said.

I knocked harder and even harder when I thought of Marni laying dizzy and weak in a hospital bed because of me. Finally, some girl I kind of recognized opened the door, with a face squinting against the light of the porch.

"Hi, sorry, I was sleeping. Come in."

I knew it wasn't her house, but she seemed to want the knocking to stop.

I gave my dad the "no judging" face and walked on in. To the right was a formal living room with a navy tufted couch. "That is where Marni was found," I explained to my dad. I was going to say "attacked," but I couldn't.

"Only an outsider would have come this way through the front. Someone who came to the party late. We would never come this way." I cried, which made me madder.

My dad put his arm around me and said, "Are you sure you want to do this? Why don't you go sit in the car and I will look around?"

"Thanks, but no. I'm doing this. Let's look for a red plastic cup with my name or Marni's name and anything else." I walked over to the side of the couch and under, and my dad checked the cushions. We walked further in and passed the space where Declan grabbed me. I could hear some people milling around outside and I headed toward the noise, my dad behind me.

I turned toward the game room and saw Jake walking around with a trash bag cleaning up.

"Hey, little Gardiner, what are you doing here? Whoa, hey Mr. Gardiner, sir, up what…" he tapered off.

"Jake, I am looking for Marni's red cup. It had her name. Actually, my name is really big and was probably in the game room."

"So weird, my friend from Pemberley just asked me the same thing. I think he found it and left. Did she leave her retainer in it?" asked Jake.

"Is Declan Wickham still here?" I asked.

"No, I never saw that dude, but Darcy asked me about him, too. He also asked me if we had security cameras."

"Good idea, do you?"

"No, just the doorbell," said Jake. "So, what happened?"

"Declan tried to hurt Marni… little Norland, Eden's sister. I think he roofied her drink."

"What a sick-ass! Sorry, Mr. Gardiner," said Jake.

"No need to apologize, he is quite a sick-ass. He is a predator and needs to be in jail," said my usually eloquent father.

"Agreed. Is she okay?" Jake asked.

"Yes, upset and dizzy, but she will be okay. She just needs the poison out of her system, but please don't tell people. It's her story to tell," I said.

"Sure, no I won't mention her name, but, ummm, do you think the police need to come here?" Jake asked.

"I am not sure there is anything they could do if they did. You don't have security cameras," my dad said.

"Let me look in the game room, just in case Owen missed something," I said.

"And I will clean up some, just in case the cops need to come," Jake said, more awake now.

If I hadn't been so upset, I would have smiled at his attempt to act calm about the cops potentially showing up.

"Give us a bag and we will collect garbage in the game room as we look," I said.

The game room was trashed, but my dad and I waded through it all and turned over cushions and checked every cup, found an earring and some headphones, but no cup and nothing like pills.

"Well, we tried. Hopefully, Owen found something. I have no idea what else to do. This is all my fault."

"Honey, there is no way any of this is your fault."

I told him what happened, and he tried to say all the right things, but I knew for sure that if I hadn't been channeling my inner Elizabeth Bennet, this would have never happened… and Marni would not be crying and hurt in a hospital bed.

25

The sun was so bright when I woke up. I could hear the neighbor kids playing in their yard and my mom vacuuming downstairs. My mind was cloudy on the details, but I think we drove home at around 4 a.m. Marni would come home today, and I had planned to hang out with her if she wanted company.

I pulled on my silky pink bathrobe over the gray t-shirt I had apparently slept in. Pulling out the tangled, painful elastic hair tie, I massaged my aching scalp and finger combed my hair back on top of my head with the scrunchy from my bedroom door handle. The vacuuming was finished by the time I reached the bottom of the stairs and I got squeeze-attacked by my mom.

"My poor sweetheart, what a scary night," said my mom, hugging me tightly.

"Mom, I'm still asleep," I tried to say, but I was too smooshed against her shoulder.

"You are too young to deal with this kind of thing. My baby, what is the world coming, too?"

"Mom, I'm okay," I said, though it was comforting to be

wrapped in her warm arms and take in the faint smell of her lavender soap.

"Helen, let go of the child. You are smothering her," said my father, coming out of the family room.

"She's having to grow up too fast."

"Okay, but let her breathe."

"I have just the thing," she said, holding me at arms-length to examine my face. I used to make you grilled cheese and tomato soup when you were little and would get a boo boo," she said, letting go of me and heading to the kitchen.

"Thanks, mom, that would definitely help. Dad's looking like he has a boo boo, too," I said, smiling at my dad, who looked tired from our quest last night.

"Sit down, you two," she smiled.

"How is Marni? Did I miss anything while I was asleep?" I asked them both.

"Marni is fine. Maggie says she is a little tired this morning, but not dizzy or nauseated anymore, and Jade went to brunch with Finn about an hour ago," my mother said. "I watched out the window when he picked her up and he helped her in the car, very gentlemanly. They look happy, but they have talking to do… if she listens to me."

"And I got a call from Tom Norland thanking us for our help last night. Apparently, the Darcy kid brought them the cup last night for testing in case they wanted to press charges. I told Tom we had looked for video or anything else and had no luck."

"Did Owen find Declan?" I asked.

"He told Tom he looked everywhere he could think of but couldn't find him and didn't know where he was living these days."

"Did they test the cup? Are they pressing charges?" I asked as my mom poured the soup into a bowl for me and my dad and handed me a bottle of Tabasco sauce.

"All know now is they are bringing Marni home today, I don't know what they decided about the police, but Ellie," my father said looking at me with the most serious face I had ever seen, "it is really unlikely anything will happen. There is no hard evidence to use against him. Even if his prints were on the cup, and it tested positive for drugs, there is no legal way to prove he did the drugging."

"I'm not letting it go. It's not right!" I said. "She did nothing wrong. You expect consequences for bad choices. Like Lydia Bennet, not to victim blame, but she totally deserved to be married to a creep." Noticing my parents' look of confusion, I added, "Never mind. I have *Pride and Prejudice* on the brain these days. Marni is even nice to spiders; she doesn't deserve this. I am devastated this happened to her, and I could have prevented it."

"We have been over this. It wasn't your fault," my dad said, "dunk your grilled cheese and you will be able to think more logically."

Text:

~~Ellie: Owen, this is Ellie. I wanted to thank you so much for helping Marni.~~

~~Ellie: Hi Owen, this is Ellie. Thank you for helping Marni and for taking the cup to her parents.~~

~~Ellie: Owen, this is Ellie. I wish we could do something about Declan, after what he did to Georgie and now Marni.~~

Text:

    Ellie: Hey, you home? Side faced kiss emoji

    Marni: Yeah, got home at 11 a.m. At kitchen table with Mom and Eden. Wanna come over?

Ellie: Is it okay with your mom?
           She want me around?

Marni: Of course, stupid question. I kinda want to
           take a nap, but come for dinner? Yes, I asked…
           she said she is making spaghetti and meatballs.

Ellie: I'll be there! side face kiss emoji pasta emoji

******

"Are you crying?" asked Marni when I walked into her bedroom. My eyes filled with tears.

Marni was sitting cross-legged on her bed, holding Ted E. Bear to her chest. The wall behind her was covered in twinkle lights and pictures showing us laughing, trusting, and having fun.

"Sorry, I want to say something. I practiced, but I wasn't planning on crying," I said, taking a deep breath and biting hard on my bottom lip.

"Dude, I'm fine," Marni said, brushing off the seriousness.

"That's not it, I mean, I'm glad. I am so sorry this happened to you and I know it is my fault. When you are ready, I will explain why it is, and I want to fix it," I blurted out.

"How could it possibly be your fault?" she asked with a very Marni furrow between her brows.

"I am pretty sure he put the drug in your cup when you asked me to watch it. When you went to the bathroom. I was so preoccupied with being on the microphone and being obnoxious with the seniors that I didn't see him come near the cups."

"He must have been fast because I didn't take very long. I didn't want to interrupt you when I came and grabbed it and went back to dance more."

"See? I didn't even see you grab it. I should have been paying attention! But there's more."

"More?"

"More proof it is my fault. Do you remember your cup had my name on it? He meant to do that to me. If he wasn't angry at me, you wouldn't have gotten hurt. All the things I said I wanted, attention from older boys, getting noticed, and the self-confidence of Elizabeth Bennet thing… all lead to this. I am genuinely sorry, and I am done trying to be different. I just want to be with my friends and keep them safe."

"I didn't think about the name on the cup thing. He is the only one at fault, though. He came prepared to mess with someone or anyone."

"I'm not trying to make it about me, but I should have been more careful with you. I knew who he was," I said lamely. "Marn, do you want to talk about it? I mean, you don't have to," I asked, sitting on the foot of her four-poster bed.

"Owen was talking to me. I was in his car, like the night we were going to Pizza Hut. I tried to say, 'I don't want pizza,' but words wouldn't come out. Before that, I remember trying to push someone away and having no strength, and feeling a heavy weight on me, but if Owen hadn't found me, I wouldn't have known who. I feel like some pathetic little girl. I honestly do not know if people are talking about me behind my back, or even how many people know. It's just so humiliating, you know?"

I started to cry again, silent tears rolling down my face as I listened to her talk. My strong and sensitive friend who rescued injured animals when we were in grade school and pretended she was not in pain when she broke her leg in Junior High, and who would go to war each time someone hurt my feelings, would not be okay for a long while. I was so angry that this boy took something from her.

"I'm sorry, it must have been so scary."

"I think the thing that scares me the most is that I didn't do anything wrong. I was just out with my friends and my sister, in our hometown, with people we know. Tons of people around. And no one saw a thing," Marni said, flat and almost emotionless.

"I know, I'm so sorry," I said, and I finally hugged her and cried hard. I am not sure how long we cried together, but we got a little embarrassed and stopped to grab some tissues off her dresser.

After blowing our noses and wiping our eyes and taking a few deep breaths, I said, "let's figure out a way to tell the world who he is so he can't do this again! We could get him expelled or kicked off his basketball team or we could do a video…"

"Ellie, no. YOU want to feel better by doing something, by getting all Jane Austeny. You mean well, but this happened to me. I get to decide what I do. I just want to move past this. Maybe paint up a storm, and then not think about it anymore." She said firmly.

"But," I said.

"No, 'but,' and I don't want to hear you say this was your fault again. If I have to accept it wasn't my fault, you do too. I'm serious," she said, standing up and looking determined.

"Okay, I will stop saying it, and I am also done trying to be someone I'm not. I'll leave Elizabeth Bennet to the pages of literature, and just be Ellie who doesn't put people in their place and stays next to her bestie at parties."

"It was better staying invisible," sighed Marni, putting her arm over my shoulder and leading me to the kitchen.

26

The evening with Marni and her family, had disturbed something inside me. They couldn't have been more loving, nor the spaghetti more delicious, but the secret looks I saw shared between her parents made me feel uneasy. It was as if we looked different to them and they were watching to see if we noticed it, too. Marni, of course, was more subdued and had zero planetary or astrological commentary. I was trying to act upbeat for her sake, but I felt like I was living in slow motion. Maybe what they knew was that we would never be quite the same.

I felt a little disloyal to Marni, but when I got home, I texted Ava to help me interpret what I saw in Marni's parents. She called me right away. Obviously, none of us were sleeping easily these days.

"Hey, how was Marni?" Ava asked.

"She was Marni, and not," I said, not making much sense even to my own ears.

"Catt told me her family and Emma's dad had a long family meeting today. She said it was like 'group therapy for the old people.' Catt's words, not mine. They were all upset and talking about keeping us safe in this world today."

"Marni said she couldn't believe it happened in her hometown, surrounded by friends, and when she wasn't doing anything wrong. It shook me."

"That's so scary. It literally could have been any of us. Can you imagine?"

"I don't want to imagine it. It traumatized her enough without her being able to remember many details. I'm doubly thankful not much technically happened," I said.

"True. Not much physically, but emotionally, this is going to last a long while. Was she able to talk about what happened, how she feels and stuff?" asked Ava.

"Yeah. A little, and we hugged and cried about it, and then she yelled at me."

"Yelled at you?"

"I mean, she was firm with me because I kept suggesting we get back at him or tell the world about him. She just wanted to stop talking about it. I kept telling her she would feel better if she did something. And she told me it was me that would feel better if we did something. Anyway, she told me to stop planning. She gets to decide, which, I know is true."

"She does get to decide for herself. And she is right, you would feel better doing something. You have always been the one to take action when things get bad."

"I have?"

"Yes, remember when my lunch box was missing in fifth grade? You found a picture of it on-line and plastered the locker area with 'Have you seen me?' posters. Finally, Sally Mitchell realized she had taken it by mistake since we had the same one, only she had not brought her lunch that day. And when Mr. Sanders had his bike stolen, you rallied the entire seventh grade class to buy him a new one, and more recently you came up with our summer 'make Ellie a more confident person and speaker' project Jane Austen style."

"About that. I think I am over it. I think I took being Elizabeth too far," I said.

"Don't be ridiculous, you were really her all along. You have always taken action and spoken your mind on behalf of others. You just needed to be reminded you can stand up for yourself as much as you do for your friends."

Tears sprang to my eyes, and I couldn't talk for a minute.

"So how was the rest of your visit after she didn't actually yell at you?" Ava said with a soft smile in her voice.

"We talked, and we cried. I was glad she could. You know she holds tears in. Then when we went to eat dinner. Her dad joked as usual and her mom tried to stuff us to death with food. But they definitely kept watching us like they knew something. Like they knew Santa wasn't real, and they were watching to see if we had figured it out. Do you know what I mean? Do you think something else happened they aren't telling us?"

"I'm guessing her parents are sad and angry this happened. My mom's comment was, 'This, unfortunately, is growing up. Seeing life has ugliness.' So maybe that's it. They know their daughter is growing up?"

"I think we all are," I said.

"True. Are you going to be okay? You know standing up for yourself is not why this happened, right?"

"I already told Marni I'm done with thoughts of being anything other than happy, invisible Ellie Gardiner."

"As I said, you are being ridiculous. You were never really invisible, and you were not especially happy taking a back seat all the time."

"Nope, no Ava logic will work on me tonight. I am going back into my cocoon until college!"

"Okay, caterpillar, I have to go to sleep. Talk tomorrow?"

"You're the best Avary davery dock," I said.
"Night weirdo."

******

Group Msg: The Invisibles

Marni: Hey, the police just left. They say there is not much they can do. Not enough evidence. Blah Blah Blah… I don't really want to talk about it anymore, I'm over it. But side kiss emoji and heart you guys. xxo

Ava: side kiss emoji pink heart emoji

Emma: thumbs up emoji red heart emoji

Catt: blue heart emoji pink heart emoji

Ellie: cursing emoji side kiss emoji

Group Text: The Invisibles

Emma: Anyone feel like watching the meteor shower tonight?

Catt: Yay, park?

Marni: Not sure. Just us or others invited?

Emma: I was thinking the original 5, the OG, the founding sisters of cool.

Marni: Dude…

Ava: I have Fallon, but I'd love to come. Would she be okay, tho not OG?

Ellie: If you girls are in, I'm in, lmk. But we need bug spray this time!

Catt: I'll be in charge of bug spray! Bug emoji

Marni: Fallon is okay, she's a nice kid. No promise you guys, but I'd like to try.

Ellie: No promise needed. lmk and I will come walk with you.

The night breeze was warm, and the crickets were singing as I spread my favorite blue and aqua beach towel in the middle of the Emerson Park field next to Marni's boho fringe blanket.

"My dad said this is the perfect night for stargazing. He said it's a new moon tonight. So it will be extra dark," said Marni.

"Oh good. I am going to wish on every shooting star, and I need to see them all!" I said. "Where is everyone?"

"Probably having to wait on Emma's dad for a ride. I can't wait until we can drive," said Marni.

"Driver's Ed next summer! I hope we get Mr. Silbaugh. He is supposed to be the easiest and lets you stop at Dairy Queen," I said.

"I'll probably get stuck with Mr. Graves. He makes you change a tire and get all dirty and he is so slow, but Eden said she heard he is retiring. So maybe he will be gone by then."

"Speaking of which, I think it might be them coming. The car is going really slowly over the speed bumps, said Marni.

"You're right, Dr. Hartfield is nice, but he is the slowest," I said in a slow-motion voice and we both laughed.

"It's weird more people didn't come to the park tonight. There are no softball games, and the moon is new, or whatever your dad called it. I thought the park might be crowded."

"A new moon. I guess it's the same thing," said Marni. "There are people playing tennis still, but the lights don't really reach all the way over here."

"Hey you guys!" yelled Emma. "Thanks, dad! I'll text you later. Is that okay?"

"Catt gassed us all out with the bug spray in the car and we had to roll down the windows, so we didn't asphyxiate," said Ava, coughing and laughing.

"I got it in my mouth," Fallon said, as she licked her tongue on the arm of her sweatshirt.

"Ewwwww," I laughed.

"I didn't mean to. I leaned over on it when I was looking for my flashlight. Anyway, you will all be glad when we aren't covered in bites tomorrow," said Catt.

"Spray me," Marni said, and I jumped in line next to her.

"I hate the smell of bug spray. It is nasty, but do my hair because mosquitoes always get me there," I said. "Do you think we should put our blankets in a line or in a square?"

"Square!" yelled Emma.

"Or circle heads all together?!" suggested Ava.

"Oh, good call! We've never done the circle," said Emma, moving her blanket over.

"If we had a really humongous selfie stick, this would be a great photo," Marni said, folding her arms behind her head as we finally settled and laid head to head facing the sparkling night sky.

"That would take someone with a freakishly long arm," I said, giggling.

"You kinda have freakishly long arms. I've been meaning to tell you," mocked Emma.

"Shut your face, rude," I said and tried to flail my arm over my head to smack her noggin, but I couldn't reach her. "You better be glad you are wrong, or I could have popped you."

"Fallon, is your tongue better now?" Catt asked.

"Yes, Ava gave me purple gum."

"Sorry about the spray."

"Sokay," said Fallon.

"If I stare at the sky long enough, I can't tell if it is individual white stars in a black sky or one huge white light covered by a black sheet with little holes," I said.

"Trippy," said Catt.

"Whoa, did you see that?" I said, closing my eyes for my first wish.

"Whoa, it was so pretty," said Marni.

"Wow, that one was long. Hang on, I gotta make a wish," Emma said.

"Make a wish on the falling stars, Fallon," said Ava.

"And don't tell anyone what it is or it won't come true," said Catt.

"There was one, a baby one," I said, pointing as if anyone could see my hand.

"I think it was a moth," said Emma

"That was not a moth. Oh, wait, yes it was. Gross."

"There… like three together over by the pool," said Ava.

"I don't want to close my eyes for each wish and miss one!" said Catt.

"You have to be quick. I have at least twenty memorized," I said.

"Oh, you don't do the same one over and over?" asked Catt.

"I'll do it," said Marni quietly, but clearly.

"Do what, Marn?" asked Ava cautiously, probably because she was, as always, a step ahead of everyone else.

Though I couldn't see her well, I looked next to me at her form lying still and staring up as she said again, "I'll do it, Ellie. I want to take action."

"You do?" I asked at the same time as Emma asked, "What action?" And Ava asked, "are you sure you're ready for that?"

"Yes, I'm sure. I feel small and closed. And I want to feel this," open armed gesturing to the sky, though I was probably the only one who could see her, "sparkly and free and open."

"No one is sparklier than you," said Ava with a catch in her voice.

"I need to paint this feeling," Marni said.

"We can figure out a way to tell the world who he is so he can't do this again. We could get him expelled, make a video," I said.

"I could just hunt him down and beat him up. I can get Kyle

211

and those guys," said Emma.

"No. Wait. While I appreciate your enthusiasm, tonight is not for planning. Tonight is for wishes," said Marni and after a long pause, "I love you guys."

"We love you, too," I said, my eyes welled with tears making the stars multiply and blur. My brave friend wanted to fight back.

"Love and smooches," yelled Catt, moved to express herself in signature Catt style.

"Don't even think of it, Kit Catt! No rolling! Emma, help! She's starting. Get her off of me," laughed Marni and we all laughed with her; in relief, in happiness, and in the sheer joy of watching our wishes streak across a glittering sky.

27

"Why don't you come with me?" asked Jade while passing me the toothpaste. "I'm going over to Finn's. Owen is there."

"Really? Why are they here?" I asked, sounding mumbley with a mouth full of whitening toothpaste.

"Finn's parents are coming back from Europe this weekend and they wanted to get the house ready. Finn is mowing the lawn, and Owen is trying to help him. I don't think they know what they are doing, but he is enjoying it."

"What doesn't he enjoy? He is the happiest person I know besides you," I said, spitting my toothpaste.

Jade rolled her sparkling eyes. The world could barely contain her happiness. She was bubbling over. It was infectious.

"So, he is really moving back full-time? What about basketball?" I asked.

"He talked to his Pemberley coach and our Meryton coach and transferred schools," Jade said.

"What?" I spit again and rinsed my mouth.

"I know! I would have never thought," said Jade, bursting with happiness.

"Brooklyn isn't, though, is she?" I asked, my mouth suddenly dry with terror at the idea of dealing with Brooklyn daily at school.

"No, put your eyes back in your head," Jade laughed. "She is staying at her old school with Georgiana and Owen. Finn said his transfer will help their parents afford to send Brooklyn so she can still go to private school."

"Also, Finn is a legacy at Penn, so he thinks he can still get in with me, hopefully. This way we get to do our senior year together! Homecoming, prom, everyday lunch!

"That is so awesome, Jade. I am so happy for you. And for me, too. He has a cool car to drive us to school."

"I know. He is the best. I am so glad we saw each other at the hospital. I mean, I'm not glad about the hospital, obviously."

"I know what you mean."

"Finn told me the reason they were at the party. Owen was going to find me and tell me he was the jerk that kept us apart and beg me to forgive Finn."

"He was?" I asked.

"I guess being yelled at on the city street helped him see the error of his ways, eh?" Jade said. "Regardless, I am glad you yelled at him and glad he listened to you. I think Owen likes you."

"If by 'likes' you mean 'completely ignores,' then maybe," I said as Jade rolled her eyes again.

"Let's see if he ignores you today. But go change, you are not wearing this robe, lazybones."

"Okay, but I have my gala rehearsal with Ms. Lemon this afternoon so I can't stay long."

I quickly changed into my overall shorts and pink tank top and grabbed my converse. I brushed my hair in front of the full-length mirror in the corner of my room and paused. A

214

month ago I had felt humiliated to be in front of these new people in this outfit, and now I didn't care. As Aunt Cassie would say, "Thank you, I like it, too!" I finished my side braid and smiled at myself. Maybe Ava is right. Maybe I am like Elizabeth Bennet, now just more comfortable with the role. I look the same, I just feel less... "

"ELLIE, come on!!!" Jade yelled, a little louder than I thought necessary, but she was a girl in love with a cute boy who was waiting down the street.

"I'm coming, rude," I said and jumped down the last three stairs like I had done every day until I turned twelve. It had felt undignified to be almost a teenager and still jumping stairs, so I stopped. Now, I was happy to be undignified once more.

******

As the daughters of a professional grass mower, we could tell that something was not quite right on the Bingley lawn. It looked like the mower Finn had used did not have a basket to collect the grass clippings, and grass carnage was everywhere. Jade laughed at the consternation on Finn's innocent face.

"It looks so good, just a few more steps and it will be perfect. We need a rake and the green barrel," said Jade.

"Excuse us, Ellie, we will be back once we find the proper tools, so your capable sister can teach me the finer points of lawn maintenance. Owen, please be civil to our guest," said Finn as they went to the shed behind the house.

"Look," he said at the same time I said, "I wanted to thank you."

We laughed awkwardly and looked at each other.

"Please," he said, "you go first."

"Thank you for helping Marni. I am so grateful you found her... in time. I actually can't believe you were there."

"Last time we spoke, was in a driveway, just like this...

215

remember?" he said, smiling, but still reserved.

"I do. I mean, I remember."

"You told me you were going to Jake's party, so I called him and asked if I could come."

"You did?"

"I did. I knew I needed to make things right with Finn and Jade."

"You are a good friend to Finn."

"I was really only thinking of you."

"Oh," I said lamely as he looked into my eyes and then down at my lips. My heart raced, and I began to ramble. "Did you know I went back to Jake's house? I got there right after you did. Hoping to find evidence. Such a miracle you arrived when you did. He had grabbed me earlier in the night and that's why you saw me sitting on the wall, being loud. I was announcing the game because Benji helped me get away from Declan. I was practicing."

"Whoa, Ellie, are you saying Declan grabbed you that night as well?" He looked furious.

"Yes. He was trying to intimidate me. Then I lashed out and told him I knew the story about his scholarship was a lie and he threatened me."

"Why would you put yourself in danger like that? I warned you he was bad news. What were you thinking?"

"Why are you yelling at me? Maybe if you had actually told people what he was like, instead of giving cryptic warnings, maybe none of this would have happened!"

He looked hurt at my sharp tone. I guess I had been holding on to some anger. If Owen hadn't been so reluctant to expose Declan's character, none of this would have happened. No way Jake would have let him come to his party.

"It's like you girls can't see past his supposed looks and charm. My sister fell for his sob stories because he had 'sad

216

eyes.' So ridiculous."

"Oh, please. As if girls are the only ones who fall for looks. 'She is tolerable, but not handsome enough to tempt me,' said Mr. Darcy."

"I'm not THAT Mr. Darcy!"

"You SO are. But anyway, your sister is what I was hoping to talk to you about. I think she and Marni should meet and talk about what happened to them. The police won't press charges against Declan with only the word of a girl who doesn't remember any details of the drugging, since it wasn't an actual... you know, assault." I shuddered at the memory, but pushed on. "The cup wasn't enough to convict him, but if many girls testified, or at the very least came together to warn others, or form a support group..."

"No way. I will not let you talk to Georgiana about this. It devastated her once, and I swore to protect her."

"So you get to protect your sister, but no one else gets protected? Is that fair?" I asked angrily.

He said nothing, but looked like flames were shooting out of his eyes.

"That is so sexist. We don't always have to be saved by a boy. We have some ideas of how we can get the word out and at least warn other girls so they don't have this happen to them. I think Georgie could contribute and it might even empower her."

"You want me to ask my sister to expose all her shame and pain to people she doesn't know so that... what? So I can stop being a sexist pig?"

Georgiana came walking up the path from the side of the house and it was obvious she had been there for a few minutes.

"I can't believe you told people," Georgiana said to Owen. Turning to me she said, "and no, I'm not interested in talking about my private business with anyone."

217

"My friend Marni could use a listening ear, someone who has been there? She…"

"I'm sorry, Ellie. I can't," she said. She ran into the house and up the stairs. I heard a faraway door slam shut.

I waited for Owen to say, "I told you so," or "get out," but he just looked at me. I felt my face flush as I read disappointment and something else in his eyes. His gaze was so intense. It felt like he was trying to memorize my face.

"I won't make her," he finally said.

"I know. But her anger proves to me I'm right. No one should suffer alone. Goodbye Owen," I said with finality. Once again, walking away from him when I really wanted to stay.

Text

> Ellie: Why are boys the worst?
> Ava: Owen?
> Ellie: I hate his guts.
> Ava: If you did, you wouldn't be so mad.
> Ava: You want to tell me what happened?
> Ellie: Yes, but not now. Just hate him with me right now.
> Ava: Done. He is dead to me.
> Ellie: Tnx! Heart emoji

Text

> Ellie: Hey, I have ideas.
> Marni: Oh no, lol
> Ellie: It involves all of us, and I think next Friday, the day before the fundraiser.
> Marni: Whoa, okay, that's soon.
> Ellie: Can we have a planning meeting at your house?
> Marni: My mom has bowling league tomorrow, at 11 a.m., then?
> Marni: Wait, one condition. Will your mom make

the chocolate drop cookies again?

Ellie: I will tell her they are for you, you may get a double batch!

Ellie: Mkay, I will text everyone.

Group Msg: The Invisibles

Ellie: Any chance you can all come to Marni's tomorrow at 11 a.m.? Planning meeting.

Ava: I can, I won't have Fallon tomorrow.

Emma: Yup.

Catt: Yup Yup dancing girl emoji

Marni: See you then sideface kiss emoji

28

My mind was all over the place as I walked through the woods and across the park to get to Marni's house. Ideas for our big mission were swirling alongside the equally powerful visions of how we could get in major trouble with each one. Questions about what was illegal and what was worth the risk haunted me, and so did thoughts of Owen and Georgie. He had looked so disappointed in me and hurt for his sister. I was pretty sure I would never see him again, and that thought made me sad.

I pushed away the image of his face with planning ideas for Operation Inform. That was what I had been calling it, to remind me our main goal was to give information. Sharks were out there, circling, dressed as charming boys. I'm guessing most girls were like us and didn't know how easy it was to "get bit." They, like us, believed people were who they seemed to be on the outside.

Rounding the bend, I saw Marni walking down her driveway to the mailbox.

"Hey, woman! Fancy meeting you here," I said.

"Good timing," she said. "I see you brought your payment," she said, pointing to the Tupperware box under my arm. "Yup, but I may have had to munch on one midway here. I got weak with hunger."

"Hey Marni, Hi Ellie," said Seth Stephenson, a junior, and popular kid, pulling out of his driveway in his vintage 1993 Mustang.

"Hey, Seth!" we said simultaneously and then burst out in giggles when he was out of earshot.

"What just happened?" I asked.

"He forgot he doesn't talk to us," laughed Marni.

"Maybe we really aren't invisible anymore?" I mused, "Or Seth has just lost it."

"He's lost it," she said, linking my arm and walking me through her creaky gate and into the game room.

"So, are you ready for this?" I asked, taking in her messy bun, light blue t-shirt, and teddy bear print pj shorts.

"I am, I mean, I am not a hundred percent sure what we are going to do, but all the things we talked about seem like something I could do. Honestly, it feels good to be doing something positive," she said.

"I…" I started.

"I know, I know, you told me so!" said Marni.

"That wasn't what I was going to say!" I laughed, "I swear! I was going to say I hope you'll be inspired to put on actual clothes instead of pajamas," I teased.

"Jellooo ladies," yelled Emma as she pushed the door open and walked in with Catt and Ava close behind.

"Helloooo, I brought chips and salsa," said Ava.

"And I brought puffy Cheetos!!" said Catt.

"Yum, I love it all," said Marni. "Thank you!"

"There is nothing I would not do for those who are really my friends. I have no notion of loving people by halves, it is not my nature," said Catt out of nowhere.

"Catt, is that from your book?" asked Ava, recognizing

Northanger Abbey.

"Yes, I've finished and am now just memorizing a few of my favorite quotes. Thanks for the recommendation," said Catt.

"You are welcome. I knew you would like her view on life. Catherine Moreland is totally you," I said.

"You were right. She is just like me; she loves her friends, and she is always looking for adventures that she can't find in her own village. It's like me. Going away to college, probably in a city, maybe NYU and go crazy there... like the book says, 'If adventures will not befall a young lady in her own village, she must seek them abroad.'"

"I didn't know you were thinking NYU," said Ava, getting quiet. "Everyone is going to be so far apart."

"New rule! No thinking of that right now," said Marni. "Erase your sad face, delete your thoughts! We are not allowed to think anything about college and life after graduation until junior year. And even then, not until after Christmas!"

"Agreed!" said Emma, grabbing a napkin full of Cheetos and popping one in her mouth.

"So, we should get started," I said as my phone lit up and vibrated. "Hang on."

Text:

Georgie: Ellie, this is Georgie. So sorry for how I acted yesterday. I'm so torn, but I want to maybe help. I know I'd like to stop being so angry. Again, I am sorry, and I hope we can still be friends.

"Oh my gosh you guys, I just got a text, I have to respond. We may have help. I'll be right back.

Text:

 Ellie: Hi! I am so glad, and I am not mad. I am sorry I
   pushed at you; it wasn't right. I am right now at my
   friend's house and we are deciding what we should

do. Are you still here or back at home? I know you
don't know these girls, but do you want us to
Facetime you into our meeting? You could help us
decide which plan to do. I have one idea I think is
the best, but it's a little risky.

Georgie: Yes, I'm back home. I'll feel like a dork
on Facetime, but okay?

Ellie: Oh, and I haven't told anyone your story,
it's yours to tell. I will say you have had a run-in
with D yourself and want to join us. Cool?

Georgie: Cool.

Ellie: Okay, I will Facetime you in just a minute.

Georgie: See you in a minute.

"Okay everyone, let's begin discussion of our plans for
Operation Inform," I said, heading to the whiteboard where
the Nolans kept score for dart board championships and wrote
"Operation Inform" in blue erasable marker on the top.

"Today, we will make a plan to be executed on Friday, the
day before the fundraiser gala. I figure this way, it is behind us
and we can really enjoy ourselves on Saturday, hopefully
having been totally successful.

"Good idea, but what are we doing? The suspense is killing
me," said Emma.

"Before I tell you my idea, I want to introduce you to
someone. Someone who has been through her own incidents
with Declan and has decided she wants to work with us. Her
name is Georgiana, or Georgie, Owen Darcy's sister. I'm going
to Facetime her in."

"Hi Georgie," said everyone as her face popped on the
screen and I showed her the entire room. She looked
embarrassed but smiled at all the faces waving and smiling
back at her.

"I'm Catt."

"I'm Emma."

"Hi, I'm Ava."

"And hi, I'm Marni. I'm the one who, well, had a problem with Declan."

"And obviously, you know me. Um, I need to put you somewhere," I said, juggling my phone and marker.

"Give her to me," said Emma, taking the phone and pointing it at the whiteboard. "Georgie, let me know if you can't hear something."

"Okay," said Georgie, "thanks."

"Okay, proceed," said Catt, "wait, do I get to wear all black like a cat burglar. A Catt burglar! I swear I didn't mean to say that. So hilarious," said Catt, practically crying at her accidental pun.

My eyes rolled in my head dramatically and I said, "I am going to apologize to all of my teachers in the fall. I totally get why they are always annoyed."

"Welcome everyone. I have an idea. I have run it by Marni and now I need to see what you all think. Do you think we can do it all in one day, and if you are up for taking a risk? We could get in trouble."

I explained my vision. We discussed and tweaked the logistics and we doled out tasks. If we were going to pull off something this big in one day, especially while remaining anonymous, then it was going to take planning. We would have to be "Invisible" for just a little longer. I had the job of finding us a ride that wouldn't ask too many questions or tell our parents. It was a tall order, and I knew it couldn't be Jade or Eden. They would talk us out of it. Aunt Cassie would, but she was in the middle of another big case, and she was also in the city. The city. I had a sudden burst of genius and yelled "Monica!" super loudly in the game room.

Everyone was working in groups on their assignments. They all looked at me, but then went right back to work. I should have been offended, but I was too excited. I guess they were used to random blurts from me.

I quickly texted Monica.

Text

Ellie: Hey Monica, it's been a week or so since I've texted, but my friends and I are doing something crazy next Friday and could use your help. You can absolutely say no. It's asking a lot, but I kinda think this would be more your cup of tea than a BBQ at the Camden Club.

Monica: Great timing! I was just thinking city life was getting a little dull. I'm in if I can help. What is it you need?

Ellie: I'll call you tonight, with more details. For now, we need a driver on Friday who can keep a secret.

Monica: I like the sound of that!

Ellie: We are not robbing a bank.

Ellie: or anything.

Ellie: No robbing.

Monica: Bummer lol

Monica: Call later. Mom and I are taking a tennis lesson. I know, I'm a walking stereotype!

Ellie: Side kiss face emoji

"I'm so excited for you guys to meet Monica. She is nothing like us and exactly like us," I said.

"You know that makes no sense, right?" said Emma.

"I mean because she is from a very wealthy family and has traveled all over the world, yet she finds people different from her interesting, nothing like the Brooklyns of the world."

"Okay, that does make sense," Emma said.

"Anyway, she just agreed to be our driver. The mission is a go!"

29

It was 8 a.m. and everyone was sitting on my porch waiting for our ride. Monica said she had the perfect vehicle and would be our getaway driver for our big adventure. Our friendship was new enough that as my phone showed 8:01 a.m., I got worried. All of our planning would fall apart if she didn't show. Without her, we couldn't get to any of the schools on our list. I looked over to where Georgie and Marni sat talking, looking like they had known each other forever rather than just a few days. I had high hopes our mission would give them the feeling of control again, or would at least be a big step forward.

A heavy rumble disrupted those thoughts, and I turned to look back at the street. A Presidential motorcade-looking black Escalade with tinted windows passed us and turned around in the cul-de-sac then pulled up along the curb in front of me. The passenger window slowly and dramatically rolled down to reveal Monica, lowering her sunglasses halfway and looking quite pleased with herself.

"You girls ready to do this?"

"Yes," everyone cheered as they opened the back doors and hopped in.

"Nice," said Emma, appreciating the snazzy SUV.

"Yay, Monica!" yelled Catt as she bounded in the back door and over the back seat.

"Wait, you have a license, right?" I asked, pausing before I jumped up into the passenger seat.

"Yes, of course. I have a license. I mean, it's not from this country, but I'm sure it's still legal," said Monica, smiling at my wide, panicked eyes. "Come on, get in, and before you ask, yes, the gas tank is full."

I jumped in, laughing at the audacity of what we were doing and the utter joy of doing it with my friends.

"Okay Ellie, I know you have a checklist," said Ava, "so let's hear it."

"Shut up, but yes I do," I smiled, pulling out my notebook and turning around in my seat to face the back two rows of excited faces.

"1. Are we all dressed in boring, nondescript clothes?" I read.

"Some of us are worse than others," Emma said, looking at Catt's oversized yellow t-shirt and faded jeans in disgust.

"I'm blending in!" Catt said, pulling on her sunglasses.

I assessed the group and noted everyone had dressed in plain t-shirts and jeans.

"Good job. You all look great."

"2. Ponytail holder and hats. I have extra ponytail holders and a few baseball caps if we need to change up our look between schools."

"You're like an evil genius!" said Catt in admiration.

"3. Map. Ava, do you have the address for all six schools, and have you checked they all have summer school classes?" I read.

"Check," yelled Ava, a little loud so I could tell she was both nervous and excited, too. "Monica, do you want me to give you the address for your GPS or do you want me to just direct you?"

"You are right behind me, so just direct me as we go. I don't know the GPS in this car."

"Cool," affirmed Ava.

"Wait, you didn't steal this, did you?" I asked Monica.

She smiled wickedly and said, "no, but I have given an IOU to an Argentinian Polo player named Marco, who is obsessed with American culture. Who knows what he will have me doing in payment."

"Oh boy," I said, shaking my head at the Monica-ness of it all.

"4. Fliers. Marni, do you and Georgie have the fliers printed up that you designed?" I continued.

"Check, and we ran it by your aunt, on the 'DL'," she whispered, "on the DL," which made me smile. "You know, for the legal check... no libel, but we need to remain anonymous just in case. Obviously, she will not tell a soul," said Marni.

"We printed up a box of 300, a little overkill," said Georgiana, still a little shy but warming up to the group.

"That should cover it," laughed Monica.

"5. Tape," I read. "Emma, you brought the tape?"

"Yes, I brought us each a roll of blue painter's tape so we can't even be accused of wrecking the stall doors," said Emma.

"Good idea!" said Ava.

"Thank you. It came to me yesterday at the store when I overheard cheerleaders saying they got in trouble by school maintenance for using duct tape on the walls. It apparently ripped a hole when they took it down. I didn't even buy all ten rolls at the same place, so I didn't raise suspicion," Emma smiled, feeling very smug.

"You've watched too much true crime," Catt said.

"6. Ellie, go over the plan for the first stop," I read.

"Okay, so Monica drops three of us off at the back. And three off at the front entrance of Adams High School. Walk in like you own the place, find the restrooms, and do your thing. I think we can make this happen in less than thirty minutes depending on how much evasive action we have to take," I said.

"Evasive action?" said Catt, looking nervous.

"Just faking like we are doing our makeup or acting like we are texting while witnesses are there," explained Emma.

"But don't be your usual talkative self," I said, looking at Catt. "You don't want them to remember you."

"Monica will hang in the area, but not be obvious," I said.

"In this thing?" Emma said, gesturing to the huge Escalade with a raised brow and a smirk.

"Well, be as inconspicuous as possible, I guess, by driving away until we text. Monica and Georgie are officially on our group text now, so let's use it to check in."

"Yay," said Catt, high-fiving Georgie and pushing Monica's shoulder from the back.

"Okay, that's it. Are we ready?" asked Monica.

"What team is going first?" asked Ava.

"We will," said Emma looking at Catt and Ava for confirmation. Both nodded solemnly.

"Wait, I add #7 to my checklist. 'Ellie, give pep talk.'" I said, making quote fingers. "Not to be too mushy, but we friends have been through a lot. We have watched two of our friends, as they felt hurt and helpless because they couldn't get justice in the normal way. You know everything points back to Jane Austen for me. We have a privilege Jane's characters didn't have. They could not take matters into their own hands like this."

Ava added, "Maybe if they could have jumped out of the

books and worked together like we are, it would have been different. I'd like to think they would all be with us on this mission, and Jane would be proud of us."

"We are doing the best thing we can for girls like us," I said.

"… girls who need to be warned that creeps like Declan are out there," added Marni.

"… and how to protect themselves," said Georgie, nodding in agreement with Marni.

I smiled at them all, my crew, my ride-or-die, "I am proud of us for taking this action to keep others safe and for being smart and stealthy… and I will treat us all to Dairy Queen when we succeed!"

"Woo hoo!!" We all cheered and kept cheering and singing as Monica blasted the radio and we headed to Adams High School.

We got to Adams just as students were streaming onto campus for summer school classes. Monica dropped off group one at the back, where the entrance to the gym and locker rooms were. Ava, Emma, and Catt jumped out and just blended into the crowd flowing into the building. Then Monica stopped along the curb a little way down from the main entrance. I momentarily panicked and was frozen in place.

"Are you okay?" Monica asked. "You look a little pale."

"I am more nervous than I thought I'd be," I confessed. Taking a deep breath, I grabbed my backpack and jumped out. "Thank you," I said to Monica as I shut the door.

"We simply have to walk in talking to each other like we know what we are doing. It will be fine," said Marni.

"I'll demonstrate," Marni said with a devilish grin. "So, Georgie," Marni said a little too loudly, "think we'll see your handsome brother anytime soon?" I glared at her and she and Georgie giggled arm in arm at me as we walked past teachers and students we didn't know.

Once inside, we acted casual and headed to the first girls' restrooms we found. There were six stalls, so we each took one and closed the door. I heard the zip sound of our three backpacks opening at the same time and I heard the rip of tape from either Marni or Georgie. I took out one of the white fliers and pulled off two small pieces of blue tape and affixed the flier right at eye level behind the door. Any girl coming into this stall would see the sign.

I hurried out of the stall and headed to the next open one, finishing in minutes.

"That's it for this one. Let's get out of here before someone comes in," said Marni.

"I'm worried girls will read this, while we are still on campus, and figure out who we are," said Georgie.

"Yeah, me too. Let's hurry, but act casual," I said.

We continued wandering the halls and found four more restrooms before we got a text from the others.

Group Msg: The Invisibles

Ava: Hey guys, done here. Got locker room and four
         restrooms, I think that's it. Meet at pick up spot?
Monica: Same as drop off, on my way.
Marni: We are finishing the last one, heading to our
         drop-off.
Monica: Thumbs up emoji

We thought we were caught coming out of our last restroom when a teacher headed our way with a determined walk, but she then yelled "Dylan, Dylan Pampas, come back here," and hustled after what looked like an 8th-grade boy who dove into the boys' restroom.

Monica stopped at the curb and we jumped in, out of breath

and elated. Everyone started excited- screaming and talking at once as Monica peeled away from the curb.

We pulled into the McDonald's to compare notes and calm down... and to eat hash browns.

"We did it!"

"One down, 5 to go!"

"That felt good!"

"Oh my goodness, I thought they caught us a few times. This one girl would not leave the locker room. She must have been ditching class in there," said Ava.

"And then Catt runs into a stall and starts fake throwing up, hoping to make her leave," said Emma, pride clear in her voice.

"Gross," I said.

"Did it work?" asked Marni, amused.

"Yup, she almost ran," said Catt proudly.

"Amazing," said Monica.

"Monica, thank you so much. There is no way we could have done this without you!" I said, and everyone agreed.

"This is a blast, way more fun than the country club. I kinda wish I could join you on the inside," said Monica wistfully.

"Why not?" I said.

"Maybe on the last one," she conceded. "We don't want to get too confident after only one."

"Yeah, I really don't want to have to puke again," said Catt. "I almost did for real."

We moved on to Belmont, then Coalmont, then Tipton, Putnam, and we ended at our own school, Meryton High. This would be the riskiest because people knew us and might realize we had no reason to be on campus.

"It is pretty dead, not too many cars around," Ava said as we sat in the Escalade.

"But the good news is since we know our way around it should go faster," I said. "Monica, you in on this one? If we get caught, I can just say you are my cousin and I wanted to show you my school."

"So, Catt doesn't have to puke?" she laughed, giving Catt a wink in the mirror.

"Exactly, you can hang the flier as I hand you tape," I said.

"You know, I haven't even seen what this entire mission is about," said Monica.

"Oh, sorry, we never showed you one?" asked Marni.

"Here." I handed her a crisp white flier with a picture of Declan playing basketball in the middle of the page. It said "This guy is a CREEPER - Don't trust him" across the top and the words at the bottom said "We want you to protect yourself, he was an abusive boyfriend to one of us, and roofied another at a party, but got away with both. Don't let you or your besties alone with him and never leave your drink at a party. Your friends, the No Longer Invisibles."

"Let me see that," Monica said, reaching for the flier. "Domkop! This is the guy?!"

Everyone froze.

"You know him?" I asked. "You called him Don Cop?

"No, I just called him a domkop, a stupid person. I never knew his name, but he tried to put his hand up my skirt last summer at a lake party," said Monica.

Georgie and Marni gasped.

"No way," I said in shock.

"We need to stop this predator," Monica said as she turned off the car. "Let's do this!"

"Wait, one more thing," I said, feeling overwhelmed with gratitude for these friends. "These fliers out our group name, and we really aren't those 'Invisibles' anymore. I'd like to suggest we change a few letters and become the 'Indivisibles.'"

"Oh, I love it," said Ava.

"... with liberty and justice for all!" Catt quoted from the pledge of allegiance with her hand over her heart.

"Well yeah, allegiance, too," I laughed, "but mostly because we can no longer be divided."

"You are getting mushy today," said Emma, nudging my shoulder. "Let's go make trouble one last time!"

30

I was comfortably upside down on my bed staring at the script Ms. Lemon and I practiced yesterday when the doorbell rang. My mom was talking with someone, but I was too exhausted from the adrenaline-filled mission to think much of it.

"ELLIE... you have a visitor!!!"

"Coming," I yelled before looking in my mirror to check that I didn't have ink on my face or something else weird. I grew curious as I descended the stairs. It wouldn't have been any of my friends or mom would have just sent them up.

In the hallway, dressed like a fashion model, as always, stood Brooklyn Bingley. She had her usual look of annoyance that I now realized was just her face... or at least the one she wore when around me.

"Hello, Brooklyn," I said, my voice sounding weary and guarded. I scanned her face for signs of what this visit was about, trying to quell the paranoia her judgmental face brought out in me. Had Georgie told her what we did today? Had Georgie told Owen, and he sent Brooklyn to yell at me?

"Would you girls like some lemonade? I can bring it to you

in the family room if you want to go sit down."

"I won't be here that long," Brooklyn said to my mom like she was dismissing a servant.

"Thank you, mom. I appreciate it," I said, glaring at Brooklyn for her rudeness, "but I agree, Brooklyn will not be here that long."

"So, why are you here?" I asked, dispensing with pleasantries after my mom left.

"Can we go talk out there in the backyard, in the little gardeny area I see out there?" asked Brooklyn, pointing past me and the French doors to the deck outside.

"Sure. It's a deck, not a garden, but after you," I said, noting the tension in her jaw as she moved past me.

The day was warm and humid, but her glare turned icy once I shut the door. She focused her gray eyes on me like a praying mantis would an aphid whose head she was about to rip off.

"Did I catch you napping?" she said as she looked me up and down, just like the first day I met her.

"Brooklyn, what do you want? I'm busy."

"Oh, I am sure you are so busy with your little country friends planning a country fair, but I don't care. Your sister now has her claws in my brother, and I just want to make a few things clear."

"I'm all ears," I said and felt an odd need to laugh with relief that this was nothing to do with Operation Inform.

"You may not take this seriously, but it is true. You will never be able to fit into his life," she said through gritted teeth.

"Who's life? What are you talking about?" I asked, not understanding her meaning but noticing her anger building.

"I saw you talking to Owen the other day in the driveway. Do you deny it? What were you talking about?"

"No, I won't deny it, but it's none of your business what we were discussing."

"You come along and insert yourself into our lives and have the nerve to say to me it's none of my business?" she spat.

"In the words of my mentor, 'I am only resolved to act in that manner, which will constitute my happiness, without reference to you, or to any person so wholly unconnected with me,'" I said with no attempt at an accent.

"What? I don't know what movie that is, but let me make something clear, you do not belong in our world!" she said as imperiously as a Queen.

"Are you sure *you* belong in that world anymore?" I said, meeting her with an equally cold and haughty stare. I felt the confidence of Elizabeth well up and erase any lingering insecurities. I knew who I was and I no longer cared what this petty, angry girl thought of me.

Her eyes virtually sparked as she yelled, "How dare you! You don't get to judge me and my family when you have a loud and nosy mom spying on us from the kitchen window and all your friends are so, so... public school. I go to Prep school and I will not be talked down to by some no-fashion country girl."

"And I'm out... as Elizabeth Bennet would say, 'You can now have nothing farther to say. You have insulted me in every possible method. I must beg to return to the house,'" I said as I turned to go inside.

"Stop quoting movies!" she spat and pointed in my face.

"Brooklyn, I don't really understand what you want from me. You can keep your world. I'm not trying to invade it. You do you, and maybe read a book."

"He got kicked off the basketball team for you, you know."

That stopped me in my tracks. I had been about to walk inside, but turned to look at her instead.

"Wait, what? Are you talking about Owen?"

"Yes, he told the police and his coach that he saw Declan at your townie party. He had to admit it to prove Declan was there. All for you. So it is all your fault he will miss playing basketball, his favorite sport, his senior year."

"I didn't know," I said, feeling shocked at his sacrifice for Marni and me. He had put something he really loved doing on the line to help us prove Declan was guilty. "So now you've told me, is that what you came for?"

She paused in her pacing to look me straight in the face. Her cheeks were flushed and her eyes narrowed in barely contained hatred. "What I want from you is to know if you are dating Owen?"

I really wanted to lie because I didn't want her to give her the satisfaction, but I had told him the last time he asked that he was the last man on earth I would ever date. I was sure he would never ask again. Honestly, I couldn't blame him.

"Well?" she pushed, "answer me!"

"I am not," I confessed.

She looked so relieved, but still skeptical. "He will be with Finn a lot. Do you promise to leave him alone? Not date him? Not pursue him?"

"Look, that is absolutely none of your business. I answered your question. You can just let yourself out through the side gate right there," I said.

"Promise me you won't date him!" she nearly shrieked.

"No, I won't promise. He is trustworthy and kind, and I like hanging out with him. He is not your property and if we want to date in the future, again it is none of your business," I said, realizing it was true. I would like to spend more time with him. And my mind couldn't help but wander to our all too brief kiss, and his soft lips.

"But, according to you, I could never get a guy of his caliber, so you have nothing to worry about, right?"

"He is supposed to be mine, and I am going to tell him I

forbid it," she said, hands on her hips, punctuating her command with the stomp of her foot.

"Angry people are not always wise," I said, quoting Jane Austen again and smiling, knowing I was irritating her. "I imagine that conversation will go well. Good luck to you."

She stood there seething, trying to stare me down.

"You know Brooklyn, it surprises me, but I am not intimidated by you anymore. I am truly sorry your world is upside down, I am, but go take it out on someone else," I said and headed toward the patio door.

"My world is only upside down because I am in this horrible town with you!" she yelled behind my back as I walked inside.

"I can see you are upset, but that has nothing to do with me. I have important real-world stuff to deal with. Goodbye," I said, shutting the door.

31

I watched Finn open the car door for Jade, who was dazzling in her off-the-shoulder white organza print dress with dusty pink peonies. The light breeze was whispering through Jade's hair and fluttering her dress as Finn turned her for one last kiss before she climbed into the car and they headed to the gala. Looking at these two, one could believe in happily ever afters, soul mates, and the whole romantic fantasy. I was so happy for them both. My face hurt from smiling. I didn't realize my mother was also watching them next to me in the doorway until I heard her sniffle.

"Aren't they so beautiful together?" she asked dabbing at her eyes.

"Yes, they are," I agreed.

"You need to get your dress on if you are riding with us. We are leaving in thirty minutes."

I hadn't wanted to ride with Jade and Finn, though they asked a million times. I wanted them to have this night to themselves, and besides, my emotions were all over the place. I felt happy about the mission yesterday, but something inside me felt unsettled. If Brooklyn and her judgmental face no longer bothered me, then why had her visit left me feeling this way? Something felt off. Maybe it was because I had held the fundraiser in my mind as the celebration of all the awesome changes I would have made this summer, and as a special night with a special someone.

I pulled my dress on over my head and slipped on the blush sandals that matched my dress perfectly, just like Emma said they would.

"Mom, will you zip this?" I asked, coming down the stairs.

"Oh Ellie, you look so pretty."

"Thanks, mom. Is my makeup okay?" I had added eyeliner and a darker pink lipstick, which was more than usual.

"You look stunning, not too made up. And when your father finishes his tie, we are ready to go."

"Finished. Best double Windsor ever," he said, meeting us in the hall. "Wow, you both look lovely."

He kissed us each on the cheek and gave a special wink to my mom not intended for my eyes. Ewww.

******

As dad turned into the park entrance, we all three gasped. As far as the eye could see fairy lights draped the trees making a fairyland tunnel all around the park. We wound through the park staring in wonder. It looked like an infinity of stars. The tunnel opened up and they directed us to park on the little league field. Dad helped mom out of the car and went to help me, but I was already out, holding on to the car door staring at the scene. The setting sun had painted the sky brilliant pink and orange and red, bathing the park in a golden warm light. It looked more magical than I could have imagined.

On each of the four sides of the field, was an enormous movie screen. Each screen was currently showing a night sky with the occasional shooting star. With the backdrop of surrounding trees and fairy lights, it really did look like we were walking among the stars. As we checked in, they gave us a blanket with the event logo "A Night Among the Stars" stitched in silver thread with several shooting stars embroidered in an arc. There was also a card with movie names and channel numbers, and they issued us headphones.

My parents looked excited, and a little confused by these offerings, and were asking a few questions when I said I was going to look for my friends.

"Love you guys. See you later."

"Good luck on stage, kiddo!"

It was weird that I wasn't all that worried about getting on stage. I looked at the card in my hand. On one side was printed: "The Meryton Community Center Board would like to thank you for your support of the Youth Center fund. Enjoy your evening among the stars."

On the other side it said:

A- Guardians of the Galaxy
B- Apollo 13
C- Hidden Figures
D- Independence Day
E - Fast Dance Music
F - Slow Dance Music

The Headphones had six corresponding channels and some funky lights on top making them look slightly like alien heads. I put it up to my ear to see if anything was on yet. I could hear classical music on all channels.

I smiled as a walked toward the center of the field, taking in the view. Everyone had agreed that once we got there, we would make our way and meet in the middle of the field. In the corners, between the movie screens, were drinks and appetizer stations.

In the dimming light, I could still make out faces and I could see people milling around the field, laying out blankets, getting snacks, and greeting friends. I saw Jade and Finn, holding hands, talking with some friends, and looking deliriously happy. It looked like the whole town had turned out.

"Hey Ellie!" an excited Collin said.

"Hi Collin, hi Charlie, how are you guys? Charlie, you look beautiful." I said, genuinely happy to see them still together and clearly happy.

"Thank you, so do you. Isn't this amazing?" asked Charlie. "I can't get over all the twinkle lights. It's so romantic."

It was hard to tell for sure, but I could have sworn Collin blushed with pride when he looked at her.

"I wish they could leave it like this forever," he said.

Looking at my vibrating phone, I laughed and said, "sorry, you guys, gotta respond to this. It's Marni. You know her patience level."

I knew they had probably heard what had happened to Marni, but they had the decency to not make the "tragedy" face and smiled instead.

"Say 'hey' for us," said Charlie.

"Will do. Have fun!"

Group Msg: The Indivisibles

Marni: Dudes, where are you? Ava and I are center field, can you see me waving my phone?

Ellie: Coming your way, surrounded by tall people, ugh! Crying laughing emoji

Catt: Just arrived with Mike.

Emma: I see you, keep doing it!

Monica: Have fun all of you!

Ellie: Wish you were here!

Monica: Marco called in his IOU. Ever heard of
                something called miniature golf?

Marni: Wow, no mini golf on the elephant preserve?
                Lol Have fun!

Monica: Send me pics! I sent you all a present.

"Hello beautiful ladies," I said as I bounded next to Marni. She was standing next to her spread-out blanket still waving her phone.

"Woot woo," said Emma when she looked at me. "I saw this dress in Indy, but it looks even better tonight. You look like a Greek goddess."

"That would be a toga," said Ava.

"Togas are on one shoulder," defended Emma.

"Togas do not have pink ruffles," finalized Ava.

"Okay, okay you guys, just thank you," I said.

"Pink in twilight is your color," said Marni.

"You guys all look great. Strike a pose and let me see," I said. "After all, this is what we have been talking about for weeks… we earned this moment!"

Ava's dress, in popsicle orange, was stunning.

"Wow, someone could snap their neck turning to look at you," I said.

"You are showing hardly any skin and you look super sexy," Emma noted enviously.

"And you miss thang… this isn't the dress we bought in Indy. I LOVE this, but I thought you were going bold red," said Ava.

"Maybe it's the heat. I was feeling more white and yellow and flowy, less va voom," said Emma, spinning to make her dress flare.

"I super love it," bounced Catt as she arrived and hugged Emma. "You look like a patch of daisies."

"And you look like a little leprechaun in this green slip," Emma teased.

"A very pretty leprechaun," said Ava.

"And last but not least, our friend, the artist, and dreamer - she who is sunshine and yellow. Give us a spin," I said.

Marni spun slowly, in her white slip dress with its sheer white overlay of mesh with white embroidered flowers, and her doc martin boots. Looking down at her feet, I smiled and my heart felt lighter. I hadn't noticed them earlier. These white doc martins with black laces were her battle boots. She wore them every time she had to slay a dragon, like a tough geometry test in Mr. Grave's class, or a gallery opening with her newest work. Her wearing them tonight meant she had battled her latest dragon and won. She would never forget, but she was taking steps to get back to her fun-loving self.

"Yours is my favorite," I whispered as I hugged her. "Just don't step on my toes," I said, and I could feel her smile in my hair.

"Selfie sesh!!" yelled Emma as everyone took out their phone and we got a million pics of ourselves… in the dark, but still cute.

"I need fortification before the movies start," chimed Catt.

"Wait, where is Mike?" asked Ava.

"I'll tell you after food. I think we only have like twenty minutes until the movie starts," said Catt as she shepherded us to the corner.

"Ellie, don't you speak soon?" asked Marni.

"Yup, I set my alarm. Ms. Lemon and I are meeting on the stage in fifteen minutes," I said, pointing to the platform in front of the nearest movie screen.

"How do you feel?" asked Emma, assessing my face. "You are freakishly calm."

"I'm a little nervous when people ask me if I am nervous,

but surprisingly, not bad. I'm excited we get to find out how close we are to our fundraising goal. They wouldn't tell us anything at practice. Monica said she sent us a present... maybe it's a baby elephant for the Community Center," I laughed.

"I hope we earned enough to get the gym fixed and still get that part-time trauma counselor. I think I get more than ever how important it could be," said Marni.

"Marni, you are the one who knows this community center the best. It should be you up there," I said, wondering why I hadn't thought of it before. She probably had thought of it before, but let me have the internship in her usual, selfless way.

"Don't be silly, you needed a thing, remember?" she said, nudging me. "You will be a community outreacher! You'll be perfect. You're a Pisces, naturally intuitive and compassionate."

Walking to our blankets with hors d'oeuvres and mock-tails, I watched couples starting to slow dance in the center of the field. I felt happy, but not content. At the beginning of the summer, it had felt so important to get this internship and to conquer my fear of speaking in front of the whole town. Now I just wanted to be one of those couples dancing under the twinkle lights.

"We have accomplished a lot this summer. I feel so proud of us," I said.

"You, Ellie, are the one who got us here. Your quest to become more like Elizabeth Bennet made us all take stock of ourselves and become more like the strong women Jane wrote about," said Ava.

"I think it worked," said Marni.

"I know it helped me channel my fierceness for good, not just for terrifying people," said Emma. "Also, I'm not trying to be funny, but something about my zombie fighting Elizabeth made me feel more confident in my decision-making. I think I have learned to trust my instincts more."

"And I told Mike 'no' when he asked me to be his girlfriend on the drive here," said Catt. "I told him I really like him, but I'm not ready to be a girlfriend. He was disappointed, but I didn't want to string him along. It felt like a very adult and Jane thing to do."

"I wasn't going to tell anyone, but I caught the boldness bug, too. I am going to send a letter to Freddy. I found his address," said Ava blushing, radiating happiness, as we all screamed.

"Because of all of you, and your unconditional friendship, I will not freeze on stage and run screaming all the way home. We are quite a team!"

"Indivisible," said Catt, raising her glass, "with liberty and justice for all!"

"For all!" we cheered.

"I love you guys. I better scoot. Do I have food on my face? Teeth check?" I asked, sticking my face toward Ava who checked and shook her head. I grabbed the lip gloss Marni handed me and stood up to cheers of "You've got this!" "Go get that internship!" "Take a deep breath." "Visualize the success." "Go Ellie!"

"Ladies and gentlemen, thank you so much for attending this beautiful event. My name is Tina Lemon, President of the Meryton Community Center Board and this is Ellie Gardiner, an outreach intern candidate. We are honored to host this evening's event on behalf of the Meryton Community Center Board and all the young people who enjoy our facilities and lunches each day."

"Woo hoo! Yeah!" came a few grade school-sounding voices in the back.

The laughter in the audience didn't make me freeze up for a change, it broke my tension, so I could smile and say, "We know you are excited for the movies to start, but we have a few people to thank and some exciting announcements. Our overall goal was to raise $300,000 to complete construction of the gym, repair a little tornado damage, and add on to the kitchen."

"It was a lofty goal, but with the impromptu tv interview on WIND after the tornado this young lady did, I'm hoping we came close!" Ms. Lemon smiled and winked at me. She had not said that in rehearsal so I got self-conscious, and I started to get blotchy.

I took a deep breath and said, "Anything for the cause," and smiled back, getting a few chuckles from the audience and cheers from my friends.

From behind us, Marni's mom, looking excited, handed us each an envelope.

"The Board would not let us know what the numbers were, so we get to be surprised along with you," said Ms. Lemon, opening her envelope.

"Oh, wow, okay, I have a few notable, wow, very notable donations to read."

"For the chair I didn't mean to broke" In the amount of $3.00, from Tommy Dillard.'

She read and I remember he had been one of the sweet 1st graders Marni tutored.

"To six new 'Indivisible' friends, and the most fun day ever, an anonymous donation in the amount of $25,000."

My jaw hit the ground, and I looked at my friends. "Monica" they mouthed. "Wow."

And into the microphone, I said, "Wow, must have been a fun day!"

Ms. Lemon continued reading her list. "Just two more, on my list...from Danners, our favorite family-owned local business, a donation in the amount of $10,000!"

People loved the Danners family, and they cheered wildly, especially the girls in front who I knew played on the Danners sponsored softball team.

"And finally, this one reads 'In gratitude from the Darcy Foundation', a one-time donation of $30,000 and a yearly donation to cover the salary of a full-time trauma counselor."

I was so stunned by the generosity, especially since the last time I saw Owen, we had fought. Maybe Owen didn't know about it, and it was from Georgiana and her dad. The unsettled feeling I had been carrying around all night surfaced again. I needed to find him and apologize. Brooklyn's visit reminded me that I wanted to get to know Owen without Declan's lies and my prejudices. I wanted to take walks, swing on swings, go to coffee shops in the city with him, and feel his lips on mine again. The shocked applause from the crowd shook me out of my fog.

I heard Ms. Lemon say, "thank you to the Darcy Foundation, that will help a lot of people, won't it, Ellie?"

I looked toward Marni and felt so many things at once. I was relieved there would be help for people who had been hurt like Marni and Georgie. And I knew the Center could continue the work people like Marni and her parents had started. I didn't deserve to be the one up here, and I felt grateful that I no longer needed to be the one up here. I would always admire Elizabeth Bennet, but right then, standing in front of the whole town, looking at my friends and family smiling from the audience, I was finally happy to be Ellie Gardiner.

Ms. Lemon looked worried that I had frozen again, but I smiled at her reassuringly and said into the mic "Yes, it will. It is beyond generous. But there is someone else who deserves to be up here to read the final total. Someone who has worked hard at the center for a long time, who devotes all her free time to it, and who should be the outreach intern. My recommendation to the Board for outreach intern is, Marni Norland."

"Marni, will you please come up here? I said into the mic, applauding along with the joyful crowd. I leaned toward Ms. Lemon and said, "I have to go. I owe someone an apology."

"A boy someone?" asked Ms. Lemon, raising her eyebrow and nodding her head toward the end of the stage.

"A boy, someone," I agreed as my eyes saw what had put the knowing side-grin on her face.

There was Owen Darcy, holding an armful of blue hydrangeas.

Marni and I passed each other as I walked toward Owen.

"It's all yours," I said, handing an envelope to a stunned, but happy-looking Marni.

"And he's all yours!" she said, hugging me briefly before bounding up to the microphone.

Owen looked like he had just walked out of a movie screen wearing a midnight blue suit and a smile that lit up his entire face.

"I got the impression you liked these?" he said and motioned me to walk with him away from the stage.

"I do, thank you," I said. Still stunned, I took the bouquet from him, inhaled the not-really-fragrant petals and set them on one of the empty high-top tables.

I could hear Marni read, "Thank you all for attending tonight and thank you to all the business partners in town. Special shout out to the hooligans in the back from our Saturday mornings group! Woo hoo! Drum roll please… as of tonight, we have raised $345,000, surpassing our goal!" Cheers went up all around and she said, "Put on your headphones and let the movies begin!"

"I wasn't sure I'd see you again," I said.

"Brooklyn came to see me."

"She did?"

"Yes," he said, smiling at my confusion. "She told me you had the nerve to think you could get a guy like me. Whatever that means, and you apparently wouldn't promise to stay away from me. She stomped her foot and forbade me from ever hanging out with you."

"Yet here you are. Very brave," I smiled slightly, still unsure of what was happening.

"It did not scare me away like she hoped. The opposite, actually. It gave me hope. I knew if you still hated me, you would have told her so very clearly."

"You know me well," I laughed and almost snorted.

More quietly I said, "I don't hate you. I never did. I was leaving the stage to find you and tell you I am so sorry for how I behaved. Not because of your family's amazing donation, but because I am so ashamed that I took all my guilt and anger and threw it at you."

I could feel a slight breeze catch my hair and flutter the hem of my dress as a similar flutter started in my stomach.

"I felt guilty, too, because of the secrets I asked you to keep," he said, stepping closer to me.

"I know you saved my friend and you were trying to protect your sister from more pain. And I know you sacrificed your place on the basketball team to get them both justice. And… I'm sorry I called you a sexist pig."

"Like my namesake, I have been a prideful, snobbish fool," he said. "And I don't care so much about not being on the team. As it turns out, I have this girl I'd like to spend more time with and she lives a few minutes out of the city in this delightful small town."

My stomach continued to flutter, and I couldn't stop smiling at this gorgeous boy.

"You look so beautiful, by the way," he said.

He smiled mischievously at me and held up the book he had been hiding behind his back, a new copy of *Pride and Prejudice*.

"You read it?" I asked, smiling into his handsome face, wondering how I could have ever thought it harsh and prideful. I took his free hand in mine, our fingers interlacing automatically as he read a marked passage.

Ellie, "you are too generous to trifle with me. If your feelings are still what they were last April, tell me so at once. My affections and wishes are unchanged, but one word from you will silence me on this subject forever."

The crowd and the noise melted away when Owen looked at me with both vulnerability and hope in his eyes. The twinkle lights sparkled just for us as I pulled him closer. I felt very lucky to be Ellie Gardiner; a girl who loved her friends, admired Jane Austen, and knew with all her heart that being Ellie was her "thing." She was already enough to be a "someone" in high school. And, excitingly, she was clearly enough to make her a "someone" to this very cute and thoughtful boy.

"I will happily silence you on this subject, Mr. Darcy," I teased. Leaning into his chest, I slid my hands up his arms, cupped his face, and kissed him. With his hands in my hair and my body tingling from his answering kiss, my mind added one last quote… I'm "completely and perfectly and incandescently happy."

ACKNOWLEDGMENTS

Some people dream of embracing the golden Oscar statue while they recite their acknowledgments to thousands of adoring fans. My dreams have always been of a less public and flashy occasion for thanking those who have helped me along the way. And, more importantly, one where I didn't have to wear Spanx to do so.

Writing a book was fun because I was able to do it with a village of writers and dreamers. Thank you to my fellow warrior women in this battle of writing and indie publishing, N.M. Garrison, Jennifer J. Coldwater, and S.F. Henne. You have my deepest gratitude for your friendship and all the honesty, encouragement, and prodding to make me better at the craft we love.

Thank you to my ever-present confidants, my mom Linda Tipton and lifetime friend, Jamie Newth. Thank you for listening and uplifting me in this, and all my other dreams. I finally finished one!

Thank you to my family for sharing Saturday morning breakfasts in the bay window. While Ellie's family was not like ours, the love and laughter were the same. Love to my brother and sister who made growing up a laugh a minute. We were always each other's best audience. Sorry I was (certainly not now) so bossy. I didn't want Ellie's mom to be as annoying as Mrs. Bennet, so I softened her to merely being a little too much. My mom was only similar in that she was a great cook, but not the nosy, loud person Ellie's mom was. It was easy to make Ellie's dad as likable as Mr. Bennet was in P&P because my dad was easy to laugh with, said ridiculous things like "I was born ready," and definitely mowed up a storm.

Thank you to my first-ever editor, Alice Sudlow, for your gentle advice and book-changing developmental edits. Another thank you to Joe Bunting and Sarah Gribble from The Write Practice for providing the signposts I needed for this journey.

Shout out to the members of my writing groups. The Order of the Quill: Natalie Garrison, Noah Fratello and Jamin Fratello and those from The Write In: Jen Bladen, Daniella Ellingson, Anamaria Ayala, Ann Gardner, and Natalie Garrison. No one is as fun to obsess with as other writers, possibly because the others are sick of us talking about books.

I'd also like to thank my childhood friends, the Radical 8, or was that 7? Lol. (Kim S., Rhonda, Jeannie, Maria, Shannon, and Kim B.) Much like Ellie in this book, I grew up with good friends who supported me, and laughed with, and at, me at all the right times. You are loved for the fun girls you were and appreciated for the wonderful women you have become. Special thank you to Mrs. F. for the iced tea and for letting us invade your house the summer before we could drive.

Thank you to both David Burney at Burney Design Co. for the artistry behind my website and branding and to Jen Bladen for my book cover design. Your combined creativity and talent made the grueling process of starting this journey fun.

Thank you to everyone who listened patiently to my obsessing about writing, publishing, and this story in particular and to people, like Keith Jordan, who helped me "young up" some of the tech lingo over lunch.

Thank you, reader, for persevering through this lengthy acknowledgment, and for reading my first YA novel *Kissing Owen Darcy*. I really appreciate you.

And, finally, to Winston and Willy. Thank you for all the snuggles and distractions. You are good boys!

Please, please write a review of this book on Amazon or Goodreads, or both. It makes a big difference for my mom, and when she is happy, I get more treats!!

xo Willy

COMING August 2023

Kissing Freddy, Again

ABOUT THE AUTHOR

Arlys Avery writes clean, teen kissing-books with fun characters, strong friendships, and happy endings.

Visit Arlys and her characters by scanning the code below to sign up for her newsletter and receive the latest news from Meryton today!